MICKEY PRICE

JOURNEY TO
OBLIVION

by

John P. Stanley

Cover & Illustrations by Paul Forsyth

DEDICATED TO SARA
AND TO POSSIBILITIES

CHAPTERS

1

THE CAMPFIRE

With a whoosh it ignited. An intense white fireball, squat at the bottom with a tapered tongue of yellow flame dancing from the top. Like a comet, it left a trail of light against the black background as the boy jerked the stick up and away from the fire pit. It sizzled and crackled, emitting occasional sparks that leaped away from it as though they were trying to escape.

"Oh, the tragedy!" the boy exclaimed without a trace of regret, his eyes twinkling in the firelight. "The tiny space capsule passes too close to the sun and bursts into flame. The foolish space explorers should not have tried to take a short cut. If only they had followed instructions from mission control!"

"That's your third flamer in a row, Tom" said his twin sister without taking her eyes off her own marshmallow. It was nearing a golden toffee-colored perfection, just about the same color as her sun-blonded hair. "No WAY are you getting a bite of this one."

Tom thought for a moment about knocking his sister's stick, sword-fighter style, into the embers. A sideways glance at his dad, who raised a single eyebrow in warning, changed his mind. Instead, Tom lowered his stick with the still-flaming blackened marshmallow into the fire.

"An offering to the gods," Tom announced dramatically. "I hope they enjoy the taste of charcoal, or else I'm in trouble."

The three campers studied the fire for another minute when Tess suddenly jumped, as though physically hit by an idea. "Hey Dad," she blurted, "you promised us a story. Come on, it's time."

"Well..." said Dad. He checked his watch, but remembered it wasn't there. He had left it on his dresser that morning before heading out for a day of fishing and night of camping under the stars. "Well," he repeated, "I guess I can start one up. What do you want tonight ... Super Bowl adventure? Zombie attack? Maybe a good old-fashioned ghost story?"

"No, Dad," said Tess, turning to face him. "We don't want A story. We want THE story. The one you've been promising to tell us all summer. The story about the thing that happened when you were a kid, when you were around our age. The mysterious adventure. Come on, it's summertime, and Mom's not here, so you can forget about our bedtime. No more excuses. Tell us THE story."

There was a long pause. The sound of distant laughter filtered through the trees from a campfire a hundred yards away along the shoreline. Dad shifted his position and leaned back against a tree stump, while Tom and Tess both held their breath.

"Well..." said Dad as he checked his wrist without a watch again. "I guess I did promise. And I guess you're old enough to hear it. I'll tell it, but it might take a while." Tess grinned and lay down in story-telling position. Her hands were clasped behind her head, and she was looking straight up towards the starry sky, with a comfortable but expectant look on her face. Tom rolled over onto his belly with his chin propped in his hands, and his feet angled upwards.

Dad cleared his throat. "Once upon a time," he started, "back when I was young...."

"Dad," interrupted Tom. "Just checking. Is this a true story?"

"Well of course it's a true story. I told you, it's my story. It actually happened and it's true, every word. Now let me start. Once upon a time, back when I was young, there were...."

"Dad," Tom cut in again. "If it's a true story and it's about you, it's probably not going to be as exciting as your usual stories. So would you mind, you know, making it more interesting? Throw in a little mystery? A little action? Maybe a car chase?"

Dad pursed his lips and sighed. "You think all true stories are boring? You know, young Tom, it just so happens that the world's most amazing and incredible stories are the true ones. The make-believe ones on the other hand, well, they're ok. But they didn't really happen, did they? The story I'm telling you ... the one I'm TRYING to tell you ... is true. Every word. That's why it's THE story. So be quiet. Once upon a time, back when I was...."

"Dad...."

"THOMAS," blurted Tess, finally losing her patience and using her brother's full name. "Go throw yourself in the lake. Give the story some room. Let it breathe."

"Thank you, Tess. Well said. Now let's begin. Question time is over, no more interruptions. Once upon a time when I was young, just a little older than you as a matter of fact, the year was 1977."

"I know you think I grew up in a time before technology. Back then, we didn't have video games or cell phones or 3-D movies. But we

3

did have one thing that you don't have now...."

"Dinosaurs as pets?" interjected Tom with a grin.

Tess growled. But Dad hadn't heard him. He was staring up through the trees and raised his finger towards the sky.

"We had that. The moon.... I know, I know, it's still up there. But it seemed different, back then. Some of us thought about it every day and dreamed about it every night. Not just kids, adults too. We all watched on live TV as astronauts walked on the moon. Sometimes, when we looked up at the moon on nights like this, we knew that astronauts were up there, right at that moment."

"The race to the moon was one of the greatest adventures our country has ever had. Each type of rocket had a different name, and each mission had a different number. First came the Mercury program. Then Gemini ... Gemini 1 to Gemini 12. Then...."

"Then came the Apollo program," interrupted Tom. "It was Apollo 11 that made the first lunar landing in 1969. We learned all about this in school. Mercury, Gemini and Apollo. And then the Space Shuttle in the 1980s. We learned about them all."

"Well, Tom...." Dad drew a deep breath. "That's where you're wrong. You didn't learn about them all. It didn't go straight from Apollo to the Space Shuttle. There was another program in between. One that was shrouded in secrecy. And that's what this story is about."

"Whoa. Time. Out." Tom held up his hands to stop his dad in his tracks. "So, I get it. This is a space story. A complicated, top-secret, space program story." He narrowed his eyes and put on his best Skeptical Tom look. "But Dad ... seriously ... what does this have to do with you?"

Dad paused as the sound of a barking dog echoed across the glassy surface of the lake.

"A fair question," Dad replied. "What I've told you so far is what's called 'important background.' I promise you, it will all become clear if you just let me tell the story. So now, if you want, I'll begin telling the part that's about the heroes of our story. Starting with me."

2

THE ORLANDO HOME FOR BOYS

It all started when Big Linus scored a goal from all the way back behind the couches, and the ball rolled straight down the hall into the laundry room. We called him Big Linus because he was almost as tall as Sister Rinaldi, and also to tell him apart from Little Linus. It was weird, because Linus is a pretty rare name. And how we ended up with two Linuses at the Orlando Home for Boys is beyond me.

Anyway, Big Linus' shot sailed about face-high through the door and made it all the way down the hall into the laundry room on three hops. As hoots and high-five smacks filled the air, Taco, our goalie, turned to chase it down the hall. Taco was the shortest kid in the house and was completely useless with a hockey stick. Or a broom. Or a tennis racket. We used all three for our version of floor hockey. He was completely useless with all three, but he wasn't bad at getting hit with the ball. He was kind of magnetic, in a way. Which made him a pretty good goalie.

But he didn't get hit by that shot by Big Linus, so it was a goal and we were now down 7-2. Things looked pretty dark for us.

"Ball!!!" yelled Big Linus through the open door and down the hall. "Come on Taco, quit stalling. Ball!!!"

We heard Taco yell something muffled but nobody could tell what he had said. A minute later, a few of us headed down the hall to the laundry room to see what was keeping him.

It was a strange sight. We saw the bottom of Taco's sneakers, and Taco's butt was sticking straight up into the air. It looked like his head was wedged into the crack between the wall and the washing machine. And one of his arms was wedged even farther into that crack.

"Taco, how'd you do that?" I asked.

"Mickey..." he wailed back at me. "I'm stuuuu-cckk. Aw man, I'm stuuuu-cckk. I can feel the ball under here, but my hand won't come back out. Come on, help me out."

Big Linus put one hand on the waist of Taco's shorts and pulled as hard as he could. Fortunately for Taco, and fortunately for the rest of us, his shorts didn't come off. But Taco seemed to stretch out like a rubber band. His hand was still stuck firmly in the bottom part of the washing machine.

I bent down and had a look. Yup, he'd really done it this time. I could see the ball, lying innocently in the far corner by one of the washing machine's legs. To reach it, Taco had squeezed his hand through a round metal ring that might have

7

held the water drainage hose at one point. It was an old machine, probably repaired a dozen times, and the hose now just kind of dangled straight down before disappearing into the floor.

That's when Little Linus, who had climbed up onto the washing machine to peer down behind it, changed a bad scene into a total chaos. Leaning over the edge, he somehow managed to hit the START button with his knee and the washing machine whirred into action. With a hiss, water started to fill the machine and the insides started to spin. Taco's wails turned into yells.

"It's eating me alive!!! Help!!! It's going to eat my hand!!! My hand!!! My precious hand!!!"

Taco was famous for overreacting. But in this case, I think he had a point. The washing machine was a big, old clunker, and when it really got going it sounded like a jet airplane taking off, and pretty much shook the whole building. At this point, it just sounded like a small truck. We also knew that once you started it, there was no stopping it because the dial had broken off and you couldn't move it to the "off" position anymore. That usually wasn't a problem. Except for this time.

Just then, Sister Rinaldi came into the laundry room, drawn by the Taco's wails and the general whoops of excitement. Little Linus yelled "it's got his hand, Sister! The washing machine is eating his hand!"

Sister Rinaldi was in charge of the house and was the closest thing to a parent any of us had. Like Taco, she was also famous for overacting and this time she didn't disappoint. She screamed "OH GOOD HEAVENS!!!" and grabbed Taco by the legs. With Big Linus on one leg, and Sister Rinaldi on the other, they started tugging Taco with all their might. The machine was now in full gallop and it was literally bouncing off the floor as its insides lurched and bumped.

So imagine this. Incredibly, besides me, there were now 12 kids and one grown-up inside a tiny laundry room the size of a closet, all of them screaming. The washing machine was thumping and bumping away. Someone was screaming "Call 911!! Call the Fire Department!!" Someone else yelled "Call the funeral home!! He's a goner!!" Sister Rinaldi was screaming something in Italian that was either a prayer or a long string of swear words. And above it all, I could hear Taco wailing like it was his last wail ever.

How, I asked myself, did I end up in a house filled with such idiots? One minute we're playing a nice game of floor hockey and the next minute the world is ending. Twelve years old and sometimes I felt like the oldest one here.

After soaking it in for a few seconds, I stepped over to the light switch and flicked it off and on a few times. That got their attention.

Twelve faces stared at me. Sister Rinaldi plus 11 kids. The 12th kid was Taco, but I couldn't see his face, of course. Only his butt.

"Look," I shouted above the mechanical din. "First, Sister Rinaldi, you've GOT to stop freaking out. You're supposed to be in charge here. YOU'RE the grown up after all. And stop pulling Taco's leg. It's not doing any good." She gently set his leg down on the tiled floor with an embarrassed look.

"Second, nobody call 911. You know how much grief we'd get if they sent a fire truck out here for this?"

"Third, Big Linus, go down to the fuse box in the basement and pull the fuse in the bottom right corner. It's marked 'washer/drier.' Just pull it straight out, no twisting." Big Linus just stood there and looked at me doubtfully. "It's a fuse box, it's not a rocket ship or high magic or something." Still he stood there. "Look, Mr. Skidmore the electrician showed me all about it last time he was here. GO!!!!" I said with some urgency. Big Linus jumped when I yelled, squeezed himself out of the laundry room and headed for the basement stairs.

"Fourth, Frankie, go get me some dish soap from the kitchen sink area." He took off at a run.

"Fifth, everyone else…take three steps back into the hall. You're totally crowding Taco. Give him some space. Come one, out!"

The crowd moved back towards the door, but not all they way into the hall. Nobody wanted to give up their view of the action, especially if somebody was about to lose an arm.

Just then, the washing machine stopped and there was sudden, glorious silence in the room. "That good?" came a muffled yell from the basement.

"Bingo." I shouted.

Frankie came back in with a box of Cascade dishwasher powder and handed it to me.

"Come on Frankie," I complained. "What good is this? Not soap powder. I need LIQUID soap. Dish soap. Palmolive or whatever. The yellow bottle by the sink. HURRY!!!"

Taco started to wail again. "I'm stuuuu-cckk. And now it huuuu-rrtts."

I patted him on the back. If you had asked me which kid in the house was most likely to get his hand ridiculously stuck inside a washing machine or clothes drier or dish washer or TV or refrigerator, I would have said "Taco." No doubt. Don't get me wrong, I liked the kid. He was my best friend in the whole place. But just like he was a magnet for the ball in floor hockey, he was a magnet for trouble.

Frankie finally returned with the bottle of soap. I grabbed it and climbed up onto the machine. Sister Rinaldi gave me a curious look, but didn't open her mouth so I decided not to explain. I leaned way, way over, back behind the machine. I twisted and leaned and just got the soap bottle above where Taco's hand was wedged. And squeezed.

"AAGGGHHH!!! I can feel the blood all over my hand!!!" screamed Taco.

"Chill, Taco," I said. "It's liquid soap, it's not blood."

"Wait a minute. I'm stuck and I'm about to die. And all you can do is make sure my hands are clean? That's unbelievable," came Taco's voice from under the washing machine. From where I was, since I couldn't see him, it seemed like it was the washing machine talking. "Or maybe..." Taco continued, "... maybe ... you're cleaning my hand because you're worried that I'm so injured I'll get an infection? Or because ... because ... OH MY GOSH!!! You're sterilizing my hand before you amputate it!!! You're going to cut my hand off!!! Sister Rinaldi, help me!!!"

Sister Rinaldi stepped forward, as if she was worried that Taco had actually guessed my plan. Before she could answer, I put Taco out of his misery. "Taco. You must relax. I don't care about how clean your hand is, and you're not going to get chopped. Just wiggle your hand a bit and get the soap worked around. I did get the soap onto you hand, didn't I?"

"Like, you poured the whole bottle on it. It's covered. It's totally gooey."

"Okay, then," I said. "Relax your hand. Slowly. And without ... freaking ... out ... twist it out of that ring where it's stuck."

Taco squatted, frozen there, for a few seconds. He wasn't moving. Sister Rinaldi said "Taco?" Suddenly, he popped

11

backwards, like a cork popping loose from a bottle. There was a hushed silence for a moment as everyone stared at the arm that had been stuck. Everybody, including Sister Rinaldi, including me, including Taco, wanting to make sure that his hand was still attached and hadn't been left stuck under the machine.

To our relief, there, at the end of Taco's stubby arm was a stubby hand. A little red around the wrist from all the pulling and wrenching. But a perfectly good hand. It even had all five fingers on it.

Sister Rinaldi gave a shriek of thanks. The rest of the kids gave a cheer. When that died down, Big Linus said "hey squirt, did you get the ball?"

I was about to suggest that we finish the game using another ball when something caught my eye outside, through the open window. The laundry room was up on the second floor. I could see out across the front lawn, which was covered in a spiky, brown grass that hurt when you walked on it with bare feet. Out to Pickett Street, and the vacant lot on the other side.

Parked in front of the home was a brown, four-door car with a long hood and a long trunk, probably a Chevy Impala. Leaning up against it were two men wearing neat, white shirts with thin black ties and black pants. The thing I noticed about those guys most of all wasn't their car, and wasn't their clothes. It was their sunglasses. Gold. Gold sunglasses reflecting the sun, so shiny that it almost looked like they were glowing.

One of them was flipping through a pad of paper held in his left hand.

The other was staring straight at me.

3

VICTORY AT THE GO-KART TRACK

The number 14 go-kart shot forward at the drop of the green flag, squeezing through the gap between the two go-karts ahead before the first turn. Trace always got a good jump. But starting at the back, she had a long way to go. And she knew the drivers at the front of the pack wouldn't be as easy to pass.

This was only Trace's fifth race in the KF3 racing series. She finished 10th in the first, 8th in the second, and had won the last two in a row to qualify for the Junior Intercontinental Championship in Las Vegas. At age 12, she was two years shy of the minimum age cut-off. You had to be 14 to compete in the KF3 Cup Series. But nobody had asked for her birth certificate at the first race, and as far as everyone was concerned, she was a 14-year old racing whiz. So instead of racing with the other kids her age in the 10-lap "Speedy Tykes" race in the morning, she was racing with the big kids in the 50-mile main event.

After making some easy passes right at the start, Trace settled into the pack and took it easy for the next few laps. She needed to get a feel for her kart and for the race course. She experimented a little on some of the turns, getting a sense of which ones she could approach with some speed, and which ones were too sharp to fool around with.

At the half-way point, after twenty-five miles, she was comfortably in 10th place, right in the middle of the field.

This race had been different from the others she had driven so far. She was the top driver in Ohio, but this race had drivers from California, North Carolina and Florida. They had driven with their families to the race in pick-up trucks or SUV's pulling shiny trailers with their names on the side. Or even better, with the names of big-time sponsors. Trace had met a kid from Hickory, North Carolina, who had posed for photos before the race standing next to his "Jupiter Oil Company" trailer. He even had two people from the Jupiter Oil Company walking around handing out autographed pictures of him. Several of the other kids had big sponsors too.

But not Trace. She and her best friend had painted some sponsor names onto the side of her ride, just so she wouldn't have to race in a blank go-kart. But they weren't exactly famous companies. They weren't even real companies.

But that didn't matter now. With 10 laps to go she was still in 9th place. It was time to make her move. She realized that most karts were driving too fast into turn three, meaning that they had to drive to the outside then brake hard in the middle of the turn and lose valuable speed. If she entered the turn a little slower, she could stay more to the inside, cut the corner and hit the gas sooner.

At turn three, she passed three cars that way. She held her position and then again, the next time through turn three, she passed two more. The next lap, two more.

This got her all the way up to second place, right behind Jupiter Oil. She soon realized that her trick on turn three wasn't going to work on this driver. He was too good. Just like her, he held back a little going into the turn, so she couldn't get inside of him.

With just one lap remaining, Trace knew there was only one thing left to do. If you can't pass someone, sometimes you have to move them out of the way.

It would happen on turn four, the last turn before the checkered flag.

Trace came down the last straightaway and into the final turn right on Jupiter Oil's back bumper, and just a little too fast. She knew she could rely on the go-kart ahead of her to slow her down, though. She gave his back bumper a little tap, slowing herself down just enough to keep her tires gripped to the pavement, but giving his go-kart just a bit more speed at exactly the wrong time. His tires screeched and his back end skidded. For just a split second, he had to ease up on the gas. But not Trace. She pounded the accelerator all the way to the floor and shot past him.

Believe it or not, she could hear him yell "hey, no fair!" as she zoomed just inches past him on the inside and roared past the checkered flag and over the finish line in first place.

The surprised track announcer stumbled and fumbled for the right words. "And it's the number ... the number 14 kart, I think, passing number 1 right at the line!! The number 14, driven by Tracy Daniels … I mean, Trace Daniels. Trace Daniels wins the Cup! Newcomer Trace Daniels wins the Cup!!!"

▲ ▼ ▲ ▼ ▲

"Yoo-hoo!! Trace!! Wonder-girl!!" A woman carrying a pet Chihuahua in one hand and a small tape recorder in the other toddled towards Trace on high heels. "I need to talk to you!!"

"Unless you're offering a sponsorship I'm not interested," said Trace, flipping her black hair over her shoulder, and setting down the enormous trophy as the victory ceremony ended.

"Oh, Wonder-girl, I'm better than a silly sponsorship. I'm going to put you on the front page of my newspaper. I'll have a special article all about you, you, you and only you. How about that?? I'll do a big photo shoot of you at your house … your bedroom … your closet with all your race fashions in it. It will be fancy-marvelous, don't you think?"

"Um, I'll have to check with my mom. And I don't think you want to take a picture of my closet, it's a total disaster."

"Oh, good good good," the dog-lady interrupted, not listening to a word Trace had said. "I'm Lacy McKenzie, Editor in Chief of the Weekly Tattler newspaper. And," she said, lowering her voice as though she didn't want other people in the area to be jealous, "we're going to become best friends."

Trace narrowed her eyes and looked at the adult standing before her with disdain. "The Tattler? Isn't that the one they sell at the supermarket checkout counter? The one with fake stories about aliens and ghost ships and five-headed pigs?" As her words hung in the air, Trace reached out to pet the dog, and was promptly bitten.

"Oh, Mr. Poopito, no, no, no, that's not how we treat our cover-girls." Lacy McKenzie kissed her dog on the head and, still facing Trace, stuck out the dog backwards and sideways. Like a running back taking a hand-off, a short man with a mustache stepped forward and plucked the dog out of Lacy's hands. In addition to the dog, he was now carrying a briefcase, a bag with pictures of Chihuahuas all over it, a cup of coffee with lipstick on it, and a large red leather purse that obviously wasn't his. He gave a small sigh, as though he often found himself in this unfortunate situation.

"Now," said Lacy McKenzie, suddenly business-like. She popped a fresh tape into the recorder and brandished a reporter's notebook and pen that seemed to have materialized out of thin air. "The Tattler is a very successful newspaper. It just so happens that people like reading about aliens and ghost ships and five-headed pigs. But just wait until they read about my Wonder Girl. I will make you a star." She snapped on the tape recorder and purred, "darling girl, tell me about your race today."

"Well..." said Trace. Despite her misgivings, she was excited about facing the very first real reporter in her racing career. She took a deep breath and prepared to give the kind of speech she had heard so many race car drivers deliver on television.

"The Number 14 'Rachel's Lemonade Stand and Ed's Lawn Service' go-kart was really running great today. I'd like to thank my Mom ... I mean, my Crew Chief ... and I'd like to thank our neighbor Mr. Henry for letting us borrow his trailer, and ...."

Trace noticed that Lacy McKenzie was no longer standing still. She was walking in a slow circle around Trace, staring at her racing suit.

"Darling Wonder-girl. I know one thing you'll need before

our photo shoot. A new little jumpsuit! Hot pink with black trim and yellow stars on the shoulders and down the arm. How can you win wearing that grey thing with ... oh my gosh ... are those oil stains?"

"Um, y-e-sssss." Trace drew out the word so that it dripped with sarcasm. "Sometimes you might find some OIL in a GARAGE at a RACE TRACK!"

"Well, my cover-girl doesn't get oil stains or dirty fingernails. Really...." Lacy McKenzie clucked and shook her head. But then, as if she just remembered something, her face lit up again. "So Wonder-girl. Tell me what makes you so fast out there. Did your mommy and daddy buy you a bigger engine so you could beat those boys?"

Trace couldn't believe what she was hearing. "Uh, noooo. All karts have the same 125 cc touch-and-go water-cooled two-stroke KF engine. The race officials do a pre-race and post-race check, and anything larger gets you disqualified." Trace paused, looking for any hint of understanding in the reporter's eyes. "You know, under Junior Indy Association rules?"

"Oh honey, you can stop talking like a mechanic. I want to write about something kids can understand. If it's not a bigger engine, then you must be the luckiest little 13-year-old girl in the world. That's what I'll write. I mean, come on. Winning three races in a row against all those aggressive boys? Have you got a little rabbit's foot in your pocket? What's your secret?"

Trace stamped her feet, and her mouth turned into a very thin red line. "Look here, Mrs. Weekly Tattler Newspaper. Maybe I won because I know my kart and I figured out the track. I know that the tires don't grip so well until they really warm up in the 10th lap. I know that number seven shock springs give too much bounce and so the car frame hits the track in the

18

straightaway. That's why we used number EIGHT springs on this track. And I know that they let cars and trucks drive across the track at turn four to get to the infield. All that traffic wears down the surface of the pavement at turn four and makes it slippery, meaning if you enter the turn too fast, or if you ... maybe ... get a little bump from the car behind you at just the wrong time, you could spin into the wall. Why don't you go ask the boy driving the Number 1 car about THAT!!?? Ask him how UNLUCKY he was!!"

Trace had said that whole outburst without taking a breath, so she sucked in a huge gulp of air. With both fists clenched, panting, red in the face, she looked like she had just run the 50 mile race rather than driving it.

Lacy McKenzie took a step backwards and was holding her small notebook out in front of her, as if to defend herself. "Well. Um. So are you telling me you DON'T have a little rabbit's foot for good luck?"

Trace gave a small frustrated scream, spun around on her heels, and marched quickly away from Lacy McKenzie, her overburdened assistant and Mr. Poopito.

She was so angry that she didn't notice the two men in short sleeved white shirts, thin black ties and black pants, wearing shiny golden sunglasses. They had been standing just around the corner of the concession stand building in the shade, listening to the whole conversation with stony expressions. After Trace stormed past, however, the shorter one showed the faintest hint of a smile at one corner of his mouth.

"Yep," he said to his partner. "Call the Director. She's the one."

▲ ▼ ▲ ▼ ▲

Trace was still out of breath when she found her mom pushing the Number 14 kart over to the flatbed trailer hitched to their beat-up red pickup truck.

"Oh my gosh Trace honey, I swear that trophy is taller than you," said her mom with a huge smile. "Go set it down on the front seat and then give me a hand pushing this little winner up the ramp, ok?"

"You got it, Mom," said Trace who had just noticed how hot and sweaty she was in her full-length Nomex racing suit. "Oil stains on a racing suit," she thought angrily. "I'd like to see that dumb reporter tune up a go-kart before the race without getting covered with oil," scowled Trace to herself. She peeled off her racing suit, folding it neatly and placing it on the seat next to her 4-foot tall Championship Cup.

When she turned to head back towards her mom and her kart, she noticed the two men in the neckties and shiny gold sunglasses walking straight towards her. Uh-oh, she thought to herself, this could NOT be good.

"Ms. Daniels, ma'am. Mrs. Daniels ma'am. We need a word with you for a minute," said the shorter one. The tall one just stood there, expressionless. With his extremely long neck, Trace thought he looked like some kind of awkward bird.

"Absolutely, gentlemen. You look like you might be lost," said Trace's mom. "Where can we send you?" Trace could tell her mother was nervous too.

"No, we're right where we need to be, ma'am. First of all, Ms. Daniels," said the shorter one, turning to Trace, "congratulations on your victory. You're a remarkable driver." He paused. "Especially considering that you're only 12."

Trace's heart sank. How could this be happening now? She

knew she had to be 14 to enter the Cup race, but that rule seemed so unfair. Without thinking, she looked back to the truck and could see the sun reflecting off the top of the enormous Championship Cup. HER Championship Cup. With a sinking feeling, she pictured the two men walking off with this prize … or worse, wheeling her kart away too.

"Now you hold on now, just one minute," began Trace's mom. "Just you wait. Maybe you should ask someone who knows a thing or two about how old my daughter is. I think I have a pretty good idea."

"Roger that, ma'am. I don't mean to argue. But I think we all know how old your daughter is."

"Mom, wait," said Trace. "It's ok." She paused, enjoying the last seconds of feeling like she was a 14-year-old KF3 International Go-Kart Champion. "You're right, I'm 12. And if that means you have to take away the Cup, then take away the Cup. But I won out there," said Trace coolly and calmly to the men. "You can't change the fact that I beat every one of those drivers out there today."

The shorter one looked again like he might smile, but then it faded as quickly as it had come. "You're right, you were the best. And you can keep your trophy. We're not here to talk to you about racing."

Trace tilted her head to the side and shot a look at her mom, who looked just as confused as her.

"Truth be told," continued the man with gold sunglasses, "if you really were 14, we wouldn't be talking to you right now."

4

SMOKE AND MAGNETS

"A practical study of magnetic force, in three parts," proclaimed Jonah Trotsky in a steady, clear voice. It wasn't exactly an exciting title for a science fair entry. But Jonah thought it was an accurate description of his project, and he believed accuracy to be a highly desirable characteristic.

"Part one, using magnets to perform work," Jonah continued.

The small crowd continued to shuffle over towards his experiment area, having just watched Billy Johnson's model volcano burst into flames and set his table on fire. Sadly, the janitor and two teachers had whipped out fire extinguishers immediately, so the blazing inferno lasted about four seconds. It was as if the teachers had been expecting one of the experiments to catch on fire. Come to think of it, that made some sense. The experiment was called "The Incredible Erupting Volcano," after all.

Jonah cleared his throat and continued. "On the table are three simple coil magnets. Each has an iron core wrapped with boron wire. Lying next to them are three metal donuts. Using only the incredible invisible force of magnets..." at this point, he paused dramatically. His mother had been an actress in college and had told him, as he was rehearsing the night before, that sometimes silence, rather than words or music, produces the biggest dramatic effect.

"Using only the incredible force of magnets..." he repeated again and paused again, "I will cause three heavy metal donuts to float in mid air." Jonah carefully placed the three metal rings above the magnets and gave each a spin. The audience clapped politely as the metal rings fluttered and spun, floating about 4 inches above the coil magnets on the table.

"Now, by flipping this switch, I will send an electric charge through each coil magnet. Based on Faraday's Law, the poles of these magnets will be reversed. The metal rings will no longer be repelled. They will be...." Jonah paused again, for maximum dramatic effect... "ATTRACTED!!" he exclaimed. He flipped the switch, and the three rings came crashing down with a loud "TWANK" onto the coil magnets.

The applause this time was louder and there were several "oohs," one "aah" and a distinct "oh my goodness!" from one of the judges.

"And now," said Jonah, with the audience's full attention on him. "The GRAND FINALE."

He moved over to the far end of his table where a strange contraption sat. Bolted to the table was the front wheel from his sister's tricycle. It had a large gray block of dark gray metal wedged into the spokes. Placed a few inches apart, all around the outside of the wheel, were ten coil magnets. Each one was about the size of a can of soup, just like the kind used in the last experiment. A series of colored wires poked out the top of these coil magnets and led back to a block of wood with a single light bulb attached to it.

"A magnetic field is a force created by electrical current," explained Jonah to the attentive audience. "Through a process called 'induction,' by adding just a bit of motion energy, you can release some of the electrical current produced by the magnets. And if you do it right, you can get enough electricity to power this 100 watt light bulb."

"Not just any magnet will produce enough electricity for this. Strapped to this wheel is the strongest magnet found on earth, Neodymium." Jonah looked right at the judges. "I had to order it from a company in Utah. It cost nineteen dollars and seventy cents and it took six weeks to arrive in the mail."

One of the judges raised his eyebrows and made a note in his book. He was clearly impressed.

"Look," said Jonah, waving to his experiment. "No plugs. No electrical outlet. No batteries. Just a few hunks of metal and wire and a spinning piece of Neodymium will power this light bulb."

The audience shuffled closer. Some bent over to look under the table for any hidden plugs or wires. People in the back row stood on their tip toes.

"Okay, young man. Let's see your cure for the energy crisis," exclaimed one judge, stroking his beard. "If this works, I'll buy one of these contraptions for my house!" A ripple of laughter passed through the crowd.

It was time.

"And now," said Jonah, spinning the tricycle wheel with a small handle attached to one side. "By spinning this wheel...." He paused to catch his breath as he strained to spin the wheel faster. "Let there be...LIGHT!!!"

All eyes turned to the bulb. All three judges were beaming. But as the wheel spun and spun, their smiles slowly drooped into frowns. Their happy expectant faces turned curious. The bulb was not lighting.

Jonah spun the wheel faster and faster. Nothing.

The wheel made a thunketa-thunketa-thunketa sound that echoed through the quiet gym.

After a while the thunketa-thunketa started to slow down. Jonah's arm felt like it was going to fall off.

"Well, young man," said the judge with the beard. "You might not have invented a way to make electricity. But you invented a humdinger of an exercise machine! I still might want one of those in my house!"

Jonah stopped spinning the wheel and sat down on the floor. He felt like a balloon after all the air had just whistled out the end.

How had that happened? Lighting the bulb was the easy part! It had worked 100 times in a row at home. And it had worked right before the Science Fair had started. UGHHH!!!

Jonah's concentration was suddenly shattered when the auditorium lights went off and a single spotlight illuminated the tall girl at the table next to him. She was wearing a white scientist's coat and her blonde hair was gathered into a tight ponytail. Peppy pop music pumped out of the large speakers hanging from the ceiling. The girl's silky English accent cut in above the music: "Okayyyy, who's ready for a spot of Science!!??"

UGHHHH!!!. Jonah thought again. He wanted to throw up.

It was Tiffany Berber Timkins. Everyone called her Princess Tiffie for short. Her parents were both big-shot doctors at the University of Chicago hospital. And from the appearance of her science project, Princess Tiffie had received A LOT of help from one of them. Probably both.

Her parents were standing just to one side of her table, beaming at the audience and at the judges. Jonah saw her dad wink at one of the judges and give the thumbs-up sign.

Princess Tiffie tugged a black velvet curtain hanging behind her table, revealing brightly-colored posters that said things like "Science Rocks!!" and "Kool Kidz Luv Science."

She proceeded to deliver a carefully-planned presentation about how awesome science is, and how awesome England is, and how awesome America is. She explained that she was going to mix some chemicals together in tribute to these two great countries.

Bo-ring. Thought Jonah.

Princess Tiffie poured the first two chemicals together. Red smoke.

She poured the next two chemicals together. White smoke.

"And now," she said. "I shall mix together two more." With her perfect English accent, the word "together" sounded like "two-getha."

"The first one is sodium nitrate. And the second one...this one in the other jar is um … uh … um…."

Sweet, thought Jonah. Please goof up. Pleasegoofup. Pleasegoofup. Oh, if life is fair you will TOTALLY GOOF UP!

Suddenly, Tiffie's dad coughed hard. Except it wasn't a real cough. The cough sounded a lot like the word "Chromium." Right afterwards, Tiffie's mom sneezed explosively, except the sneeze sounded strangely like "aaahhh ..... aaahhh ..... aaahhh - Carbonate."

"Oh I remember! Chromium Carbonate," said Princess Tiffie brightly. "The second one is Chromium Carbonate." And this time SHE winked at one of the judges. The judge returned her wink and then nodded approvingly at the other judges.

Princess Tiffie mixed the two chemicals together and, guess what, they created a blue mist. Now, red, white and blue smoke bubbled out of the three containers, flowing down onto the table and then off the table in a kind of smoky waterfall.

Jonah had to admit, for just a second, that it looked pretty cool. But it was NOT what he called a science experiment. I mean really, how hard was it to mix together six tubes of liquid!!

"Red, white and blue! Red, white and blue!" sang Princess Tiffie. "God bless America and God bless the Queen! Thank you, thank you, thank you!!"

Princess Tiffie curtseyed to the crowd. She was getting thunderous applause from her parents and...oh my gosh, thought Jonah...thunderous applause from the JUDGES!! One of the judges strode up to Tiffie and took the microphone. He said "I think we all know who gets first prize here today at the Griffin Middle School Science Fair! Tiffany, very entertaining. Congratulations!" To Jonah's horror, the judge placed a heavy gold medal around Tiffie's neck.

Boy, that was fast. It was all over. The boy who loved science more than pizza had been beaten by Princess Tiffie

Timkins in a Science contest.

The lights flashed back on and a small crowd surged forward to walk around in the smoke that was still flowing down off of Tiffie's display table.

Jonah turned back to his table. Why hadn't it worked this time? Why hadn't the bulb lit? He ran his experiment again in his mind. The Neodymium sample was pure. Everything was set up right. The magnets had generated a good charge. The principle of induction was a force of nature that never changes. Why hadn't it lit the bulb?

Jonah was concentrating so hard, he didn't notice the two men picking their way through the crowd surrounding the winner's table.

One was tall, the other short. They were wearing white shirts, thin black ties, and black pants. Remarkably, even indoors, they were both wearing sunglasses with reflecting gold lenses.

Jonah didn't notice them when they stopped in front of his table. He was too absorbed in his own thoughts.

"Don't knock yourself out, Jonah," said one of the men with the sunglasses. "Even the best-planned missions can fail because of something completely unexpected."

"Yeah, yeah," Jonah mumbled, without turning around. "Thanks, judge. But I don't want the second place ribbon."

"I'm not the judge," laughed the shorter sunglasses man. "And besides," he waved a hand over towards the other side of the room. "It looks like they gave second place to the boy with the erupting volcano."

"Look," the sunglasses man said as Jonah turned to face him. "We don't want to talk to the first or second place finishers. They don't interest us. We want to talk to you. You just had

28

some bad luck."

Jonah stood up straighter and looked at the two strangers with suspicion. "I don't believe in luck. There was a reason why the bulb didn't light. And I'm going to figure it out."

Jonah leaned closer to his experiment for a better view of the light bulb. He looked closely at the inner workings inside the light bulb and his heart sank. That was the reason. How simple. And how stupid! The light bulb's filament ... the super-thin wire that glows white-hot when electricity passes through it ... the thing that makes the light bulb light ... it had broken in half. The light bulb had simply burned out. His spinning magnets HAD generated enough electricity. It was the light bulb that had failed him.

"Jiminy Christmas," whispered Jonah, feeling deflated like a limp balloon. "Can you believe that?"

Jonah removed the broken bulb and screwed in a replacement bulb. With only two cranks of the tricycle wheel, the bulb flickered to life, giving a bright yellow glow. Jonah stopped spinning the wheel, closed his eyes and hit himself square in the forehead.

"Very good, Jonah Trotsky. And why do you think the bulb burned out?" asked sunglasses man.

"The filament is thin and fragile," groaned Jonah. "The spinning bicycle wheel shakes and rattles the table like crazy. All the shaking and rattling loosened the filament and ended up breaking it. That's what happens when you shake a regular grocery story light bulb like this. That's why they use different, stronger bulbs in things like machines or cars or motorcycles. And that's what I should be using."

"So it wasn't luck," continued Jonah. "I don't believe in luck. I could have figured this out."

"Very good again," said the sunglasses man. "Not only are you a scientist, you're a detective too. You know," he continued, quieter now, "if you used an even stronger magnet, you could power a hundred light bulbs."

"Yeah, right. Stronger magnet," said Jonah as he adjusted the wires on his experiment. "I'm using Neodymium, and it's the strongest magnet there is anywhere."

"Oh, it's a strong magnet. The strongest magnet on earth. But we've seen stronger magnets, Jonah."

Suddenly, Jonah stood up straight and looked closer at the two strange men talking to him. "Wait a minute. What do you mean, 'you've seen stronger magnets.' And how do you know my name?"

5

OPERATION BREAKOUT

I flicked my wrist and sent the brightly colored "fly" sailing through the air. The fishing rod gave a satisfying clicking whir as the line played out. This time, the fourth try, the fly and hook passed right through the center of the large black tire.

"Bulls eye," whispered Taco. "Nice shot, Mickey."

Leaning out the bedroom window up on the third floor, I had just hooked the tire swing hanging from the giant Cyprus tree in the side yard. I started to reel it in.

"No way it's going to hold. That rod will snap in half," grumbled Big Linus.

"Have faith," I said. "It's a 75 pound line and a Bass-Max

rod. This thing's strong enough to catch a dolphin, so it'll bring in that tire."

I wasn't half as confident as I sounded, though. The rod was straining under the weight of the tire, bent into the shape of a candy cane. My arms were straining too, as I struggled to spin the little reel handle.

The tire was almost up to the window when I had a sudden brainstorm. Instead of struggling to crank the reel with my right hand, I held the fishing rod firm and just walked backwards into the room, pulling the tire the final ten feet up to the window. I had almost reached the doorway when I saw Taco and Big Linus lean way out the window and pull the tire up onto the ledge.

"Sa-WEET!!" Taco exclaimed. "Just like you said, Mickey. Send It ... hook it ... and reeeeeeeel it in."

I ran forward, removed the hook from the tire, and clipped it safely back onto the fishing rod. I knew I would need that again later.

"Okay," I said. "We have our transportation. Operation Breakout now moves to phase two. The escape."

The three of us peered nervously over the edge of the window sill at the hard baked earth of the side yard, three stories below. It suddenly occurred to me that my plan seemed a whole lot easier when it was just talk. Now someone actually had to jump out of the third story window and ride the tire swing down to the ground.

That person would have to be crazy!!

"Piece of cake," I said. I looked at Big Linus and had an idea. I took a deep breath. "This stage will take a whole lot of skill. Real athletic skill. The first guy will need to show the others how to ride this thing." I looked sideways at the others. "Linus and Taco, step back. I'll show you how it's done." I pushed forwards to the edge of the window and grabbed the tire from Linus.

"Whoa, cowboy. Wait a minute," protested Linus. "You need an athlete for this? Who are you kidding? I'm the athlete here. I'll show you turkeys how it's done."

Got him, I thought as I fought back a grin. I gave Linus my most serious expression and said gravely, "well, you're probably right, Linus. If anyone can do it, you can." I breathed a huge sigh of relief.

Linus scooted up onto the window ledge and put his legs through the tire swing.

"Um, Linus?" said Taco. "If you don't make it, can I have your bed? And your Miami Dolphins jersey?"

"Taco, stop talking," I said quickly as Linus eyed the ground nervously. "Linus is all over this, no problem. And besides, I'll get the Dolphin's jersey when he dies. I mean, IF he dies. But you can have his bed, Taco. It smells like butt."

"That's enough, pipsqueaks," said Linus. "I'm gonna be buried in my Dolphin's jersey when I die, so nobody gets it. And nobody gets my bed either. They'll send it to a museum in Washington D.C. and people will line up for hours just to see it. So get outta my way, I'm going…."

"WAIT!" I said, grabbing the back of Linus' shorts. "Some advice before you go." I put my head next to his and pointed out into the yard. Both of us looked out along my outstretched arm. "If you jump straight, you'll swing into the trunk of the tree, right? Horribly, directly, smack-tastically into the trunk?"

Linus squinted out at the tree, and then his eyes got big as he pictured himself hurtling headfirst into the enormous tree.

"Here's what you do, though," I explained. "Jump out sideways. Put your feet on the ledge and shove off as hard as you can to the right, off towards the road. That should spin you out in a circle. Instead of swinging straight at the trunk, you'll go out over the grass, curve around the tree, and end up ... right ... over ... the sandbox."

Linus followed my index finger, turning his head to the right, tracing the big, swooping path. And he grinned when his eyes finally landed on the giant sandbox.

"Remember," I said, "if you land safely...." I caught an angry glare from Linus. "Okay. WHEN you land safely ... I'll cast the hook back down, and you can attach it to the tire. Try to do this from the other side of the tree, though. Keep out of sight. Mrs. Finley is on guard duty. She's old and feeble, but she isn't COMPLETELY blind and deaf. If she catches us, this is all for nothing. And we'll get in huge trouble. And we won't get our ice cream. And that's not ... going ... to ... happen," I added, poking my friends in the shoulder with each word.

Mrs. Finley lived next door to the Orlando Boys' Home and often came over when Sister Rinaldi had to leave the house on an errand. Right now, she was sitting at the foot of the stairs in the front hall as all the boys were supposed to be reading in their rooms for an hour. Which gave the three of us just enough time to execute Operation Breakout, walk a mile to the Dairy Queen, get a Deluxe Banana Split Supreme, and make it back to our room before the good Sister came home.

With that, Taco and I started the countdown. "Mission control," said Taco, "we're clear for launch of Meatball One."

Linus shot him another one of his classic dirty looks, but Taco didn't notice. Or didn't care.

"10, 9, 8, 7 ... lighting main engine ... 6, 5, 4 ... digging a grave for this fearless astronaut ... 3, 2, 1, zero ... zero ... zero. Come on Linus ... I said ZERO!!!"

And with that, Linus launched himself out into the open air, pushing far right and away from the window. It was a beautiful sight. It seemed like he was sailing in slow motion. He curved down, down, down and out and around the tree to the far side. And with perfect timing, Linus let go of the tire at just the right moment, as it zipped low over the sandbox. Linus landed feet-first and executed a perfect summersault, with a spray of dry, white sand.

"Touchdown!!" shrieked Taco, as I clamped my hand over his mouth to muffle any further celebration.

Linus gave a wave and scrambled off to retrieve the tire as it continued to swing around the tree. I grabbed the fishing rod and cast the fly off again into the yard, where it landed in the short grass just to the right of the tree trunk.

As I reeled up the tire for a second time, I started coaching Taco, who was suddenly silent as he eyed the 3-story drop to the ground below.

"Taco, you got it. Piece of cake with a cherry on top. You saw Big Linus do it."

Taco looked slightly green and was gripping the window sill so hard his nails were scratching into the paint.

"Taco. You see Linus down there. You know what he's thinking? He's not thinking about Operation Breakout. And he's not thinking about his banana split."

Taco gave me a curious look.

"He's thinking about how totally AWESOME it would be for him to be the only one to do the swing. How totally AWESOME it would be for you and me to chicken out, right after he jumped. You can't give him that satisfaction. You just can't."

"Be the man, Taco" I said. "Be the man. And don't look down."

Taco turned back to face the giant tree and grabbed onto the rope. "Be the man and don't look down," he whispered out loud. "Be the man and don't look down. Be the man and don't look down."

With his eyes tightly shut, he scooted his feet into the tire, curling himself into a ball, holding tight to the rope. The tire tipped gently forward and started to scuff off the ledge.

"And don't forget..." I said quickly. But it was too late. "Don't forget to push off to the right." My words floated out after Taco as he plummeted down towards the yard. Streaking straight towards the giant Cyprus tree trunk.

The tire hit the tree, dead on, with a deep, echoing "BWOMPPP!!" At first, I thought the tire had split into two pieces on impact. Then I realized that the part bouncing far to the right was the tire. It was rubber, after all. The part bouncing to the left was Taco. And he was ... well, he was kind of rubbery too. He sailed over a bench and went crashing into the enormous blackberry bush about 20 feet from the base of the tree and disappeared.

It was like the bush had swallowed him whole.

And then the bush talked. "I'm ok," it said. "It'll take a while to get these branches out of my side. But I'll be ok."

Linus was doubled over in silent laughter. I was giggling so hard I could hardly reel up the tire.

By the time I made it out the window and had swung down to the sandbox, Taco had escaped from the blackberry bush, but not without scrapes on every visible bit of skin. And a large branch was still sticking out of his hair at an angle.

"Operation Breakout, phase three," I said as the three of us crouched behind the tree. We moved silently along the edge of the yard out to Pickett Road. Down the road, through the edge of the park, cut through the shopping center parking lot, then straight to DQ.

We were so focused on staying low that we hadn't noticed the brown Chevy Impala sitting across the street. Or the two men wearing shiny gold sunglasses, watching our every move.

▲ ▼ ▲ ▼ ▲

Walking back from the Dairy Queen, all three of us savored the rare feeling of complete freedom. Life at the house was always chaotic. Always crowded. Often fun. But never free. It was even sweeter than ice cream to be walking along the road in the hot sun, setting our own schedule, completely free. And I still couldn't believe we had executed the escape so perfectly. Well, except for Taco's not-so-perfect swing into the tree.

Peeking from between the branches of the large pine trees lining the road was the moon, sitting pale against the bright blue sky.

"Moon's out," I said. "I thought it was Tuesday, but I guess it's Moon-day."

"Oh, no," said Taco, stopping dead. "Oh, this is not good. This is bad. A bad, bad sign. The moon should NOT be out during the daytime. It's crazy. It's backwards. It's upside down!!"

Linus and I had heard this one before. Taco would soon be talking about dogs and cats and ....

"Moon and sun, sharing the same sky. Dogs and cats getting married. Fish walking on the land, bears diving into the ocean deep. Everything is backwards!" His hand went to his forehead, and he threw his head back for great dramatic effect. Leaning forward towards us, his voice almost a whisper, he continued, "peanut butter fighting with jelly."

"The Detroit Lions winning the Super Bowl!!" shouted Linus, feeling the spirit.

"Hold on," said Taco, "that's too far. Not THAT crazy."

"Come on, Taco," I said. "The sun and moon appearing together isn't crazy at all. Of course they're in the same sky. The moon spins around the earth." I made a fist with one hand, and circled my other fist around it. "And they both move around the sun. You're the sun," and I walked in a circle around him, still spinning my fists. "Sometimes the moon is on the back side of the earth. Sometimes it's on the front side, the side closer to the sun."

Taco looked skeptical.

"Sometimes, the moon actually blocks the sun," I said, setting Taco and my two fists in a straight line. "That's a solar eclipse."

Taco looked alarmed.

"Wait. Are you telling me that the moon and sun are whipping around together out there together in the sky? So they could, like, run into each other??" Taco stepped forward towards me. "Just a little off-course, then whoomp," he bumped his sun-chest into my moon-fist.

"The moon whoomps into the sun. And there's a giant SUN-SPLOSION. End of life as we know it! Kiss yourself goodbye!" screamed Taco. "This could be the big one. Impact in ten minutes!"

"Taco," I said. "You are so wrong in so many ways. How did you get this way? Did Sister Rinaldi find you at the dog pound before you came to the Home?" I asked. Taco was laughing too hard to hear me.

That didn't last long, though. We had turned the last corner and were now approaching our house. We stopped talking as we crossed the road and moved quickly and silently across the big, grassy yard.

My plan for re-entering the house was simple. We would just wait in the bushes next to the porch until we heard the sound of the other boys coming downstairs at the end of reading time. When they came outside into the yard, we would just blend in with the crowd. Foolproof.

Or maybe not.

We hadn't counted on the Brown Impala.

As the three of us crouched behind the bushes beside the front porch and listened to the sound of the house coming to life again after reading time, I heard the slam of one car door, and then another. To my surprise, I saw two men in white shirts and thin black ties, wearing shiny gold sunglasses, walking straight towards us.

I stood up as the shorter man with sunglasses reached us.

"Hi there, Tarzan. Nice job with that tire swing. How was the ice cream?"

I was stunned. I had to come up with something fast.

"Would you believe, we always have permission to do that if we finish our books early?" I asked, without any real hope of being believed.

"Not even close, Tarzan," said short sunglasses man. "Why don't you come inside with us. Sister Rinaldi is expecting us at three o'clock, so we're right on time."

Turning to the other two, he said "Linus, Taco, you're free to go. Believe it or not, that old lady watching the front door had no idea you had gone, and neither does Sister Rinaldi. Operation Breakout was a success."

Linus and Taco stared at the two men in disbelief.

"But … the … you … how … Operation Breakout … what the …" said Taco, his voice trailing off into nothingness.

I took a deep breath and stood up straighter. "You're not from Department of Children's' Services," I asked, "are you?"

"Negative," said the two men at exactly the same time, as they walked past us into the house.

6

THE MYSTERIOUS INVITATION

My mind was racing as I led the two strange men down the front hall towards Sister Rinaldi's office in the back of the house. Not from Children's Services? But then where?

The police? Oh, come on. An ice cream run in the middle of the day was not something that would bring out the police. But then who?

Sister Rinaldi must have heard us coming. As I approached her office, she suddenly burst out of her doorway and put her hands on my shoulders, steering me into the room.

"Gentlemen, please come in, come in. I see you've met Mickey. Come in, come in. Let's find you a seat."

The two men did not introduce themselves to Sister Rinaldi, as though they had met her before. Once inside her cluttered office, they both stood, upright, just inside the doorway. They removed their gold sunglasses at exactly the same moment, and slipped them into their shirt pockets.

Sister Rinaldi, her hands still protectively on my shoulders, steered me to a chair at the edge of the desk. She gestured the two visitors towards the two chairs with tall wooden backs which sat on the oriental rug facing her desk.

The two men paused, waiting for Sister Rinaldi to sit down first.

Sister Rinaldi took a long look at me and pursed her lips tensely before starting. "Mickey," she began, "these two special visitors asked to meet you. They talked to me this morning about a special ... well ... a special school ... or a special opportunity for you. It's a ...."

"Ma'am. Ma'am, if I may," said the shorter one. He had short-cropped hair, just like the other man's. His eyes were cold, steel blue, but had friendly wrinkles around the edges.

"Mickey, we need to introduce ourselves. I'm Major Jackson. And this is Major Austen." The taller man nodded his close-cropped head at me, without smiling.

"Nice to meet you," I said warily. "Exactly what kind of Major are you?"

Jackson looked at me with approval. "Good question. I'm a Major in the United States Air Force. But I'm not working for the Air Force right now. I guess you can say I'm on loan to NASA."

I looked at him with surprise. "NASA? The space program? You're an astronaut?"

"I'm an astronaut. And so is Major Austen here. And that's why we're here. We have been sent on behalf of NASA to give you a special invitation. We're inviting you to come to the

Kennedy Space Center for a kind of camp. An explorers camp, you could say. To learn about the space program. To go through some training exercises, just like a real astronaut does."

I hadn't moved during this whole conversation. I suddenly realized my mouth was wide open, so I closed it.

"You've got to be kidding me," was all I could say. Seriously. It was like the coach of the Dolphins had just dropped by and asked me to be his quarterback. Or like President Ford had strolled in off the street and invited me to come to the White House. "Are you kidding me?"

"That's a negative," said Jackson. "It's a two or three week program. And it's not just you. You will be joining a class of other kids your age, from all around the country."

I thought about that. "So, why me? Why was I picked?"

"There are things I need to know, and things I don't need to know," said Major Jackson. "You asked about one of the second things. All I know is, your name's on my list. And the invitation … the opportunity … is up to you now. The camp starts tomorrow, so you don't have much time to decide. But go ahead, talk it over with Mrs. Rinaldi."

"Sister," she said sharply, correcting the man in the uniform.

"Sorry ma'am. Talk it over with SISTER Rinaldi. But do you want some advice, young man?"

I nodded my head.

He looked at me hard for about ten seconds straight. "Say yes."

▲ ▼ ▲ ▼ ▲

There was a long silence as Dad got up to put another log on the dying camp fire. Tom and Tess were still speechless as he flopped back

43

to a sitting position and took a long drink of water from his Miami Dolphins cup that had been sitting in the pine straw next to him.

Tom finally broke the silence. "Dad. Um, first of all ... WHOA. This is a crazy story. Seriously. Second of all, did this seriously happen?"

"Well, Tom," said Dad, "think about it for a minute. When I was thirteen, I started going to St. Paul's School in New Hampshire and spending my summers in Connecticut. But before that, you remember where I lived. Orlando. You've seen the pictures of the Orlando Boys' Home."

Tess sat up excitedly. "And pictures of your friend Taco! Tom, we've seen his picture, right? The funny chubby kid in those pictures with Dad?"

"That's right, Tess. You've seen pictures of him. And pictures of Sister Rinaldi too."

"But, Dad...." Tom was nowhere near convinced. "What's up with those other kids. Trace and Jonah? Why are they in the story? I don't understand how they fit in. And also," he continued, "that girl Trace. That's not Trace McGuff the NASCAR driver, is it?"

"Well, they only made one Trace, that's for sure," said Dad with a grin. "Yeah, that's Trace McGuff. Daniels was her last name before she got married. I haven't seen her in a few years but we still keep in touch. How d'you think we got the great seats and special tour of the garage last year at the Daytona 500?"

"And the guys in gold sunglasses? And Jonah Trotsky? And the space camp?" Tess fired off his questions quickly.

"Hey, it's all true. But I'm just getting started. This story is just about to kick into high gear." Dad pulled a camp clock out of his backpack. It was 11:45.

"Don't ... you ... dare ... stop," warned Tess, rising slowly up to a standing position on her sleeping bag. "I'm serious, keep talking and keep telling us about this space camp."

Glancing one more time at the clock, Dad sighed and leaned back against the tree stump. "Okay. Just because it's summer. And just because we're getting to the good part. And," he paused, reflexively looking over his shoulder, "just because Mom's out of town. Don't tell her I kept you up so late, okay?"

The two kids nodded earnestly.

"Okay, I'll keep going."

Tess flopped back down on her sleeping bag. She and her brother were lying on their stomachs, facing their Dad, their elbows on the ground and their chins in their hands.

"All right," Dad continued. "We came back from the Dairy Queen. The strange men in gold sunglasses gave me a mysterious invitation to some sort of camp at the Kennedy Space Center. And I said yes."

7

THE ADVENTURE BEGINS

It was a strange feeling when I walked into the dining room the next morning at breakfast. Everyone had pretty much left me alone as I packed my clothes, so I was the last one to come downstairs. The usual chaos in the dining room was replaced by a strange stillness. The usual din of talking was replaced by an eerie silence. The usual happy familiarity was replaced by an odd uncertainty.

And everybody was staring at me as I walked in.

Of course it was Taco who broke the silence. "Hey space cadet," he called, "you'll be saying 'That's one small step for a doofus ... one giant leap for doofus-kind!'" With that, it was like a dam burst. Kids started laughing and asking me questions all at once. Plates of pancakes and bacon appeared from the kitchen. This day, spare no expense, we had fried eggs too, with pitchers of Orange Tang to mark the occasion. I felt like I was king of the world, even though I had no idea what was coming next.

The time since the two astronauts left was a blur. While the two visitors from NASA were in Sister Rinaldi's office with me, the rest of the boys had kept their distance, probably waiting in the living room for the meeting to break up. But as soon as the two men left, the crowd of boys had slowly crept down the hall until we could hear them whispering loudly outside the door ... and then thumping against the door, probably as they jockeyed for a position closest to the key hole so that they might catch a stray word coming from Sister Rinaldi or me.

Not that I was saying much. There wasn't anything to say.

Sister Rinaldi kept telling me to think things over carefully, and that I didn't need to go if I didn't want to. But I had already made up my mind to go.

The two men had explained that part of the Space Program's mission was to give young people an opportunity to experience what astronauts experience. The Young Explorer's Program was part of this. They explained that there were spots for twenty kids to participate in the program, and that kids had been selected from all around the country. But one of the spots had just opened up when somebody had dropped out. A boy from Nebraska, said Major Austen.

And so I had decided to accept the invitation.

I had barely gulped down a couple pancakes and some orange juice when Sister Rinaldi came bustling in from the front hall to tell me my ride was here. There was a sudden hush again, as kids scrambled from their chairs to the front windows and into the hall to catch a glimpse of the helicopter or limousine that had arrived.

I must say I was a little disappointed to discover that NASA had sent a white van with an enormously fat driver to pick me up, instead of a helicopter or limousine, but I didn't have time to stay disappointed. Sister Rinaldi was raining a storm of information and questions onto the driver as he carried my suitcase to the van. This gave me a chance to walk behind her with Taco by my side.

"So, Mickey," said Taco, tugging on my sleeve as we walked. "If you don't send me a post card from rocket camp I'll be crushed. And you'd better bring back a space helmet or jet pack or something when you're done. Okay?"

"You got it, Taco." He looked like he might cry and all of a sudden I felt it welling up in me, so I quickly started talking. "Look, you take my bed while I'm gone. It's WAY better than yours because it's right by the window. AND you have total control over my comic books while I'm gone. AND I'm back in two weeks."

That seemed to boost Taco's spirits. The next thing I knew, the van was backing out of the driveway and the entire population of the Orlando Boys' Home was in the front yard shouting last-minute advice and waving goodbye.

Taco ran alongside and then behind the van as it picked up speed down Pickett Road. A few seconds later, the van turned the corner, and my house and Taco disappeared from sight. I sometimes think back to that moment and imagine Taco, the few moments after I lost sight of him. He probably kept running for a while, then slowed to a jog, and finally stopped in the middle of the road. Staring at the empty corner where my van had just turned.

But back then, in the van, I had other things to consider.

"Kennedy Space Center please," I said to the driver as though I was in a taxi.

"Not so fast, kid," came the reply. "We're heading to Orlando International Airport. We have another pick-up."

▲ ▼ ▲ ▼ ▲

It was barely 15 minutes from my neighborhood in Holden Heights to the airport. The driver bypassed the area clogged with Disney buses and the area for regular passenger pickup, and pulled into a small lot at the end of the terminal with some police vehicles and other white vans. On cue, a woman in a neat blue uniform opened a door and ushered out a boy with shaggy black hair carrying an overstuffed green backpack and a tall, skinny girl with a ponytail wearing a baseball cap and pulling a red bag on wheels.

They both craned their necks to see who was in the van. I decided to sit back and play it cool. The two kids climbed aboard as the driver exchanged some papers with the woman in the uniform and then quickly pulled out towards the highway.

"And then there were three," said the boy. "I'm Jonah from Chicago. This is Trace from Cleveland." The girl nodded her head as she slid into the back seat and Jonah plunked down next to me. "And that makes you...."

"Mickey from Orlando. Nice to meet you," I said.

"MICKEY from ORLANDO? You've GOT to be kidding me," said Trace. "Does Disney World know you escaped? Where's Minnie?" Her sarcastic look slowly turned to one of embarrassment. "Sorry, you probably hear that all the time."

"Not as much as you'd think," I said, trying my hardest to appear confident. "We usually let the Magic Kingdom crowd do their own thing. We kind of forget they're around after a while."

"So, what's CAMS?" I asked, quickly changing the subject and pointing to the letters on her hat.

"That's what I asked," said Jonah. "Apparently, it stands for Cleveland Area Motor Speedway. Trace and I were on the plane from Chicago together and she told me all about it. Turns out we're riding with the fastest kid on four wheels. The go-kart champion of Ohio."

"Well, the go-kart champion of the entire USA actually," said Trace. She said it with pride. But without bragging. I liked her already. "And this guy," she continued, "is some kind of Albert Einstein scientist. Seriously. Mickey, ask him what his favorite magazine is. Go ahead."

"Okay, what's your favorite magazine?" I asked.

"It's a tie between Modern Robotics Weekly and the Journal of Advanced Metal Research," said Jonah. He was totally bragging. But I found it hard not to like him too, and had to laugh as Trace rolled her eyes.

"Well then, we have a lot in common, Jonah," I said. "I love robots!"

Jonah perked up and spun in his seat to face me. "You do? Omigosh, how many have you made? Do you have trouble with the transductor circuits and the mental remote control units? Maybe we can build one together. Did you bring your supply kit?"

Oh boy, I thought. "Um, when I say I love robots, I was thinking more about Iron Man the Movie and the Doctor Decepto comic books. I did bring those along."

Jonah's blank stare told me he wasn't familiar with Doctor Decepto and his Metal Monsters of Doom. Trace jumped in to change the subject. "So," she asked, "what's your specialty, Mickey from Orlando?"

I paused and wondered what to say. I had never thought of myself as having a specialty before. I was just good at being a kid. "Well," I said, "I'm the best pitcher on our Little League baseball team, at least now that Hudson Hooper moved away. I'm a huge fan of the Miami Dolphins. HUGE. Hate the Tampa Bay Buccaneers, love the fish." No response. "And I can eat more pizza at a single sitting than anybody else in my house, even Big Linus."

I could tell I was losing them.

"Come on, where's the love?" I asked. "I might be skinny but I can really eat a ton. You guys never had a pizza eating contest? You've got to follow the rules: if you don't eat the whole piece, crust and all, you don't get credit for the piece."

They both shook their heads.

"Well, I tell you what," I said, undeterred. "We'll have a pizza eating contest sometime before this camp is over, and I'll show you who's the king."

Jonah's eyes perked up again. "Camp?" he said with a smile. "Is that what you think we're going to? Camp?"

"Um ... yeah. Young Explorers Camp? Kennedy Space Center? Didn't they tell you?" I said.

"Oh, they told me all right," said Jonah. He glanced secretively up at the driver, who didn't seem to be paying us the slightest bit of attention. Even so, Jonah lowered his voice. "But do you think you can believe everything they tell you?"

"Oh, no. Here he goes again. I got this whole theory on the plane, all the way over Tennessee and Georgia, I think it was," said Trace, rolling her eyes for a second time. "Where's your proof, Jonah?"

"Go ahead," said Jonah, completely unfazed by Trace's doubt. "Make fun. But if you think we're here for a little kids' camp, then you're about as smart as the donut I ate for breakfast. Listen," said Jonah, lowering his voice to a whisper and glancing up at the driver again as he leaned closer to me. "You probably haven't been paying attention to the special science magazines like I have, and the recent rumors about NASA's lunar project? Mysterious launches, unexplained missions? Well, if you have been reading those articles ... like me ... then you'll know that NASA is having some serious problems. Something is going wrong."

"Fine," I said. "Maybe that's true. But what makes you think that has anything to do with us?"

"Well," admitted Jonah, "that part I can't figure out. It just seems like the space program should be awfully busy with other things, rather than worrying about a space camp right now. It seems like a funny time to send a couple top astronauts out to round up kids from across America, doesn't it? And that's another thing. Isn't this an odd time for a camp? Don't they normally do camps in the summer?"

I hadn't really thought about that. It was the end of October, right in the middle of school.

"And *another* thing," said Jonah. He was on a roll. "This whole invitation came out of the blue. Just like Trace, I just heard about this last week. They told me they were inviting me late because some kid from Nebraska dropped and there was an open spot. How about you, when did they invite you?"

"Um. Like, yesterday," I admitted. "But wait, they told ME that I got the Nebraska kid's spot!"

Even Trace looked surprised now. "That's weird. They told me I got the last spot. But it was a kid from Kansas who dropped out."

Jonah let out a low whistle, and I didn't have an answer.

But to be honest, it didn't bother me in the slightest. I was just excited to be off on an adventure. "Nebraska, Kansas, whatever," I cut in. "I just think this sounds awesome, whatever it's called and why-ever they're doing it."

Jonah sank back into his seat with a sigh and our conversation turned to our homes, our schools and then to Trace's recent go-kart victory. She was telling us about her thrilling pass on the final lap when she realized we were no longer listening and her voice faded away .... She realized Jonah and I were craning our necks to stare out the front window.

The van was heading due east and had passed over a long causeway over water. The expanse of land in front of us was hard baked and treeless, with clumps of shrubs and clumps of buildings. Visible now, in the distance, were several hulking towers rising up into the hazy sky. I knew right away what they were. They weren't radio or TV towers. We were looking at the launch pad towers at Cape Canaveral.

We were looking at the home base of the American space program.

We passed under a large sign that said "Welcome to the Kennedy Space Center at Cape Canaveral." A guard waved us through. We were travelling slowly now. A line of cars and RVs clogged the road leading to a large parking lot and a shiny visitors' center.

Our van turned out of traffic, however, taking a small, unmarked road to the right, and headed for a low one-story building at the edge of a tall fence. I realized it was actually two fences, about ten feet apart. And both had barbed wire on the top. As the van slowed to approach the gate, the driver said over his shoulder "Welcome to Kennedy. That's the public area over on the left. We're heading into the restricted area. Not many people get to go through this fence."

"I think I've died and gone to heaven. This is awesome," said Jonah.

"I think I've died and gone to Weird-issippi. This is bizarre," said Trace.

They both looked at me for the deciding vote.

"Give me a little more time," I said. "I'm on the fence."

As the van rolled forward, Jonah said "too late now, Mickey from Orlando. We're THROUGH the fence. And Trace ... I have a feeling this is going to get even weirder before it's all over."

8

THE SECRETS OF THE
SPACE PROGRAM

Once inside the gate we pulled into a small parking lot on the other side of the guard building. A tall woman in a white shirt and pants was waiting for us. She emerged from the shade of a palm tree when she saw us and took a few quick steps forward. She pulled open the door while the van was still rolling and hopped skillfully into the passenger seat as the driver hit the gas again and pulled back out onto the road without stopping. Black letters on a shiny white road sign spelled out *Apollo Drive*.

"Trace, Mickey, Jonah," she said as she nodded at each of us, "welcome to Kennedy. I'm Amanda Collins, and you can call me Amanda. I'm assigned to the Moon Project Task Force, and I'll be spending a lot of time with you three, and the others, for the next few weeks."

"The others?" Jonah interjected. I was beginning to understand that Jonah was never afraid to speak up.

"Yes, the other kids in the program. 17 others, 20 total." Amanda saw that Jonah was about to interrupt again so she held up a hand making a quick "stop" sign. "Now wait, wait, I know you all have a ton of questions.... Or at least YOU do, Jonah. You'll get a chance to ask them very soon. Just..." Amanda pushed her hand forward again as Jonah opened his mouth. Jonah sank back in his seat, almost as though she had used some magical force to propel him backwards, "...relax. And let me tell you about where you are."

I turned my attention back to the windows of the van as we rolled along Apollo Drive. Bushes and short trees a little taller than the van were growing on either side of the road, but they soon gave way to shorter, stubby bushes, giving us a better view of the buildings that scattered the area. "This is the John F. Kennedy Space Center at Cape Canaveral. There are almost fifteen thousand employees here, all working together on the space program."

"There are engineers who help design and maintain the rockets, the landing vehicles and other space craft. There are specialists who run our computer and communications systems, and thousands of others who keep everything else going. We're like a small city. And of course, there are the astronauts who live here and train in the weeks leading up to their missions."

"We're heading towards the...." Her words were suddenly drowned out by a thunderous rumble of sound. My head quickly spun left, right and up to see what was making the noise. I saw a flash of grey out the left window quickly disappear over the roof and then reappear on the right side of the van. It was a plane … a jet plane … flying extremely low. It must have been some kind of air force fighter jet.

"And how could I forget," said Amanda after the rumble had died down. "We also have an airport. The Cape Canaveral Air Force Station."

"Whoa. Now THAT plane was fast. And I know fast," said Trace, awe-struck and impressed.

"Well, you'll get used to those. Most of the astronauts come from the Air Force, and they like to show off by flying their toys. Anyway," Amanda continued, "NASA's other major facility is the Johnson Space Center in Texas. A lot of our design and training takes place there. But this," she waved out the window, "is where the action happens. Kennedy is where the rockets are launched. All our missions start from here … but they don't end here. As you know, a command module carrying the astronauts reenters the earth's atmosphere and then is slowed down with huge parachutes before splashing down in the ocean."

"Some day we'll have a rocket that can return to dry land, just like an airplane. Our scientists are working on an exciting new program called the 'Space Shuttle.' It looks more like an airplane than a rocket, and will land on a regular runway rather than splashing down in the ocean."

"I'll believe THAT when I see it," Jonah snorted, sarcastically.

"Some day soon, you'll see," said Amanda, smiling. We pulled up to a group of one-story buildings. Painted white rocks lined the circular drive way in front of the first building, and there was a flagpole with a large American flag. They obviously watered the grass here, because the lawn between the buildings was smooth and green as a golf course. There were flowers lining some of the pathways.

"Welcome to the Astronaut Center. Camp Alpha, we call it. It has classrooms, a cafeteria, sleeping quarters, a gym, and a swimming pool. You will be calling it home for the next few weeks. You three are the last ones to arrive, but don't worry, you haven't missed much. Follow me. It's time to meet the other kids here. Your fellow campers."

Amanda sprang out of the van, again before it had stopped. She told us to leave our bags ... those would be taken where they needed to go ... and motioned for us to follow her.

She led us down a hall, then stopped at an open door and pointed inside, smiling. Jonah walked in first and stopped short so that I crashed into his back. It looked like a class room, with several rows of chairs and tables facing a chalk board. The front rows were filled with kids, each of them wearing a dark blue jump suit. It looked a little like the one my friend Mackie wore at the Sunoco gas station near the Dairy Queen, except without the stains from grease and last week's burrito. Each jumpsuit had a small American flag on each arm. A glittering "USA" patch sewn onto the left side in the front. And a NASA patch with an eagle on the right side.

I glanced down at my green striped shorts and cartoon T-Shirt that said "Dirt Bike Racer." Nice choice, Mickey, I thought to myself. I crossed my arms and shuffled into the room.

The other kids stared at us and there were a few whispers as we came in. Then they quickly swiveled to face forward as Amanda walked briskly to the front of the room. Jonah, Trace and I scooted quickly into three empty seats in the third row.

I noticed there were five men standing at the front, behind a large table. All five had short military-style buzz cut hair. Each was wearing a blue jumpsuit just like the campers. And they were all wearing those incredibly cool gold sunglasses. One of them had a toothpick hanging out of his mouth and gave me a scowl, then sighed and checked his watch. He obviously wanted to be somewhere else.

"Welcome to Young Astronaut Academy," announced Amanda in an official tone.

Jonah leaned towards me and whispered "Young Astronaut Academy? Young Explorers' Academy? Astronaut Adventure Camp? See, they can't even keep the name of this camp straight! Very fishy. Am I right, am I right?"

Boy, that kid was suspicious about everything.

More men and women in uniforms were filtering into the back of the room, and now filled every seat behind the kids in the first three rows.

"First of all, congratulations. There are about 3 million 5th graders in America. NASA could have invited any one of them. But they picked 20. They picked you. You're lucky to be here, and we're lucky to have you."

"This week will be full of surprises, just like the space program," Amanda continued. "We will be treating you like real astronauts. You will sleep where they sleep and eat where they eat. You will receive some of the training they receive and take the tests that they take. There are three main parts of training for our astronauts: physical, technical and mental. And you will receive all three."

"We want you to feel like real astronauts. We want you to follow our rules, but we also want you to be curious. We want you to ask questions. We want you to...."

As Amanda kept talking, I noticed that Jonah's hand was up in the air. Trace noticed too and turned to look at him. The table on our left noticed too and started staring at him. Finally Amanda noticed what we had noticed and stopped talking.

"Okay, Jonah, shoot," she said.

"You meant what you said about being curious and asking questions?"

"Absolutely Jonah, go ahead."

"Can you discuss the problems faced by the recent lunar missions?" asked Jonah. "It was the third mission in one year and it seemed like there was a big hurry to get it up there. The newspapers had almost no information about the purpose of the mission. NASA said the mission was just collecting rock samples. But I think there is something else going on. Can you explain?" Jonah looked at Amanda intently. I shot a look sideways at Trace, who rolled her eyes at Jonah for the fifth time today. We were afraid our new friend might be a little crazy.

"Well…." Amanda looked at her feet. "That's a very good question, and I think we will be discussing the recent missions at some point during your camp experience. You see, it's true, there was a … well … a small, you know … a problem that …." Amanda Collins looked very relieved when she was interrupted by a voice from the back of the room. The voice wasn't loud, but it was strong and deep and southern and filled the room. Everyone in the room swiveled back to face the speaker.

"Some people might call it a problem. But for the space program, it's a CHALLENGE. Do you understand what I'm saying?" A tall man with piercing blue eyes and wearing a dark blue uniform stood leaning against the open doorway.

His question was hanging over the room, as he scanned the kids in the front three rows. None of us answered. The man turned to the five adults in the front of the room. "Do YOU understand what I'm saying?"

"Yes, sir," came the response from the adults, speaking as one.

"Good," said the man as he strolled forward. "Our newcomers may not understand it now. But you will all appreciate and understand, before too long, that we don't see things as PROBLEMS here. We see them as CHALLENGES that have to be overcome." He spoke slowly, and gave certain words extra punch for emphasis.

"I'm Director Marshall. I'm in charge here. This is my base. I run the United States Space Program. I'm responsible for the success of our missions and the safety of our astronauts. I'm responsible for everything that goes on HERE," he pointed around the room, "and up THERE," he gestured to the ceiling and beyond. "I'm responsible for every brilliant idea and SUCCESS. And I'm responsible for every bad mistake and FAILURE."

"And I hope you'll all fall into the first category, and not the second," he said, mumbling the last few words. Then he continued firmly, "the men standing behind me are astronauts who will be leading the next expedition to the moon. This is Team Varsity, led by Commander Riker."

The man with the toothpick took a half step forward and nodded. He still looked sour.

"And now, young..." Director Marshall glanced down at a piece of paper in his left hand, "...Jonah Trotsky, I will address your question."

Director Marshall told us about the history of missions to the moon ... the first missions that simply got close and took pictures of the moon ... the ones that orbited the moon ... the first mission to actually land astronauts on the moon in 1969 ... and other trips to the moon in the early 1970s to do experiments and to gather moon rocks. Then, he told us about how, on one trip, the crew had discovered a very special, highly magnetic metal called Pleurinium. It was far more powerful than the strongest magnet found on Earth. He told us about the mining center that had been built last year to dig for the special rock.

And he told us that nothing about the Pleurinium and the special mining center was in the newspapers.

It had all been kept secret.

The public had been told that the recent trips to the moon had been to make maps and gather samples of moon dust.

I looked over at Jonah. His mouth was hanging open and his eyes, wide open already, looked like they were getting bigger and bigger with every word by Director Marshall.

"But now, here's where it gets interesting," said Director Marshall. At that point, there was a crash to my right side as Jonah fell straight out of his chair. I think Jonah had been listening so hard that he forgot … well, as crazy as it sounds … I think he forgot how to sit. He scrambled back up into his seat, having somehow managed to close his mouth. The Director raised one eyebrow and seemed about to smile before he continued.

"As I said, the interesting part. After the first large load of Pleurinium was pulled to the surface, something happened. Our astronauts got sick, and fast. We had to evacuate the first group of astronauts within one day. We sent another group a month later and the same thing happened. We sent a third group three months later and the same thing happened again. Each time, they started getting sick only a few hours after arriving. After about twelve hours, some of them couldn't stand up any more. After eighteen, we had to evacuate them, every time. Nobody has been able to stay there for even one day."

"I bet I know what causes the illness," Jonah interrupted. "It must be that highly magnetic rock. The Pleurinium. It's the Pleurinium, isn't it?"

All eyes were on Jonah, who was dangerously leaning forward in his chair again.

Director Marshall raised his eyebrows. "Good guess, Jonah. That's what our scientists guessed also. And it's more than a guess. They have proved it by bringing some of that special rock back to the laboratory and watching how people react to it. We now know that it's the Pleurinium that causes the strange illness. Something about its extra strong magnetic force. And the moon base was built right on top of a huge deposit of Pleurinium, the largest one on the moon."

"Our top scientists and doctors ...." At this point, Director Marshall paused and waived at a row of women and men in white coats standing in the back of the room. Marshall frowned and continued, sounding frustrated. "At least, people TELL ME they're best scientists and doctors we could find. They have been trying to figure out why the Pleurinium affects our astronauts this way ... and how to prevent it ... and how to send astronauts back to the moon base without having them get sick. Any luck?"

We all turned to look back at the row of doctors and scientists who were now shuffling nervously from one foot to the other. One of them mumbled something that sounded like "not yet."

"Well," barked the Director, "KEEP WORKING! We're kind of in a hurry!" He waved his hands like you do when you shoo a cat, and the adults in white coats scurried out of the room.

"So anyway," the Director continued. "Last month we sent a final mission to shut down the facility and turn off the nuclear reactor that powers the mining station. We sent five of our best, Commander Riker led the team, along with Jackson, Austen, Reimann and Strider. They ... they ran into some unexpected challenges. With nobody there to keep things running right, some of the machinery had started to fail."

He paused. "Commander Riker's team was unable to turn off the nuclear reactor that generates power for the moon base. Nuclear reactors can create a lot of energy if they're working right. But if they're not working right, you'd better watch out. Our moon base reactor is broken and is now in danger of exploding, which would shower the moon with dangerous, radioactive material. If you know anything about dangerous, radioactive material, you know that's not a good thing."

There was a stunned silence in the room.

None of us could believe what we were hearing. Especially me.

Just one day ago at this time, I had been sneaking out of the Boys' House to get ice cream with Taco and Big Linus. The biggest secret I knew was the location of my special stash of comic books, stored under a squeaky floor board in the northeast corner of our attic. And now, less than a day later, I was learning the secrets of the U.S. space program.

Director Marshall was looking around the room again, his eyes passing over each one of us in the first three rows. Finally, he broke the silence.

"Again, this is a CHALLENGE. Not a PROBLEM. We are working hard on the next mission. The next mission will get it RIGHT. The next mission will SAVE THE MOON."

"Darn right we will," barked Commander Riker, causing Director Marshall to jump a little. "Team Varsity is working 24-7 on the preparations. 24 hours a day, 7 days a week. We don't take a break. We don't sleep. We're ready to go as soon as you say the word, sir!"

"Good man." Director Marshall looked a little uneasy, faced by Commander Riker's intensity. "You ... um ... you have my permission to sleep once in a while, though."

Riker didn't crack a smile. He just stared straight forward. The only thing moving was the toothpick, which he jiggled between his front teeth.

9

SOME KIND OF SUPERCAMPER

Amanda led us out of the main building into a grassy courtyard with a white cement pathway cutting diagonally across the grass in an X pattern. In the middle of the X was a paved circle surrounded by stone benches. And in the middle of the paved circle stood a huge flag pole with an enormous American flag flapping at the top. We walked across the X towards another two-story building that looked a lot like the first one. Amanda explained that this was the training dormitory, where astronaut candidates lived during their training. We would have the "East Wing" all to ourselves.

She showed us to a large common room area with tables and chairs, a ping pong table and a big TV. "Girls down the left hallway, boys down the right," said Amanda as she clipped quickly into the room. "The bags you brought with you are already in your room. You won't be needing those, though. In your rooms you'll find your camp supplies: your uniforms, your books, everything you'll need for the next week."

Jonah and I were assigned to share a room at the end of the hall. It was a little smaller than my room at home, but everything was spotless and shiny. I saw that the neatly made bed was stacked with piles of clothes.

We raced over to our beds. It was like a birthday or Christmas, except all the presents were opened. Just like my birthday, there were new socks and underpants. But next to those were two dark blue astronaut jumpsuits. And grey shorts and grey T-shirts with the NASA badge on the front. And baseball hats. One said "Kennedy Space Center," and another that had the letters "NASA" underneath a rocket that was arching up, up and away.

I glanced over and saw that Jonah had moved right past the items on the bed and was flipping through the items on his desk. There were stacks of notebooks and pens and a tower of thick, heavy books.

I picked up one of the heavy books. It looked promising. There was an awesome full-color photo on the front showing a gleaming black and white rocket blasting off, shooting yellow flame and white clouds out of the bottom. The inside of the book did not live up to the promise. There was page after page of tiny text, with confusing diagrams of machinery – probably the inside of the rocket engine. It looked absolutely, completely, impossibly complicated.

I put down the book and turned back to the bed. Shoes. A small bag of bathroom supplies. And then, sitting on the brown blanket next to the hats, was a pair of sunglasses. Just like the ones worn by the two recruiters. Gold.

"Jonah," I said, "put down that book. Look what we GOT!" I slipped the sunglasses on and squared to face the mirror. Totally cool.

"Mmmm-Hmmm." Jonah glanced up from his book. His eyes were on me, but his mind was obviously still deep within the book's pages. "Nice."

"*Nice?* Is that all you can say?" I looked at the mirror and saw myself, wearing gold sunglasses, reflected in the lenses of the sunglasses. As I said, totally cool.

"Okay Mr. Italian-Supercool-Model-Fashion-Boy," laughed Jonah. "Your sunglasses go well with your Dirt Bike Racer T-shirt."

Gah! I grabbed my astronaut jumpsuit and started to climb in, covering up my former self.

"You know why those sunglasses are gold, don't you? And why the helmet visors used by astronauts in space are gold?" asked Jonah, watching me fumble with the snaps on my jumpsuit.

"Because gold is totally cool and better than silver, and WAY better than bronze," I said quickly, stating the obvious. "Don't you watch the Olympics?"

"Um, not exactly, Mick. It's all about protection. They use real gold on the astronauts' visors to block the most harmful of the infra-red rays coming from the sun. It just turns out that gold does that better than just about anything else. These sunglasses probably have a micro-thin layer of gold on them, too."

"Man, how do you get so smart?" I asked. "You're a walking library. You must have one heck of a science teacher!"

"Science class? Well, that helps. But I read the really cool stuff outside of school. I found out about how the space program uses gold in my International Journal of Advanced Science Research magazine. You should really check it out. It's not as complicated as it sounds. It's even got a comic strip section."

"Now you're talking," I said.

"Yeah," continued Jonah, chuckling, "the comic strip stars this subatomic particle named Zippy. He has adventures with other subatomic particles and different types of energy and electromagnetic forces. His best friend is a charm quark named Ray. In one episode, they surf this cosmic wave through the outer galaxy, and then suddenly they get bombarded by electrons...."

"Dude," I interrupted. "You're frightening me. I feel like you're actually sucking intelligence out of my head to feed your giant brain." I shook my head. "You're reading comics about complicated science. Last Sunday morning, I had to ask Sister Rinaldi to explain the Charlie Brown comic strip to me."

▲ ▼ ▲ ▼ ▲

Jonah and I were still putting away our new stuff when I heard a voice in the doorway behind us. "Come on, y'all, it's lunch time. Ya hungry? And hot dang, will you take your sunglasses off indoors? You're fixin' to walk into a wall with those on. Save 'em for the sun, friend."

A tall boy with dark hair and freckles had leaned into our room from the hallway. He had the thickest, heaviest southern accent I had ever heard.

"Yeah sure," I said as I quickly took off my glasses and set them carefully on my dresser. "By the way, where's lunch?"

But he had already turned and was sauntering down the hallway. "Just hurry up," his voice floated back to us. "And follow your ears to the noise."

Jonah threw on his jumpsuit and we tore out of our room into the hallway. We heard the chatter of boys' and girls' voices coming from the direction of the common room, and when we got there we followed the stragglers down the main hallway to the stairs and then into the cafeteria.

We caught up with the tall boy with freckles who introduced himself as Dale from Texas. And then introduced us to his friend from Texas, whose name was also Dale.

"Dale and Dale? Two Dales?" I asked.

They both laughed. "Nah," said the tall one. "I'm Dale. He's DALE."

I looked at Jonah, who seemed just as confused as me.

"Come on," the tall boy drawled. "You boys from the north got the same ears they give out in Texas. I'm Dale, D-A-L-E. This here's Dell, D-E-L-L. Big difference, you hear?"

The two boys from Texas grinned broadly at us. I got the feeling they enjoyed introducing themselves to people.

I figured out pretty soon that everybody just called them "The Texans," so their exact names didn't matter anyway.

The Texans led us over to the lunch line where we grabbed a tray and silverware. The cafeteria was filled with a mix kids and adults. Some adults were wearing astronauts' jumpsuits, others were dressed in dark pants and white shirts, and a few were wearing military uniforms. As we walked through the line, the chefs behind the counter slid plates of cheeseburgers, chicken sandwiches and grilled cheeses into rows, along with paper containers of fries, bowls of canned fruit and Jell-O. There was also a salad bar and machines where you could fill up milk and soda. I grabbed two cheeseburgers, a plate of fries and a shiny red apple.

After I had poured out two glasses of milk, I scanned the room and saw Trace waving from a table by the windows. She was sitting with three other girls, but there was still room for me along with Jonah and the Texans. Trace introduced us to her roommate Katherine Obando from Cupertino, California.

"Boys, you'll like Katherine," said Trace in her excited, eighty-mile-per-hour way of talking. "She says, call her Kat. You won't believe this. She actually has her own computer. And she brought it with her."

I gasped. "No … way. An entire computer? Did you drive it here in a truck or something?"

"No, silly," said Kat, a girl with small features and a huge bloom of tangled, frizzy brown hair. "Come on, it's 1977. Computers are small as can be now. My whole computer fits into a suitcase."

"Yeah, it comes in a suitcase! It's cute," Trace explained. "It's called a … what is it… a Plum?"

"An Apple, the Apple One," said Kat. "It's incredible. My neighbors in California are trying to start a company to sell them, and the Apple One is their first computer. My dad says they'll never make a dime, but he doesn't know anything. I think they'll be famous one day. I can write programs on it. It's incredible what you can do with a computer."

"I don't see that thang catchin' on," said one of the Texans, shaking his head. "Why would ordinary folk want one?"

"You'd be surprised," said Kat quietly. "Do you like

baseball?"

"Well, heck yeah. My daddy and I drive to Dallas every summer to watch the Rangers play. They're going to win the World Series next year, you mark my words."

Kat shook her head and frowned. "Sounds like you could use a computer. See, it's like this. My mom loves baseball, so I wrote a program for her that will predict the winners in baseball games. I enter all of the information I can get about the players: their batting averages, how they hit against left-handed pitchers and right-handed pitchers, how they play in the daytime and at night, how they play at home and away, how they play at the beginning of the season or the end of the season. If it's a number, I put it into the computer program. Then you tell the computer who is playing and…."

"And it tells you who's going to win the game!?" I gasped.

"Well, kind of," continued Kat. "It doesn't know for sure. But it's usually right. And I hate to break it to you Dale or Dell or whichever Texan you are, but I don't think the Rangers have much of a chance next year, unless they replace their entire team."

"Awww, come on," yelled the Texan. "That's a bunch of cow pookie if I ever heard it. You're telling me your computer can predict the future?"

Kat blinked and seemed to shrink a little bit, against the force of the larger boy's yelling.

"Hey, Tex, calm down," Jonah jumped in. "She didn't say anything about predicting the future. But she said it can help you make sense of the numbers and it can make a pretty good guess."

The Texan saw Kat hang her head and quickly apologized. "Pardon me for raisin' my voice, ma'am. Mighty unkind of me.

I didn't mean any disrespect to you, or to your Pineapple computer."

"All I'm sayin'," he continued, "is that I'll do just fine without a computer in my life." He proceeded to entertain us with stories of his ranch back home. He and the other Texan told stories that were more and more incredible. How they would rope cattle and drive off wolves and ride their horses with the buffalo herds under moonlit skies. I started to suspect that both of them lived in a regular neighborhood in the suburbs and went to a regular school. But I didn't want to say anything because their stories were so entertaining.

I was just finishing my dry, stiff cheeseburger when I saw Trace and Jonah sit up straighter, looking at someone approaching the table behind me. As I turned, I saw a tall boy with short, buzz-cut brown hair. He pulled up a chair, spun it around and sat down on it back-to-front at the end of the table. He smiled broadly as he grabbed a French fry off my plate and popped it into his mouth.

"So, it's the new kids," he said, chewing with his mouth open. "Hi, new kids. Welcome to Kennedy. You must be overwhelmed. Totally confused." He dipped his head so he could see Jonah's eyes. "Right, new kid with messy brown hair?"

Although his words were friendly enough, they were as fake as a cardboard penny.

He was wearing the collar of his jumpsuit turned up in a cool way. I noticed he had the letters "Lance M." stitched onto his uniform under his space program patch. This guy thought he was some kind of Supercamper.

"I'm going to give you the lay of the land here," said Lance M. "You know, explain who's who. What's what. Which end is up. You're playing catch-up, you know?"

"You see that kid with the blond hair sitting against the wall?" He gestured towards a big kid across the room, who was leaning back casually with his feet on the table, laughing loudly at something. "That's Brad Stimple. Sitting next to him is Mandy Rockwell. Maybe you've heard of her father, Senator Rockwell from Tennessee? The three of us have been here training for three weeks. Pretty intense stuff."

He paused for a moment to let that part sink in before continuing, in a lazy tone of voice. "I think it's great they invited you other kids to come along. You know, to watch and learn. But let me give you a little advice, okay new kids? Stay out of our way. There's some important business happening here, and we can't let you ... the space campers, that is ... mess things up. I know you get it," he said, nodding at me. "You're a smart kid, right?" As he said the last part, he casually reached for another one of my fries.

But I was too quick. I slid my tray quickly to the left so that the boy's hand missed my fries and landed in a puddle of ketchup.

"Easy old-timer," I said. If I had learned one thing at the Boys' Home, it was how to protect my food. "I guess you're still figuring things out too. These are MY fries. But you can get your own up there. For free. Pretty good deal." I tipped my head toward the food counter and gave him my best ear-to-ear grin.

His eyes narrowed for just a second before he returned my grin with one of his own. "Nah, keep your fries, Mickey Price from the mean streets of Orlando." I must have looked surprised that he knew my name because he gave a satisfied smile. "And Trace Daniels, the bumper car champ. And Jonah

74

Trotsky, the mad scientist. And, frizzy haired computer girl and two guys from Texas whose names I can't be bothered to learn. No offense, y'all. Nice to meet you. I'm Lance, in case you didn't know that already."

With that, he spun around and strolled back towards the table where Stimple and Rockwell were telling jokes.

One of the Texans was the first to speak. "That boy's got a bad attitude as big as the Texas sky. When I see a horse with a bad attitude like that, I just keep out of its way. Same for him. Best just to let him run wild." The other Texan nodded his head in agreement.

Trace was fuming. "Bumper car champ? Who does he think he is? Called me a BUMPER car champ!!? GAH!!"

"Easy Trace," I said. "He might be a jerk, but don't turn him into an enemy. It's only our first day. Keep your cool."

I wasn't convinced by my own words, though. I didn't like Lance M. the Supercamper either.

10

AN UNPLANNED ENCOUNTER
WITH CHIHUAHUAS

It sounded like a door-bell. Bling, blong. Pause. Bling, blong. Pause. Bling, blong. I blinked and noticed that the overhead lights in the dormitory room had clicked on automatically. I guess this was their way of waking us up.

They were starting us early on the first morning of space camp. There was only the faintest glimmer of dawn in the sky outside our bedroom window.

Back at home, I usually woke up to the sound of Taco's voice. Taco was the first one to fall asleep at night, sometimes right in the middle of things while we were all watching TV, or curled up on a couch in our common room while the rest of us were playing a game. And he was ALWAYS the first one to wake up. He usually woke me up next, just by talking at me until I finally gave in and talked back.

Sometimes I'd pretend I was asleep as he kept talking. And he'd say things that were more and more ridiculous, just to get me to admit I was awake.

One time, it couldn't have been much past 6:00 in the morning, I counted how many times he said my name. Seventy two. I managed to lie perfectly still and not move a muscle as he said "Mickey, Mickey, Mickey" seventy two times. He must have known I was awake, because Mickey fifty through Mickey seventy-two were pretty loud.

But instead of saying Mickey a seventy-third time, he started to tell a tall tale about how the Cyprus tree outside our window had become haunted during the night and had tried to reach in through the window and attack me and drag me out to my doom.

"It was stealthy at first," Taco had said, almost in a whisper. "Sliiiiiidin' the window open and streeeeeetchin' across the room in the pale moonlight. That's when I heard it, with its leaves going flick flick flick as they slid over the windowsill. Then I realized the eeeeeevil tree was goin' after you, Mickey. Slowly, steadily across the floor towards your bed. So I grabbed my TRUSTY AXE and started attacking that creeping branch."

I lay still, trying to suppress a giggle, trying to keep my breathing normal. Taco continued.

"I cut the sucker right down the middle, but it kept coming. The more I cut, the faster it moved. And then came a second branch. And then a third. Like an unstoppable army of snakes, sliiiiiidin' in through the window."

"So there I was, screamin' my head off, whackin' at the branches with this huge axe as it tried to grab you and pull you out the window. It had you around the ankle, Mickey, but I finally distracted it, and it turned to attack me. I was backed up into the corner. My axe was useless against its mighty force. So I grabbed my TRUSTY CHAINSAW!!!"

This wasn't easy. I refused to give in, but it was almost impossible to keep from cracking up.

"Brrr-AWWW, gug-guh-guh-guh. Brrr-AWWW, guh-guh-guh-guh," Taco had screamed at the top of his lungs. "I was loppin' off branches left and right. But the tree kept comin'. Brrr-AWWW. You kept sleeping but I was hard at work. Wood chips and sawdust were flyin' everywhere. Branches and leaves all over the place. I was covered with sap. Oh, the sap, the horrible sap! The tree was ... it was ... and ... oh geez, come on Mickey. Will you wake up already?"

Right then, I had jumped out of bed. "YES!! I win!! You gave up, you stopped your story!! Victory!!" I danced around the room. "Victory is mine!!"

Taco was grinning from ear to ear. "No, Mick. I won. Look who's out of bed."

I realized I had a smile on my face, lying in a strange bed a hundred miles away from Orlando as a chime that sounded like a doorbell kept ringing over and over and over. I sighed. But then my mind quickly returned to reality and I was jolted by curiosity.

What on earth was going to happen at space camp today?

Jonah and I jumped from our beds at the same time, just as the chiming stopped. I heard voices in the hallway and a piece of paper came sliding under our door.

GOOD MORNING CAMPERS
Monday, October 23, 1977
Kennedy Young Astronauts' Adventure Academy
Day One Schedule

6:30AM Wake up
Shower – Breakfast
8:00AM Morning Classroom Time – Meeting Room B
10:00AM Flight Simulator
12:00PM Lunch
1:00PM Games and Free Time
3:00PM Swimming Pool
5:00PM Dinner
6:00PM Evening Classroom Time – Meeting Room B
9:00PM Lights Out

"There you go, Jonah," I said with a grin. "Are you satisfied now? This looks like an official camp schedule to me. All perfectly innocent. Nothing sneaky, no mystery. Just a plain old fashioned camp. Right?"

Jonah scowled at me. Maybe he wasn't a morning person.

▲ ▼ ▲ ▼ ▲

After a breakfast of waffles and eggs and grapefruit we all reported to Meeting Room B to start our training.

We had assigned seats. On my left was Mandy Rockwell,

one of the supercampers. She turned her back on me as soon as I sat down and continued talking to the boy on the other side of her, bragging about how she and Lance had gone on a special tour of the local Air Force base the day before. The empty seat to my right was soon filled by Kat Obando. I asked her a few more questions about her prized computer. We didn't have much time to talk, however, because the class started as soon as everyone had found their seats.

The training started with a movie about the history of the space program. It described how scientists had developed rockets with longer and longer ranges. It explained how the scientists eventually figured out how to send rockets up out of the earth's atmosphere ... and then back down again. There were lots of fiery crashes back then, so the rockets didn't have people in them.

The first animal successfully launched into space was a monkey named Ziggy 2.

They didn't explain what happened to Ziggy 1, but I could guess.

They launched mice. Dogs. More monkeys. Guinea pigs. Frogs. A cat named Felix. And then, finally, a human.

After the movie, the lights came back on and we blinked at each other under the bright overhead lights. Team Varsity was lined up along the side wall. They must have entered while the movie was playing. Commander Riker and the other four members were standing at attention as they were reintroduced by Amanda.

"We're lucky to have our best astronauts here for a few minutes this morning, campers," said Amanda. "You are among the first to hear this. It hasn't been announced yet to the newspapers. Team Varsity is in their final week of preparation before they leave on their important mission. The launch is scheduled for next week. Next Monday morning."

Commander Riker puffed out his chest as a ripple of excitement spread through the classroom.

"Each member of Team Varsity has a special job in the mission," continued Amanda. "There are five seats in the launch vehicle. And five very special jobs." She explained how Riker was the Flight Commander and Pilot. He was the leader, the quarterback, the astronaut in charge. Number two on the team was the Co-Pilot and sat next to the Flight Commander in the front row. The other three sat in the back row of the command module. The third crew member was the Navigator who kept close track of the rocket's location and direction and maps, basically making sure the space craft stayed on course and didn't end up flying into the sun. The fourth astronaut was the Computer Engineer, and kept track of the complicated computer programs and onboard electronics.

"And number five, that's me," said a short, smiley man who seemed a little plump for an astronaut. "I'm pretty much just a passenger during the flight. But if we encounter anything strange or unexplained, that's where I come in. I'm Grover Reimann, the Mission Scientist. And I'm going to make sure we turn off that nuclear reactor if it's the last thing I do!"

The astronaut to Reimann's left gave him a high five.

Riker cleared his throat with a sharp "A-HEM," and both men jumped to attention. They quickly replaced their grins with stern scowls to match Riker's.

Amanda asked us to stand up and give them all a big round of applause. Team Varsity left the room as we clapped, off to their next important training destination. Reimann paused in the doorway, allowing his fellow astronauts to move down the hall. The smile returned to his face, and he raised his hands in the air triumphantly. Our applause grew, and several kids added whoops above the clapping.

Reimann leaned back inside and said uncertainly, "hey anyone want to do a cheer? Let's go NASA? Gimme an N?"

"ENNNN!" came the response.

"Gimme an A," he yelled, louder now, slapping his hands together above his head and making the shape of an A.

"AYYYYY!" we roared back.

"GI …. MMEE … AN … S!" He was really getting into it now, for some reason flapping his arms like a chicken.

"ESSSSSS!" we screamed, so loud that the light bulbs rattled.

"GI … MMEE … AN …." Suddenly, his cheer was cut short. A large hand clamped down on Reimann's shoulder and yanked him backwards into the hall.

Commander Riker was not amused.

▲ ▼ ▲ ▼ ▲

After two more speakers, we had a snack break of Fig Newtons and Orange Tang. Amanda then led us to a building across the courtyard and into a large room filled with computer equipment and monitors. Once we had all filed in, a bear-like man with big shoulders and a bald head started addressing our group.

"I'm Pete Looper, Mission Communications Director here at NASA. I'm the voice in the astronauts' ear during the mission. Their link to earth. I pass along important instructions, but most of all, I just try to keep everyone cool and calm. This Flight Simulator is a key part of the training for the astronauts. The simulator is built to look exactly like the cockpit area of the command module. The same seat. The same controls. The same kind of radio. We want to make it as similar as possible."

"The flight simulator is attached to a giant computer. It's like a big, complicated video game. You move the controls in the flight simulator and your capsule responds. We can practice the blast-off, flying through space, landing on the moon, lifting off from the moon, and reentering the earth's atmosphere. We can take you to the moon and back, without ever leaving this room."

As Looper talked, I scanned the wide bank of TV screens on the wall in the front of the room. Facing the TV screens were two rows of attendants at desks, about ten of them, each one sitting in front of computer monitors and dials and blinking lights. Each of the attendants was wearing a white shirt, and all had turned to listen to the speech.

The most interesting thing in the room, though, was the space capsule in the corner. It had a small ladder leading up to a door, with hundreds of wires running out of the top and sides. The wires reached across the ground like strands of colored spaghetti, leading in twisted clumps to the computers.

"Okay. You all, each one of you, will get your turn in the flight simulator. That little contraption over there. Each of you is going to go through the re-entry procedure. That's the last leg of the trip, when the capsule approaches the earth's atmosphere … re-enters the atmosphere … and deploys three huge parachutes to slow it down. And, if you follow the instructions right, you'll splash down in the target zone … somewhere in the Pacific Ocean near Hawaii where a Navy ship would be waiting."

One of the Texans had raised his hand in the front row. Looper pointed at him and said "you there, go ahead."

"Sir, I got one question," he drawled. "I can ride a horse but my daddy don't even let me drive his pickup truck. If I can't drive a pickup, how do you expect me to drive a space ship?"

"Don't you worry, son," said Looper, calmly. "There is a computer program that guides the real command modules back into the earth's atmosphere. It's called Program 64, and we use the same computer program in this flight simulator. It does all the work. You just need to trust Program 64 and the folks at Mission Control. We know where you are, how fast you're going, and where you're going to end up. We'll tell you what to do and when to do it. The test this morning is all about listening and following directions. It's that simple."

We noticed that Looper was looking off to his left, at a boy who had wandered over to the capsule and was peering in through its tiny window.

Looper cleared his throat. "Young man?" he said. "Young MAN! Did you hear me? What's the test all about this morning?"

"Um … we've gotta figure out how to fly this thing?" he said uncertainly.

"Not exactly. Anyone else?"

"I know, I know!" said a girl named Madison, waving her hand eagerly. "It's about listening and following directions." She looked very pleased with herself. She pursed her lips and nodded slowly at the boy standing next to the space capsule.

"Right you are young lady," said Looper. "And that means you," pointing at the boy, "will go first."

▲ ▼ ▲ ▼ ▲

After all the build-up, the test itself didn't seem too hard.

The campers went one at a time into the test capsule and were buckled into the pilot's chair and given radio headsets. We watched on the TV monitors as they went through a series of instructions. Read numbers from this dial or that dial ... push this button or that button ... fire thruster rockets ... make an adjustment here or there.

A couple of the kids didn't do so well. To the delight of many, Madison failed to turn off her thruster rocket, even after Looper reminded her five times to hit the big red "OFF" button. This ended up sending her out towards Saturn, so her test ended early.

One of the Texans flicked the wrong switch and shut off the oxygen, which ended his test early too.

Lance was one of the only people to do it absolutely perfectly. So were Rockwell and Stimple. As much as I hated to admit it, those three were living up to the Supercamper label.

The morning wore on and my attention started to fade. Plus, it was kind of warm in the room. And the electric lights overhead were making a nice, soothing buzzing sound. Kind of like bees.

Yeah, bees, I thought to myself. Big, fuzzy bees buzzing around lazily on a sunny summer afternoon. My head started to nod....

"PRICE!!" shouted the loudspeaker.

I scrambled to my feet, aware that everyone in the room was looking at me. I guess it was my turn. I scrambled over to the corner of the room, passing Jonah who had just finished his turn and gave me a thumbs-up of encouragement.

At the test module an engineer handed me a helmet which she helped me adjust and put on my head. It was heavy and uncomfortable. I said "hi, can you hear me?" My voice must have carried through the room's loudspeakers loud and clear because I could see Lance look up and whisper something to Stimple, who gave a mile-wide smirk.

As I strapped myself into the Flight Commander's seat, Looper's voice filled the radio headset. "Okay, Mickey, we'll get started as soon as you're ready. Just remember, follow the instructions and trust the computer and you'll do just fine."

Piece of cake, I thought, staring at the dizzying display of buttons and knobs and computer displays and switches and gauges and dials and readouts and flashing lights that surrounded the Flight Commander's chair.

Looper's voice came through the headset, issuing a set of commands. They had sounded easy when the others were taking their turn. But it was harder now that I was the one actually in the pilot's chair, doing things like "find the fifth row of switches to the left of the round glowing dial at the center and flick the first three." Or "check your speed, fourth dial from the top in Row J."

Surely all these instruments and switches weren't really necessary.

"Mickey," said Looper, "you are now 4 minutes from reentry. The center panel should say 'Program 64,' can you confirm?"

"Lets see ... center panel ... uh ..." my eyes raced over the dizzying array of numbers and lights and dials. Bingo. "Oh yeah!! Roger!!"

I had noticed that all of the astronauts, and also Lance and his buddies, used the word "Roger" to mean yes. I guess it was all part of being an astronaut.

"It says 'Program 64 Active,'" I continued. "What does that mean again?"

"Mickey, Program 64 is the final reentry program. The computer makes the final calculations and fires your booster rockets to get you at the perfect angle for reentry. It then tells you exactly when to deploy your parachutes."

"Roger that," I said, feeling confident now. "Program 64, take me home."

"Good job, Mickey, three minutes to reentry. Remember, reentry is when you hit the earth's atmosphere. You will lose radio contact for a few minutes. The radios we use to talk to you in space won't work because you won't be in space anymore. The radios we use to talk to you in the Earth's atmosphere won't work because you're not quite home yet. And the command module will shake. In a real reentry, it would shake so hard and be so loud, you wouldn't be able to talk anyway."

A gentle beeping rang out through my headset and the main screen flashed the words "Course Adjustment."

"Um, Mission Control, Mickey Price here. Can I say something?"

"Go ahead, Mickey. And you don't need to say who you are. We kind of know that."

"Oh, sorry, Mission Control. Um, the main screen says "Course Adjustment – right booster 75 percent, 17 seconds."

"Roger that, Mickey. Good job. So lets make the course adjustment."

Looper walked me through the process to adjust course, finding the right control to set the direction of the booster rocket and to fire it for exactly the right amount of time.

I thought I had done it right, but a few seconds later the "Course Adjustment" warning came on again. I fired the booster rocket again. And then again a third time.

Suddenly a shrill warning buzzer, louder and more insistent, filled the cabin.

It went downhill from there. According to Looper, I had done something wrong, even though I swear I had followed all the instructions perfectly. I was off-course, and it was apparently too late to do anything about it.

After going through the outer atmosphere, Looper delivered the verdict. "Mickey, you were lucky. A little more off-course and you would have burned up like a flaming marshmallow coming through the atmosphere. The bad news is that you'll miss your landing spot in the Pacific and will impact on land, in central Mexico. Prepare for ELCI."

"ELCI?" I asked.

"Emergency Land Crash Impact," Looper replied. "If this was a real ELCI, NASA would scramble helicopters and ambulances and get the rescue team to the crash site as soon as possible."

"Can't I steer? Change course? Zoom a little to the left or something?"

"Negative, Mickey. The Command Module has no booster rockets and no steering. I'm afraid you're falling like a brick," replied Looper.

"What's the big deal about coming down on land?" I asked. "I've got parachutes, right?"

"We always aim for the water, Mickey. It's possible to survive an ELCI, but there's a lot that can go wrong. Even with a parachute, you're going 30-40 miles per hour. It's like jumping from a high dive onto a sidewalk. Or driving your car into a brick wall. The impact is hard. There could be a fire. The door could jam shut. All sorts of things could go wrong."

My mind raced. I never gave up on anything, and I didn't want to quit, but they weren't giving me any options. "What can

I do, Mission Control. Give me instructions!"

"Mickey, Program 64 will take it from here. You might still survive the impact, so it's not a complete failure. Parachutes deploy in 5 ... 4 ... 3 ... 2 ... 1 ... main parachutes have deployed and you're now a floater. Computer is calculating the exact crash site ... it ... is ... okay, it's the desert, 52 miles east of the city of Chihuahua in Mexico."

At that moment, the hatch door opened on my right and the engineer eased herself into the cabin to help me with the buckles. She told me we could end the test a early because there was nothing more I could do, now that the parachutes had come out. "Don't worry, Mickey," she said, trying to reassure me. "At least you made it through the atmosphere."

My face burned as I walked back towards my fellow campers on the other side of the test room, knowing they had all just heard every detail of my crash broadcast over the loudspeakers in the room. Jonah gave me a slap on the shoulder and said "hey, not all that bad Mick. A lot of kids did worse."

As I headed over towards the drinking fountain, I heard some high-pitched barking and panting coming from Lance and a group of kids standing around him.

It took me a minute to get the joke.

They were being Chihuahuas. Very funny.

11

CHECKERS

An hour later, I was leaning back in my chair after devouring three cheeseburgers and a large piece of chocolate cake in the cafeteria. Jonah and one of the Texans were having an animated argument about Jonah's great idea for ranch management. Jonah proposed putting special collars onto the cows and using robots with powerful magnets to round them up, instead of using cowboys and rope and lassos.

"That ain't right. Ain't no robot alive that can rope a calf like I can," bragged the big Texan.

Jonah sighed. "First of all, robots aren't alive. And second of all, you just wait. It won't be long before you have robot ranchers. They'll be much more efficient than humans. Think about it. They could work all day and all night. And they'd be fast as anything, if you gave them backpacks with jet engines."

I grinned, thinking about renaming the local NFL football team. No more Dallas Cowboys. A huge crowd in ten-gallon hats would cheer for the Dallas Robot-Ranchers.

Over in the corner, Supercamper Lance was sitting with a few adult astronauts from Team Varsity, along with Rockwell and Stimple. They were all leaning forward, with their heads over the table, having what looked like a very important, private conversation. Commander Riker was holding a salt shaker in one hand, swooping around like a rocket as he explained something. He didn't seem to realize that every time his rocket turned upside down, salt poured onto the table.

To be honest, at that moment, it didn't bother me that Lance was over there, hearing about the trip the real astronauts were about to take. I was stuffed full of cheeseburgers and Space Camp was going pretty well so far.

Over behind the Varsity table, I noticed that Kat and Trace had just come through the food line, and were standing at the edge of the cafeteria, scanning the room for a familiar face. I stood up and waved both hands like a sailor on a ship signaling to shore.

Trace burst into a smile and started weaving her way through the crowded tables towards us, with Kat behind her.

"Hey, where have you guys been?" I asked. "We waited for you in line and now we're almost done."

"You ... would .... not ... believe ... what this girl did," said Trace, nodding at Kat as her friend sheepishly slid into a chair at the end of our table. "She's some sort of genius, I swear. Tell them Kat. Come on, you tell."

"It was nothing. I just … it was nothing," Kat mumbled into her tray. She was looking down slightly, so her bushy hair covered most of her face.

"Come ON, girl!" said Trace, her face bright and beaming. "Okay, okay. If you won't tell, I will. Listen up boys. Remember how Kat was the last one to go on the Flight Simulator, right after Mickey? And she crash landed on the North Pole, right?"

"You give my order to Santa?" asked Jonah with a grin. "A red bicycle and a microscope?"

Trace ignored him.

"She crash landed, and then you all left to come to lunch. And I was about to leave too when I saw Kat tapping away at a computer in the corner. Soon the other Mission Control engineers were gathered around her. One of them was trying to make her stop, saying she was going to ruin everything. But Director Marshall said 'No, let her keep going. Lets see what she can do.'"

"Wait, she was trying the Flight Simulator again?" I asked.

"No, not the Flight Simulator. She was trying to fix the Flight Simulator PROGRAM. You see, she had a hunch that the program had somehow gone wrong, since Mickey and she had both crashed after doing everything right? Well, the whole thing is just a video game, right? Kat said she thought something in the game was broken and she had some idea about how to fix it. Right Kat?"

"Fix the game? Where would you even start?" I asked.

Kat looked up. "It's just a computer program. A computer program is a set of instructions that the computer follows. Do this. Do that. If this happens, do this. If that happens, do that. It's not magic. A computer does exactly what you tell it to do.

And if something goes wrong, it could be because the program contains an error. A mistake."

"Yeah, go figure," said Trace with a shrug. "Anyway, this girl is sitting there at the computer in the corner. With all these NASA engineers huddled around her, whispering to each other. I'm hearing things like 'Oh my gosh, she's tapped into the mainframe.' And 'Holy Cow, she's fixing the root formula.' And 'Golly, she's fixing the whos-a-magibbit.'"

"And then all of a sudden, Kat pushes her chair back and says 'Okay, that should do it. Try it again.' Just like that. La-dee-da, I'm done. The NASA guys swarm around the computer, and one of them runs into the capsule to check something. You should have seen the looks on their faces when they realized that she'd fixed it."

"The looks on their faces?" I asked. "They weren't mad, were they?"

"Mad? Heck no," said Trace. "They carried Kat around the room on their shoulders like she'd just won the 500-mile race at the Rockingham Motor Speedway. Somebody even asked for her autograph. There was whooping and hollering and cheering. Sure, the room got pretty quiet when Director Marshall said maybe he should fire everybody and replace them with a bunch of kids like Kat. But then he laughed and said he was probably kidding. Tell you what, the party pretty much ended right there. The NASA engineers didn't start dancing around again. So we left and came to lunch."

Kat's head was still tipped towards her tray, but I could see through her bushy hair that she had cracked into a small grin.

"Come on GIRL!" Trace concluded. "You've got to celebrate your victories. Whoop it up when you win. 'Cause you're not going to win every time."

"Whoop ... hooray!" said Kat quietly.

Trace shook her head with dramatic disappointment. "We'll work on your celebration skills, Katherine Obando, Computer Genius. I'll teach you a signature Victory Dance before this camp is over."

After congratulating Kat for a while, the conversation shifted back to Jonah's robot cowboys, and how Kat could write a computer program that would control the entire ranch, so the head rancher could take long vacations in Hawaii while the robots took care of things back in Texas. The Texans were interested in that idea, of course.

After a while, Amanda started making her way from table to table and the other campers got up to put their empty trays away. "Kids," she said when she got to our table, "you've had a full morning and we still have a lot to do today. We'll start off with some relaxation. We have a special game room set up on the other side of the compound. So take care of your trays, grab your back packs and meet in the lobby."

Without another word, Amanda turned disappeared through the open door. We scrambled to follow. We met Amanda and the rest of the campers in the lobby, where Amanda had been joined by three scientists in white coats, carrying thick notebooks. When everyone was there, they led us back through the building and through an emergency exit door.

I blinked and squinted in the bright sunlight for a few steps before noticing that Lance had slipped on his gold astronaut sunglasses. I dug deep into my bag and pulled out mine.

We had turned onto a cement path that ran along a narrow drainage creek. Frogs hiding in the long grass beside the path jumped into the creek with a chirp as we walked past.

We crossed a service road and continued along the creek for

a few more minutes before I saw the small, white building. It was actually a trailer without a cab with the rear wheels still on it. A shiny new air conditioner stuck out the back, whirring loudly and dripping moisture into a puddle.

Amanda paused at the bottom of a small metal ladder leading up to the door. "Okay, you guys can hang out here for a while. You've been working hard and we wanted to give you a break. There are games inside and a movie to watch."

"Go on in, follow the instructions, and we'll see you in a couple hours."

"You're not coming along?" asked Jonah.

"Nope, I've got some … paperwork to do. As I said, this is just hang out time. In you go!"

The first kids in line piled into the trailer. It was larger inside than I had thought from the outside. There were comfy cushions on the ground and a few bean bag chairs, all scattered around 5 or 6 low tables. The air inside the trailer was cool and dry and smelled like fresh paint.

I plunked down next to Jonah who started reading aloud from a card sitting on the nearest table:

CHECKERS

Time to test your skill against your friends.
Have a checkers tournament for an hour.
Play a game, then the winner moves on and plays
another winner.
Keep going until there is a champion.
If you lose, find a friend and keep playing!
Your movie will start in one hour.

"Jonah," I said, "you are SO going down in flames. Prepare to face the checkers master."

I opened up the red-and-black checked board and placed it between us as Jonah opened the metal box containing the game pieces. The sound of clinking mixed with chatter as we all started plinking the heavy metal pieces onto the game boards.

Madison decided it was a good time to give us all a lesson in checkers. "Okay, people. Place all your pieces on the dark squares. No moving sideways or backwards, unless you're a king. And always jump diagonally," she trilled a cheerful but bossy voice.

Jonah and I were the first to get the game board set up and he moved his first piece with a thunk.

"And if your piece gets captured," Madison continued, "pick it up and place it neatly by the side."

"We know how to play checkers," came the singsong reply from Lance in a perfect imitation of Madison. There was scattered laughter for a few seconds, then a hush fell on the room again as we concentrated on our games.

I quickly realized that Jonah was going to destroy me. My stack of defeated checkers pieces started to pile up quickly and I only had captured one of his. I plinked the defeated pieces together. They were heavy, with a rubbery red coating. I found that if you stacked two together in the right direction, they grabbed each other with a pull, and if you flipped one upside down, it would push the other one away. I put my six captured pieces together into a mini skyscraper.

Jonah finished me off in an amazing triple-jump.

After a few more games, we all stopped to watch Jonah beat a boy named Elvis from Mississippi in the championship round. Most of us were pretty much through with checkers at that point. Trace and I joined a few others in the center of the room piling our checkers pieces together into a giant tower that reached almost to the ceiling.

It wasn't much longer before the movie projector in the corner jumped to life and started whirring, seemingly by magic. The lights dimmed and the movie flickered onto the wall at the far end. All of us quickly scooted the checker boards aside and jockeyed for prime position in front of the movie screen. It wasn't really necessary because the movie filled almost the whole wall and almost every position had a great view.

To my delight, the movie was Godzilla.

▲ ▼ ▲ ▼ ▲

Just as the movie ended there was a light rap at the door. The door opened a crack, letting bright sunshine spill into the room along with Amanda's voice. "All right, hope you liked the show. Leave everything in the room – absolutely everything – don't bring ANYTHING with you, just your bags. Who wants to head to the swimming pool?"

The room was suddenly thrown into chaos. After a morning in the classroom and flight simulator and then another three hours inside, the thought of a swimming pool was exactly what we needed. It was a flurry of arms and legs as everybody scrambled for their backpacks and burst through the door to the outside. This time I remembered to put on my sunglasses before heading out into the afternoon sun. Amanda led the first of us away from the trailer and over to a shady cluster of palm trees.

The three scientists in white coats walked around among us, taking attendance. Or maybe they were doctors. One of them asked me how I was feeling. He had me stick out my arms straight sideways and then bend my elbows and touch my nose. I thought that was kind of odd, but whatever.

Madison was standing next to me trying to stuff one of the checkers boxes into her backpack when it slipped out and dropped onto the ground with a flop. The checkers pieces scattered out onto the hard packed earth.

Amanda instinctively reached down to help Madison pick up what she had dropped, but then suddenly pulled her hand back in surprise and took several startled steps away.

"Why did you bring those out? You were supposed to leave them inside," said Amanda. The scientist standing beside me jumped and moved back too.

"Um ... sorry?" said Madison, as she plunked the pieces back into the box. "It's just the checkers. I'm sorry."

"You can't choose to ignore some of the rules here. The rules are important, all of them," said Amanda sharply. "Pick those up and put them back into the trailer. Right now."

As Madison fumbled with the box, all of us moved away from her and clustered tightly around Amanda. Amanda looked down at us and said, "wait, nobody ELSE brought anything out with them, did they?"

Jonah said "Um ...." He unzipped his backpack and pulled out a checkers box. One of the Texans did the same and said "I kind of need the practice."

Amanda's head spun left and right, as she took several more quick steps backwards. Amanda raised her right hand and pointed back at the door of the trailer. "Put those back! Put them back now!"

Jonah turned and took a few steps towards the trailer, but then stopped and gave Amanda a strange look. One of his looks. A classic Jonah look.

I didn't know Johan very well, way back then. I'd only met him one day earlier. But I knew him well enough to know that his brain was working overtime. He stopped moving towards the trailer and turned to Amanda, holding the checkers box right out to her.

"Here you go," said Jonah, taking a step forward toward Amanda.

She took a step backwards.

"No really, you can have them," said Jonah, advancing again. Amanda retreated again. I almost had to laugh, as Jonah chased Amanda in a slow circle around the group. She took a step backwards for every one of his steps forward.

"Ms. Collins," said Jonah. "If you don't tell them about these checkers, I will." Amanda pursed her lips disapprovingly, so Jonah continued.

"Pleurinium," he said. "The dangerous moon magnet. Tell me I'm wrong."

He and Amanda locked eyes and stared at each other angrily.

Amanda was the first to look away.

"They're made of Pleurinium," Jonah repeated. "And you were trying to see how it affected us, how it affects kids. Weren't you?"

I heard a squeaky scream and then a plonk as Madison's box hit the ground. The Texan did the same thing. They both dropped their boxes like hot potatoes and ran away from them.

"Ms. Collins? Why would you do that to us? Pleurinium is poisonous!" said Trace, angrily.

"Okay, okay," Amanda said in a frustrated tone. "Yes, they're made of Pleurinium The checkers are made of Pleurinium. You're right. But, dangerous? Poisonous? Really?

Trace, tell me how you feel. Are you tired? Dizzy? Sick? One little bit?"

Trace shook her head.

"Anyone?" Amanda pressed. "Feel bad? Strange? Anything?"

We all shook our heads.

"All right then, Jonah Trotsky," Amanda sighed. "Would you tell your friends, since you have it all figured out?"

"Sure thing," said Jonah, brandishing the box of Pleurinium checkers. "We have all heard how the Pleurinium has a negative affect on adults, causing exhaustion, dizziness and nausea almost immediately. And then, after minutes and hours, causing worse symptoms like fainting or unconsciousness. That's for adults. But for kids, it doesn't have that affect. It doesn't have ANY affect. None. Zero."

"Correct, Mr. Trotsky, correct," one of the white-coated scientists interrupted. "All of our tests show that Pleurinium does not affect kids under about 13 years old. Anyone over 13 … well, that's a different story. And this test proved it again. The funny thing is, we still have no idea why. But we're doing everything we can to figure it out. And we've got to figure it out before Team Varsity goes back to the moon."

▲ ▼ ▲ ▼ ▲

That evening after dinner and ice cream sundaes, we watched a movie about how the moon base was built and listened to a long speech by one of the astronauts who had helped build it the year before. It was almost 10:00 by the time we got back to the dormitory, but they still gave us 30 minutes until lights-out.

The comfy couches and bean bag chairs were a welcome change from the hard-backed metal chairs in the classroom. As we scattered ourselves around the room, Jonah introduced a new crazy theory about how we were being trained to go to the moon.

"Don't you see? Pleurinium doesn't affect kids? Are you finally buying it? That's why we're here. They're sending us to the moon!"

That statement was met by a chorus of whoops and laughter from the other kids. One of the Texans jumped up onto the back of the couch and cupped his hands together to make a tinny radio sound.

"This is Mission Control. We're about to witness the first kids walking in space. Hold onto your shorts. Ladeeez and gentlemen, here he comes. Jumpin' Jonah Trotsky is away from the air lock and is ... actually ... walkin' ... on the moon!"

The other Texan rose in fake slow-motion and pretended to space-walk around the room. The rest of the group laughed as he slowly churned his arms in slow circles and bounce-hopped over the back of the couch and onto a table.

The rest of the group laughed, but I didn't feel like joining them. I had a funny sensation in my stomach. And, strangely enough, I noticed that Lance wasn't laughing either.

Jonah scowled. He turned towards me, giving me another one of his pleading looks. Then his gaze changed suddenly and he stood up, staring straight at me. He must have seen something in my eyes.

"Wait ... wait a minute ..." Jonah said slowly. "Mickey, you ... you ... agree with me, don't you?"

The funny feeling in my stomach grew more intense. I ran through Jonah's arguments in my head again. Why had everybody been invited to space camp at the last minute? How had I been invited without even applying? Why couldn't our leaders seem to agree on the name of our camp? Was it really a coincidence that all this was happening while there was an emergency on the moon? Why were they studying our reaction to Pleurinium? And why was Commander Riker always so negative, so nasty negative towards all of us in the Space Camp? It was almost like he felt threatened by us.

I realized that most of the kids in the room had stopped watching the Texans and were now watching Jonah and me, as we stood facing each other. Even the Texans had stopped clowning around and were staring at us.

Then the last piece hit me.

"Team Varsity," I said.

"Team Varsity?" asked Jonah. "What about it?"

"Varsity," I said again. "You know what Varsity means?" I didn't wait for an answer. "High schools have a 'Varsity' sports team. Colleges have 'Varsity' teams too. It means the best team at a school, the top team. But you don't call it a 'Varsity' team if there's only one team. If there was only one team, you'd just call it 'Team.' Right?"

"Um ... dude ... I thought you were on my side," said Jonah, a little disappointed. "Now you're sounding like a crazy person. What's all this about sports teams?"

I scanned the crowd and locked eyes with Trace, who cracked a smile. "Oh, he's making sense," said Trace. "What he's trying to say is, the top team is called the Varsity. The second team is called the Junior Varsity. You don't have a Varsity without a Junior Varsity."

"So," continued Trace, "what does that make us?"

"Exactly," said Jonah. "That makes us the Junior Varsity.

They brought us here ... they're putting us through tests ... because they need a Junior Varsity team. A backup team to send to the moon, in case they can't send the adults. And if the genius NASA scientists can't solve the Pleurinium problem soon, that's exactly what they're going to do."

12

GREATEST. FIELD TRIP. EVER.

The next morning was sunny. Low, white clouds raced
overhead, pushed in from the Atlantic Ocean by a steady breeze.
After a breakfast of pancakes and sausage, all 20 of us loaded
into a white school bus that had pulled up in front of the main
entrance. When asked what we were doing, Amanda replied
simply: "We're going to see the rocket."

A buzz of excitement spread through the group as we settled
into our seats and then immediately pulled out onto Apollo
Drive heading north. After a while we turned right towards the
ocean, and then left again onto a broad, straight road with no

traffic on it. The land was flat and barren here, with patches of gnarly brown grass and scrub bushes, nothing taller than knee-high. Except for the row of metal towers stretching out in front of us, reaching up into the sky.

As we headed north, we passed a dusty, pot-holed cement road cutting away to the right at an angle, leading to the first tower. We passed another road leading to another lonely tower and then a third.

I watched as a row of white sea birds lifted off from the top rim of one tower, their wings flapping quickly for seven, eight, nine beats until they caught the breeze and eased steadily back down the beach towards the next abandoned tower.

"These towers were used to launch the early test rockets out over the Atlantic," said Amanda, pointing back at the launch pads we had just passed. She had turned in her seat to sit backwards, facing us. "The next ones were used by the Mercury program, to send the first American astronauts into orbit. Then came the Gemini program, with longer space flights and the first space walk. All the Gemini missions blasted off from that launch pad right over there, number 17.

My eyes returned to the towers we were approaching, straight ahead. They were enormous, much larger than the first ones.

"The next two launch pads were used for the Apollo program. These towers were bigger to support the much larger rockets – larger and more powerful because they needed enough fuel to take the spacecraft all the way to the moon and back. The first to get to the moon was Apollo 11, carrying Neil Armstrong, Buzz Aldrin and Michael Collins. It blasted off from launch complex 39, right over there."

All of our heads turned to follow her pointing finger, as

though we might still catch a glimpse of the actual rockets if we looked quickly enough.

"I didn't work for NASA back then, I was still in college," said Amanda. "But I watched the Apollo 11 launch from right over there, standing with my mom and dad at the public viewing area at Piney Point. It's something I will never forget, and it changed my life forever. At that point I realized I had to be a part of the space program."

"You see," Amanda continued, turning from the window to face us, "even from a mile away, I could feel the power and rumble of the rocket right in my stomach. It shook the ground under my feet. I can only imagine what it would be like to be actually inside the launch vehicle ... actually experiencing it myself. Few people ever do."

She had us all in a bit of a daydream, imagining the liftoff. I looked at Trace and Jonah, and the other kids in the bus too, and saw that their eyes were all turned up into the sky, tracing the imagined path of a rocket.

Amanda seemed to shake out of her dream. "Well anyway," she said abruptly. "That's your history lesson for the day. We just drove through 30 years of the early space program's history. Mercury, Gemini, Apollo. These programs were important building blocks and got us where we are today. The Artemis program."

And that's when I noticed that the final red tower in the line was not empty. It was even taller than the last two, sitting on top of what looked like a small cement hill at the end of an enormous ramp. As we pulled closer to it, I saw a huge shape appearing from behind the tower. It was smooth -- black-and-white at the bottom, with a large American flag painted on the side. About two thirds of the way up it narrowed, and was capped by a shining golden section with a thin point at the very top.

"And here's Lunch Complex 40. With the Artemis Seven, ready for launch."

We got out of the bus, which had pulled up alongside some other cars next to the launch pad. A steep cement wall angled up to the base of the rocket. I guessed that's what the "pad" was, an enormous cement slab that the rocket and tower sat on. Right now, we were climbing up a thin metal staircase to the top of that slab. A couple times I glanced up – straight up almost – at the rocket pointing up into space.

When I got to the top of the stairs, I saw that the launch pad was a bee hive of activity. There were small trucks shuttling supplies to the base of the rocket, plus dozens of workers with clipboards or tools or electronic instruments, all busy at some task.

Amanda introduced the person in charge of the Launch Complex and told us to "huddle up" so we could hear him. That was a good idea. Even by squeezing in close, and even with him barking out his words in something close to a yell, it was hard to hear him above the commotion.

I nudged Trace on the arm and pointed to an elevator creeping slowly up the heavy red metal tower to the top of the rocket.

Jonah saw what we were looking at. "Yeah, I'd give my right arm for a ride on that. That's how you get to the command module, the area for the crew. The astronauts ride that elevator on the day of the launch. Can you imagine?"

"Man," I said as I looked down the coast line. "Just think of the view from up there. I wonder if I could see Orlando." I thought of home for the first time in almost 24 hours. But it didn't last long because I heard the word "elevator."

"I see you all looking at the elevator," yelled the Launch Complex director. "It runs 36 stories up the tower to the command module, the crew compartment."

"So, does anybody want to go up?" asked Amanda brightly.

Right. That was officially the dumbest question in the history of questions.

Twenty hands shot straight up. Actually, it was twenty one hands. Our van driver had followed us up the steps and had been standing next to me, listening to the speech.

He shrugged his shoulders when I looked at him curiously. "Hey come on," he said, "I've worked at Kennedy for ten years and never got to ride up to the top. It was worth a try."

I shrugged right back, then realized that I'd fallen behind. I jogged forward to catch up to the rest of the kids who had followed Amanda under the frame of the tower and towards the base of the elevator.

"No pushing, settle down," Amanda chided the group. "We'll do this in groups of five. The elevator isn't large and there's not much room at the top. Five at a time up to the top, where you'll have a chance to look around the real command module of the Artemis Seven spacecraft. Then you'll walk down 36 stories ...." There were immediate groans from some of the kids. "Yes, WALK down the stairs, which should be totally awesome, right? I mean, how many kids in America get this kind of close look at the Artemis?"

She had a point.

"So this will take a while. While you wait your turn at the bottom here, Mr...." and she glanced down at the Launch Complex Director's name tag, "Mr. Dulmore here will keep you entertained with fascinating stories about ... well ... about

108

whatever it is that he does around here. Right Mr. Dulmore?"

"Oh, of course, right!" said Dulmore, who looked rather surprised to hear his name in the same sentence as the words "entertained" and "fascinating."

Amanda started counting heads and swept five kids to her left towards the elevator door. Her path was blocked by Lance, who was pushing Rockwell, Stimple and two other girls towards the elevator.

"Now, Lance," said Amanda lightly, "I've got my first five. You'll get your turn, don't worry."

Lance kept walking forward, with a smug grin on his face. "Look Mrs. Collins." His voice was quiet and mocking, and he used a tone and enunciation that might be used when speaking to a pre-schooler. "You don't want me to tell my ... DAD ... that you're interfering with my training, do you?"

Trace shot me a quizzical look, her eyes saying "WHAT??" I gave a tiny shrug.

"Young man," said Amanda, now turning to face him. Her face still carried a smile, but her voice was sharper than usual. "You can tell the Director anything you like. I have a job to do and I'm going to keep doing it. And you're going to wait ... your ... turn." With each word, she gave his shoulder a gentle jab with her index finger.

Trace shot me another look, but this time her eyes said "AHA!!" I gave a bigger shrug. What was Lance talking about? His dad? The Director? Wait. Director Marshall. Lance had the name "Lance M." on his jumpsuit. Lance Marshall. Director Marshall was his father!?

Lance still stood facing Amanda. He was almost her height and his chest was puffed out like a soldier at attention. But then I saw his shoulders slump a bit. He had made up his mind. He backed down. Lance gave a little laugh and made an exaggerated bow to Amanda and the 5 campers, as he waved them towards the elevator.

Trace leaned in towards Jonah and me. "Of course. Now it makes sense," she groaned, almost in a whisper. "I was beginning to wonder why Supercamper acts like he runs this place. It's because he practically does."

▲ ▼ ▲ ▼ ▲

The elevator came back five minutes later with only Amanda inside. Dulmore had been telling us about the special kind of cement used to make the base of the launch pad; and how thick the cement was; and how many cement trucks it had taken to deliver the cement; and how long it takes cement to dry. Boy, that guy loved cement.

I was thrilled that, when Amanda stepped out of the elevator, she called my name, along with Trace, Kat, Jonah and Elvis from Mississippi. Lance looked like hot smoke was going to pour from his ears.

"We'll send a postcard," Trace whispered to Lance as we stepped past him. Then she stuck her hand out behind her back to give me a mini high-five.

The elevator was different from any elevator I had ever been on. It was like a metal mesh cage, with holes in the floor so you could look down. And the walls only went up to my shoulder level, leaving the rest open to the air.

As we started the ascent, Amanda pointed out what the workers were doing. "We're in final preparation mode," she said. "With launch just a couple days away, we're working 24 hours a day, every day, on all the final details. The engineers are checking and re-checking all of the machinery and the electronics. The food is being loaded into the command module. The oxygen tanks are being filled."

"This bottom section we're passing now is called the Stage One rocket. It contains a huge amount of rocket fuel. It burns for the first six minutes of flight and gets the space craft about 30 miles into the air. And when that fuel is gone...."

"42 miles," said Jonah.

"Excuse me?" said Amanda, surprised.

"I'm sorry, Ms. Collins, I didn't mean to interrupt," said Jonah. "It's just that Stage One burns for 42 miles, not 30. At that point the space craft is traveling about 6,000 miles per hour. The empty Stage One rocket detaches and falls into the ocean ... you know, so the spacecraft doesn't need to carry the weight of the huge, empty fuel tank."

"Um ... that's right Jonah. You mind telling me how you know all that?"

"Aren't we ALL supposed to know this already?" asked Jonah, looking honestly confused. "I mean, that was covered in the materials you gave us when we arrived. You know, the green binder, volume seventeen, section six? The part about rocket propulsion?"

"Dude," said Elvis in amazement. "You didn't actually READ all that stuff and UNDERSTAND everything, did you?"

Jonah shrugged. Amanda politely asked Jonah to please pick up where she had left off, and muttered something about how she might learn something.

Jonah cleared his throat and continued. As our elevator slowly continued to climb, Jonah explained to us that we were now passing the "Stage Two" section of the rocket, which carried the spacecraft to the outer part of the Earth's atmosphere at a speed of ... holy cow ... over 20,000 miles per hour. "Exit velocity" he called it, the speed at which the spacecraft would exit the earth's atmosphere.

After a while, the sides of the rocket started to taper inwards and it got narrower. We were nearing the top.

"Here, above the Stage Three rocket are the last two sections of the spacecraft. The sections we have passed so far just store the fuel and fall away during the flight. These top two sections are the ones that land on the moon. The big lower section is called the Service Module – it contains rocket engines that are small compared to the ones needed to blast off from earth, and it also carries fuel, a bunch of equipment, oxygen tanks, and an air lock used to enter and exit the spacecraft on the Moon. The Service Module doesn't return to earth, though. At the end of the return trip, right before reentering the Earth's atmosphere, the Service Module detaches and floats away. That leaves only the Command Module – the small golden section at the very top – to come back to the Earth."

"Perfect timing, Jonah," said Amanda. The elevator slowed as it moved up and into a little building at the top of the tower. "We're now in the 'Ready Center,' the room where the astronauts gather before boarding the spacecraft."

We squeezed our way through a handful of workers. One of them was loading packages of Fig Newtons and small bags of dried apricots into a plastic container.

"These are the final preparations. The food, the special equipment, everything is being loaded for the launch," explained Amanda as we stepped outside onto a thin metal walkway heading towards the top of the enormous space ship.

I had to admit, it was dizzying to look down at the ocean and launch pad 36 floors below. I noticed that Kat had grabbed

Jonah's hand as we moved out onto the walkway. Her eyes were terrified and she stared straight ahead. Jonah looked completely embarrassed. I grinned and flashed him a thumbs-up sign, causing him to blush so that his face matched the color of the red safety railing.

We took turns peering inside the command module through the small opening, about half the size of a regular door. "Is this all there is!?" exclaimed Elvis, the first one to look. "Isn't there another room where the astronauts can, you know, move around and stretch their legs?"

"No Elvis," smiled Amanda as Trace pushed Elvis aside and leaned her head in through the entrance. "What you see is what you get. It's cramped, but it has everything the astronauts need for the trip to the moon and back."

"But come on," said Trace with her head still inside. "Why not give them a little more space? A little room with beanbag chairs? A Foosball table?"

"Jonah?" asked Amanda, realizing he was itching to give the answer.

"No unnecessary weight, that's why," said Jonah. "It's hard enough to get just this little command module up out of the atmosphere. We just came up a skyscraper worth of rocket and rocket fuel, remember? It's cramped and small, but after all, it's all they need for a three-day trip to the moon."

Trace pulled her head out and I leaned forward, blinking to get my eyes adjusted to the darkness inside the command module. I saw what Elvis and Trace were talking about. Even empty, it looked cramped. I tried to imagine what it would be like with five full-size astronauts inside.

There were two seats in the front row, facing a narrow slit window on top of an enormous display of switches and computer screens and dials, just like in the test module we had seen the day before. There were even switches and buttons on the ceiling directly above the two captains' seats. Then, squeezed in right behind them in a second row were three more seats.

"What's the little door in the back?" I asked, wondering about the little hatch door about the size of a large pizza box. I pulled my head out to allow Kat to take her turn.

"That door leads down into the Service Module," said Amanda. "When the astronauts arrive at their destination, they head through that door into the air lock, and then out onto the moon."

After Jonah had looked around the cabin, Amanda led us back across the narrow walkway to the tower and showed us the head of the staircase. While we were at the top, peering into the shining, golden capsule that would take five brave astronauts out into space, I was able to imagine that we were the ones who would be making the trip.

As we walked down the stairs, however, it was like we were returning to the real world where we were kids at a space camp. The golden capsule was, once again, far above us and out of reach.

13

THE SECOND TEST

"On your marks!"

After we returned from the launch pad, we all had lunch in the cafeteria, and then were hustled straight to the gymnasium for our afternoon's activities. We were divided into four teams of five for some sort of relay race. We were Team C – Trace, Kat, Jonah, Madison and me. We stood with our toes behind the end line of the basketball court in the gym, leaning forward, ready to spring into action.

"Get set."

The other three teams of five were clumped together, farther down the end line. The Texans, Elvis and two others were on our left. They had confidently predicted victory, but Trace had told us quietly "let them talk, let them talk." Lance, Stimple and Rockwell had been teamed with two athletic-looking girls from Massachusetts. They were on the far left, staring forward resolutely.

I clutched my sheet of paper with the instructions and noticed that my shoe was untied. I wondered if I had time to tie it. It would only take a few seconds....

"GO!!!!!"

Instantly forgetting about my shoelace, I rocketed forward with my team towards the open doors at the far end of the gym. The Great Space Race was on!

▲ ▼ ▲ ▼ ▲

"Dad. Dad. DAD!!"

Dad looked up, pulled from deep inside his story that had taken him far away ... or far back in time.

"Yes, Tom. What is it."

"Dad, the Great Space Race? What are you talking about? What's that?"

"Oh, right," said Dad. "I need to explain that part, don't I."

"Don't worry about it, Dad. This story is WAY more complicated than your usual ones, so I get it, you'll mess up sometimes and leave some parts out. So go ahead. Make up the part about the Great Space Race."

Dad couldn't see the sly expression on Tom's face in the dark, but he could hear that Tom was baiting him.

"MAKE UP the part about the Great Space Race? Come on, Tom.

This is a true story. I just jumped ahead, that's all."

"Okay, whatever, Dad. Make it up, tell it, whatever. I was just pointing out that you left something out. It's late, you're tired, no problem."

"Thanks for your great understanding, Tom," said Dad. "And it is late. You still with us, Tess?"

"Of course," came a voice from the darkness.

"All right, the Great Space Race. It was a big team competition. You know, like the decathlon in the Olympics, where the athletes have to do all of the track and field sports – the long jump, the high jump, the shot put, sprinting, distance running? This was like a decathlon of space camp activities. We started with a footrace. Then took a space trivia test. Then we had an obstacle course in the gym. Then our team was tied together with ropes ... kind of like a leash connecting each one of us to the other ... and we had to make it through a maze blindfolded. One thing after another. Each team of five competing against the other."

"And the prize?" asked Tess.

"Oh yeah, the prize. What WAS the prize? I can't even remember. I think it was a special gift bag for everyone on the team. It had a NASA jacket and a little piece of moon rock and a book about space, something like that. But we knew there was something more at stake. They were watching us. Watching how we performed."

"So Dad, is this the main point of the story?" asked Tess. "The Great Space Race?"

Dad paused and glanced over at the camping clock. 12:45AM.

"You getting tired? You want me to make this the end? The Grand Finale?"

"MAKE IT the Grand Finale?" asked Tom. "Wait, it either is or it isn't the Grand Finale. If you MAKE IT the Grand Finale, that means you're making up the whole story, right?"

Dad paused. "No.... I just meant, you know, make it the Grand Finale for tonight. This story has already happened. I'm just bringing it back from my memory."

"Fine, Mr. Space Camper," said Tom. "You go ahead with the story.

"Thanks for your kind permission," said Dad. "I'll go ahead with the story. Back to the Great Space Race. Our team was in second place. Maybe third. We had a problem in the maze. Madison kept wanting to lead and it took us a while to realize she had a terrible sense of direction. We kept walking and walking and ending up back at the beginning of the maze. So after we finally finished the maze, we were in third place with only one part to go. Our instruction sheet just called it "Final Test — Conference Room B."

▲ ▼ ▲ ▼ ▲

Kat and I came racing into the conference room together, with Jonah, Trace and Madison right behind. At first, my heart sank when I saw Lance sitting at a desk in the far corner of the room. Stimple, Rockwell and the rest of their team was in the room too, sitting at desks, already concentrating hard on the final stage of the test. But at least they were still working. They hadn't finished yet. There was still time.

I saw a red envelope with my name on it on a table in the first row. I sprinted over and tore open the cover. Kat found her envelope in the back row and ripped it open as well. I sat down at my desk I pulled out two pieces of paper. The first said simply: "WHAT IS THE MOST IMPORTANT PART OF ANY MISSION?" The second said this:

O

I shook the envelope, hoping something else would fall out, then desperately peered inside. Empty. I flipped the pages over, back and front. Nothing more than I had already seen. "WHAT IS THE MOST IMPORTANT PART OF ANY MISSION?" And then the second paper with that strange collection of dashes and a circle.

"You've got to be kidding me," I said to the ceiling.

Lance's head spun around to look at me, but he wasn't gloating. I saw a look of desperate confusion on his face before he turned back to look at his own pieces of paper.

Well, I thought, at least he was just as clueless as me.

I looked at the dashes and circle again. I spun it sideways. It looked kind of like a basketball pole and hoop.

Nah, couldn't be.

I spun it upside down. It looked like … of course … it was a word. A series of blanks and an O. Like hangman.

__ __ __ __ __ O __ __

Except how was I supposed to guess it with only one letter? The most important part of any mission. Helmet. Food. Air. Toilet. No, those words were too short.

Spacesuit. Oxygen Tank. Parachute. No, too long.

Rocket. Liftoff. Blastoff.

A jolt went through my brain. Wait a minute. That fit! B-I-A-S-T-O-F-F. That was it!! Sweet!!

But as I started to fill in the letter "B" I was hit by a second jolt. This time, it was a jolt of uncertainty. Was "Blastoff" really the MOST important part of a mission? Sure, it was important. But so was the flight. And landing on the moon. And then doing the work. And then lifting off from the moon. And coming back into the atmosphere. And of course, landing safely. After what happened in the flight simulator test, how could I forget about the crash landing. How could one of these parts be more important than the others?

I started to panic and checked the others in the classroom to see if they were having any more luck than me. By this time, Jonah had arrived and had the same befuddled look as everybody else, isolated at separate desks. Trace, sitting in the back row, had a look of determination on her face but wasn't writing anything down.

I was officially stuck. I decided there was only one thing to do. I walked down the center aisle to Trace's desk.

"Hey Trace, you got it?" I whispered.

"Yeah, of course. I got it about ten minutes ago." She spat at me with a frustrated whisper. "I just thought I'd sit here and draw a picture of a PURPLE UNICORN to waste some time. OF COURSE I DON'T HAVE IT!!" Boy, was she frustrated.

Rockwell glared over at us and said "SHHHHH!!!!" before returning to her work.

"Gee, sorry," I said to Trace.

"Yeah, whatever," said Trace. "I feel like I've come up with every 8-letter word ending in K in the dictionary. It's a pretty impressive list. Backpack ... sunblock ... doorlock. I'm not sure that's a word though...."

"Wait," I interrupted. "What did you say?"

"I said doorlock. You know, a lock on a door? But I'm not sure if that's one word or two. Doorlock. Door ... lock. You know what I mean?"

I grabbed her sheet of paper and stared at her clue. It had this printed on it:

$$\_\ \_\ \_\ \_\ \_\ \_\ \_\ \mathbf{K}$$

"Trace," I said, "Trace, YOU ROCK!"

"Wait. Y-O-U-R-O-C-K. That's not enough letters, Mick. It's

only seven," whispered Trace. I ignored her and snuck over to Kat's desk. I grabbed Kat's page, then quickly reached for Jonah's and walked over to pick up the Madison's. With the rest of the team following me, I returned to Trace's desk and lined up the pieces of paper, one above the other.

Each one had 8 blanks. But each one had a different letter filled in. Kat's clue started with a T. The next two spaces were blank on all of our clues. Madison' clue had an "M" in the fourth spot. Jonah's had a "W" in the fifth. Mine had an "O" in the sixth. And Trace's ended in a "K."

T __ __ M W O __ K.

"The most important part of a mission..." I said.

"You got it, Mick," said Kat excitedly, looking over my shoulder. She mouthed the answer at the rest of us. A feeling like electricity swept through me ... through all of us ... as we quickly filled in the blanks. Kat gathered our answer sheets and we bolted for the door, suddenly in first place, with our entire team heading back to the finish line in the Gymnasium.

We sprinted the short distance between buildings in record time and skidded as a group into the Gymnasium where we found Amanda and Major Jackson waiting with a group of scientists and engineers.

"So, it's you five. I can't say I'm surprised," said Amanda with a smile.

As Kat handed in our answer sheets, we heard the sound of heavy footsteps in the hall behind us. Lance burst into the room, red in the face.

"I got it. I got the answer on my own. But it's my duty to report that these five totally cheated."

"Cheated?" asked Amanda, raising her eyebrows.

"Yes ma'am, cheated," said Lance, standing up straight like

121

some kind of soldier with a smirk on his face. "They were talking and working together, and everybody else saw it. You can ask anyone. They officially broke the rules."

There was another commotion in the hallway and the remaining fourteen kids came bursting into the room and jostled their way to the front, pushing each other aside as they tried to hand their answer sheets to Major Jackson.

"Ma'am," continued Lance as Amanda put the papers in order and the crowd backed away a few steps, "those five will be disqualified, right?"

"Not at all," said Amanda. "I don't remember anything in the rules saying you have to work alone. Besides..." she continued, flipping through the answer sheets to find his, "you didn't get it right. 'BLASTOFF' is not the answer we were looking for."

I couldn't help bursting into a smile.

"Trace, Mickey, Kat, Jonah, Madison, you got it right," said Major Jackson with a grin. "'TEAMWORK' is the answer. There are many important parts of a mission. The blastoff is certainly one of the important parts. But each part, each individual task, is impossible without help from your teammates. It's all about teamwork."

Amanda jumped in. "You see, answering this question alone was almost impossible. But working together, you could figure it out. Congratulations to Team Three, you win. And also, congratulations to the rest of the teams. It looks like you all got it right, too. I guess you followed the example set by Team Three and figured out you needed to cooperate. Good work everybody and ... sorry ... nice try, Lance." Lance took a step back. His mouth opened and closed as though he was talking, but no sound came out.

Jonah had his arm around Kat's shoulders and they were both smiling broadly. Trace had her lips pursed firmly together and pumped her fist several times in silent celebration.

I was ecstatic. It felt great to win and even better to win with my friends.

"Okay," said Amanda checking her watch. "It's five thirty. We'll break for dinner in just a few minutes. But first, find a seat. We need to talk about what we learned."

As we shuffled back towards the chairs, two men in white shirts and walkie-talkies came bursting into the room. They spoke in low voices to Major Jackson, and Amanda leaned in to listen. I watched her face and saw a look of complete shock fill her eyes. Her hand flew to her mouth as she glanced quickly at the kids retreating to the chairs, then turned again to listen to the two visitors.

Everyone in the room realized that something was up. The lively chatter had stopped and I was frozen, half-way between standing and sitting down.

The two men took a step backwards to let Amanda speak.

Something was different. Her usual confidence and polish was gone. She looked nervous.

"There's been a change of plan," she stammered. "I'll be walking you back to the dormitory now. You'll still have some time before dinner. It's been a long day, so this is … um … this is good. Some time for you all to relax."

"If you ask me," said Jonah leaning in towards me, "it looks like SHE'S the one who could use some time to relax."

14

READY OR NOT

When we got back to the dormitory we all headed to the common room to hang out. Trace, Kat, Jonah and I ... and even Madison ... received a few high fives for winning the race. Lance had stopped calling us cheaters, at least, but instead he started loudly making fun of the whole competition.

"Yeah, they figured out that word problem, but big deal. Being good at a crossword puzzle doesn't have anything to do with being an astronaut," he sneered as he shot a sideways glance towards our group. That seemed to make him feel better, and a few other kids nodded in agreement and went over to sit near Lance and as he started to tell a story about visiting the White House with his father.

Trace was ready to burst. "That no good, arrogant, lousy attitude, bone-head, meat-head, big-head …. AAGH." She rose from the couch with her hands balled into fists and looked like she was ready to march over to Lance and kick him in the shins. Or worse.

I grabbed the back of her shirt and pulled her back onto the couch, which she hit with a thud. I think she was happy to be back on the couch, instead of marching across the room to confront Lance and his fan club.

"Trace … you know he's just doing that to get a reaction, right?" I asked. "Yank your chain? Get your goat?"

"Well, he got my goat all right. Lets see if he's still smiling after a nice knuckle sandwich." She slapped her right fist against her left hand with a loud "thwack." Then burst out laughing. "Or we could just beat him again in the next contest, what do you say?"

The response was unanimous. Jonah, Kat and I showed our agreement by piling on top of her on the couch. Then I felt the weight of Madison and a couple Texans pile on top of us too.

When I finally pulled myself free from the pile of kids I saw a pair of women's shoes with two pairs of men's shoes in the doorway. Not just the shoes, of course. They were attached to people. But it was the shoes I saw first.

It was Amanda, Major Jackson and Major Austen.

They weren't smiling.

As I stood up and patted down my messed-up hair, they stepped aside. And in walked Director Marshall.

A sudden hush fell over the room, and soon the only noise was the snorts and giggles coming from the two Texans who were still piled on top of each other, wrestling. Kat gave one of them a sharp kick with her sneaker. He howled "Hey no fair, why did you ...?" But he scrambled quickly to his feet when he saw our visitors.

"Oh ... howdy there, good evening Mr. Important Director Marshall, Sir." He couldn't stop babbling. "I didn't see you standing there. Mighty nice of you to come by for a visit. I'll ... well, um ... sorry .... I'll think I'll just be quiet now."

Marshall regarded the Texan with raised eyebrows. Then he spoke.

"Young astronauts, our engineers have received some disturbing news from our monitoring equipment on the moon. The nuclear reactor is in worse shape than we had feared. We have to move quickly. VERY quickly. We cannot wait until the planned launch date next week. We have to move up the launch ... to tomorrow morning."

There was complete silence now in the room.

I could even hear the mechanical buzz-hum of the long, skinny light bulbs overhead.

"You will all be able to see the launch tomorrow morning. For most of you, you will continue with camp as usual. You will be able to watch one of the most exciting, important and unusual missions in the history of the space program. A few of you will be ... separated ... from the main group. You will be watching from a different location."

I glanced sideways at Jonah, but he didn't take his eyes off Director Marshall. Jonah's lips were moving, but noiselessly, and I couldn't figure out what he was saying.

"Don't ask why," the Director continued. "That's not important. What's important is the mission. And the launch is just a few hours away."

There were a couple hands in the air but the Director brushed them aside. "No time for questions. Amanda will stay with you and can tell you about the evening's activities. I have to go to Mission Control. Five of you will come with Major Jackson, Major Austen and me."

He paused.

He nodded at the tallest boy in the room, who had already started to walk towards the door. "Lance," he said, "step out with us."

Rockwell and Stimple also got to their feet, and kids started to scoot out of the way, making room for them as they followed Lance to the door. But the Director closed his eyes for just a second before raising his right hand towards them and shaking his head lightly. "Trace Daniels. Katherine Obando. Jonah Trotsky. Step out with us."

Lance gasped and stared at his father in shock. "But Dad, that's crazy. What about ... you gotta be kidding me!"

The Director turned swiftly. With a loud crack he snapped his fingers and pointed sharply at Lance's nose. "Not one more word, young man. That's an order and it's crystal clear. And you KNOW how to follow orders."

Lance sagged and hung his head. Rockwell and Stimple stood frozen in the middle of the room, their mouths hanging open in disbelief.

Marshall turned back to face the group. "And...." he scanned the room as if looking for one more person. Amanda stepped forward and whispered in his ear. "Oh right," said the Director. "Price. Mickey Price. Step out with us. The rest of you, carry on."

Marshall spun on his heels and was out the door almost before his words traveled across the room to my ears. Or at least, before his words had sunk in.

Kat and Jonah were headed towards the door, but my butt was still firmly glued to the couch. I felt Trace take my hand and give it a strong tug, pulling me to my feet.

As I walked past Amanda, she said "good luck, kids."

Out in the hall, Lance, Kat and Jonah were standing next to Major Jackson when Trace and I approached.

Jackson took a deep breath. "Kids, you are the five. You're Team Junior Varsity. Lets get you ready."

"Do you mean…," I asked, unable to finish the sentence.

"Yes, Price," said the short astronaut, looking at me intensely. "We can't solve the Pleurinium problem and we need to send up the rescue team immediately. So you are the five. You're going up."

▲ ▼ ▲ ▼ ▲

We were whisked into a van for the short ride to the Mission Control complex and herded into a conference room where the Director was waiting with Team Varsity. Riker did not look happy.

The Director paired each one of us with a member of Team Varsity, who would tell us about our special jobs and give us instructions. Lance would be our Flight Commander, and was paired with Riker. I was assigned to Strider, the gruff looking Co-Pilot. Trace was paired with Jackson and would be our Navigator, in charge of our maps and direction. Kat was paired with Austen and would be our Computer Engineer, keeping track of our electronics and computer systems. And Jonah, of course, was our Mission Scientist, paired with Reimann, the scientist on Team Varsity.

For the next two hours, Strider showed me pictures of the Co-Pilot's seat and instruments in the command module. He explained what the flight would be like, and explained the kinds of things the Co-Pilot might have to do during the flight. I paid as much attention as I could, I really did. I nodded my head and said "got it" or "roger that" at all the right times.

But after a while, I began to wonder whether I would actually remember any of this. Did I remember what he had said two minutes ago? What was the first thing he had told me? Had I forgotten some absolutely critical piece of information?

"Price ... Price ... PRICE, are you okay?" I looked up and Strider was giving me a very concerned look.

"Oh, sure. No problem. I was just wondering ... I mean ... do you honestly expect me to remember all of this? Seriously?"

Strider looked startled at first and paused, then sighed and broke into a big grin. "Look Price, you'll have it easy. You're not leaving us behind, we're going with you, in a way. We'll be watching you, we'll be reading your instrument panel readouts, we'll be connected by radio. We'll be there every step of the way. I'm going through all this so it will be familiar when it happens. But you don't need to memorize everything right now."

I must not have looked convinced.

"Look," Strider continued, "imagine this. You need to draw a picture on a piece of paper. It's hard if you're drawing on a blank page, right? But it's easy if you're doing a 'Connect-the-dots,' right? Every dot is numbered. You just follow the numbers. That's what you're doing on this mission. We'll worry about the dots, you just connect them. Okay?"

"It's just like what you did in the flight simulator," Strider explained, "where you practiced following instructions. If you leave it to us, everything will turn out just right."

"Um ... you might not remember," I cut in. "In the flight simulator test, I followed the instructions but my command module missed the landing zone by a thousand miles crashed in Chihuahua."

Strider's smile vanished and he shifted nervously in his seat. "Well ... then I guess you thank your lucky stars that was just a test. We'll get it right this time, trust us." Strider finished with an unconvincing smile.

"Now look," Strider continued, "let me give you a few pointers about the Moon Base. We call it Oblivion Base. Number One, don't expect anything fancy or comfortable at Oblivion. It's like living in a factory, with metal walls and pipes and wires everywhere. Number Two, the food stinks. The chewy peanut butter sticks are pretty good, but don't get your hopes up about the freeze-dried burgers. And Number Three, make sure you watch the sun rise around the corner of the earth sometime. Make sure you're wearing your special sun glasses, because the glare can really hurt your eyes. But it's an incredible sight to see."

It seemed like Strider had run out of advice, and he looked relieved when the Director chose that exact moment to sweep back into the room. He clapped his hands twice, quickly. "Eyes up here," he barked. The room was immediately silent. The clock over his shoulder said 12:10. It was past midnight.

"Junior Varsity, I have just two things to tell you before we'll let you get some sleep."

"Number one. The primary goal of the Artemis Seven trip is YOUR SAFETY. Remember that. Our mission is to bring you back safely, all of you. Shutting down the nuclear reactor ... that is just icing on the cake. Got that?"

He pointed his finger at each of us. Lance, Trace, Jonah, Kat, and then me. We nodded.

"Got that?" He pointed his finger at Team Varsity and the other adults crowding into the room. "Yes, sir!" came the reply.

"Good. Now, number two. I'm not going to say 'Good Luck.' Luck is what saves you when you make a mistake. Luck is what saves you when you fail. Well, let me tell you something, kids. You can't rely on luck. Sometimes it's there, sometimes it's not. I can tell each one of you, NASA will not need luck on this mission. We have the best equipment, the best plan and the best people in the world. We will not need luck."

He looked around the room. The astronauts on Team Varsity were nodding their heads in agreement. The astronauts on Team Junior Varsity just looked sleepy.

"So instead of 'Good Luck,' I will just say 'Follow the Plan.'"

To tell the truth, I should have expected something a little more encouraging, coming from a guy who was about to strap us to the tip of a skyscraper filled with explosive fuel and light a match. But at least it was simple. And at that moment, sitting there in the bright conference room at the Kennedy Space Center, I had complete confidence in the man with the perfect, simple plan.

▲ ▼ ▲ ▼ ▲

Dad looked over at Tess who was now sitting up in her sleeping bag, eyes wide, mouth wide open. Speechless, but not for long. Out spilled a jumbled assortment of words. "That's ... but the ... secret ... with the ... but how did ... a rocket?? ... and then ... really?"

"Yes Tess, really. I was gonna be strapped tight in a command module atop the biggest rocket ever made. I had four companions. And

I was 12."

"Woah. Wo-wo-woah," said Tess, shaking her head.

Dad looked over at Tom who wasn't saying anything but whose mind was obviously moving 100 miles an hour behind his eyes, which narrowed slightly.

Finally Tom spoke. "No way, not gonna buy it. Good story. Great story even. But I'm not gonna buy it being real."

Dad simply cracked a slight grin and shrugged his shoulders.

Tom continued. "Just like last April Fools day, when you woke us up in the morning and told us we had missed the helicopter landing in our back yard the night before. Or the time when we were four and you told us Congress had voted to cancel Christmas because of the bad economy...."

"Hold on, Tom," Dad interrupted. "I apologized for that one. A lot. And I think Santa didn't appreciate my joke because you got a little extra that year, right?"

"True. But that's not the point," said Tom. "I'm just saying, you don't have the world's best record on truthfulness, right? How do we know this one's not another big, fat, tall tale?"

"Reason number one, Tess believes me. Right Tess?"

Tess looked from her brother to her father, then back again, clearly torn. "I dunno. I want to believe it. But it does seem, I don't know, kind of crazy. I think you would have said something about this before, right? You know what I mean?"

"Yeah, Dad," pressed Tom. "How come we've never heard about this before? Why aren't you in the space travel hall of fame? Or the Guinness Book of World Records? Why don't have old photos up on the walls? Or your space suit in the attic? Come on. This is a good story. But it's made up. Right?"

"Who says I don't have proof? If you make me show you, I'll do it," said Dad. "But there's a good reason why this wasn't made public.

Things were different back in the 1970s. The United States wasn't the only country with a space program. The Soviet Union ... the big country that later broke apart and became Russia and a few others ... they had a space program too. A great one. The Soviets were actually the first ones to send an astronaut into space. The Americans and Soviets didn't get along, so the American government was obsessed with beating the Soviets to the moon ... and beating them in finding out what the moon had to offer. That's what the Artemis missions were all about."

"So, think about it," continued Dad. "With so much pressure to beat the Soviets, with the whole world watching, the American government felt like it couldn't admit failure. And NASA didn't want to admit that it had to turn to a bunch of kids to save the day. On that morning back in 1977, there were only about 100 people in the world who knew NASA was sending kids up to the moon instead of the Team Varsity astronauts."

"Just a few dozen engineers and scientists in Mission Control. And our parents ... or for me, Sister Rinaldi. And the President. NASA told the rest of the world it was Team Varsity inside the rocket that morning. All the newspapers and TV stations reported it that way. Imagine if they had known the truth ...."

▲ ▼ ▲ ▼ ▲

"Ten." That morning, the five of us had ridden together to the launch pad in a van with dark, tinted windows. As we passed the Mission Control complex, we had slowed to weave through some TV trucks with satellite dishes on top. The news channels were probably showing the rocket on the launch pad, talking about Riker and the other four adult astronauts inside. Little did they know that Riker and the rest of Team Varsity were sitting in a small room without windows next to Mission Control, watching everything on special cameras and listening to the radio transmission.

"Nine." All across America, kids were getting ready for school. Maybe putting on their sneakers before heading out to the sidewalk or to the bus. At the Orlando Boys' Home, the older boys were just leaving to walk the seven blocks to the middle school, while the younger ones waited for the Pinecrest Elementary School bus on the corner.

"Eight." Boy, I was strapped in tight. I could move my hands freely and could jiggle my legs up and down, but my shoulders were strapped into my seat and my head was firmly wedged into my helmet. A sea gull landed on the front window. Boy was he in for a surprise.

"Seven." I rolled my eyes left and saw Lance, sitting beside me in the Flight Commander's seat. His eyes were alive with excitement and there was a faint smile on his lips.

"Six." I wondered what Jonah, Trace and Kat were doing in the back row behind me. Probably the same as me. Wondering what would happen next.

"Five." The engines must have started to ignite. I could feel the rocket shudder and there was a dull rumble from behind me.

"Four." I was actually a little hungry. I wonder when we'd get time for a snack.

"Three." Each second seemed to last forever, but the countdown was relentless.

"Two." No stopping now.

"One." Gulp.

"Main engine ignition…. We have LIFTOFF! Liftoff of Artemis Seven!"

The rumble grew to a roar and my seat began to vibrate

harder. But nothing else. The blue sky above me was still blue, and it wasn't getting any closer. I angled my eyes down to the "Altitude" meter, however, and it confirmed that we weren't just sitting still. The numbers were slowly climbing as we cleared the tower and started to pull away from the ground.

The noise built slowly and so did the pressure, thrusting us back into our seats. In a car, you can step on the gas and it only takes a few seconds to get up to full speed. In this spacecraft, the enormous, explosive rockets kept pushing us faster and faster. Just when it felt like we would break apart with any more thrust, we would kick up to another level.

After a while, I just closed my eyes. After all, there wasn't anything to see and I didn't exactly have a steering wheel. Over the roar of the engines, I heard the radio squawk: "Artemis Seven, this is Control. Power up thrusters to 100%. Over."

"Control, this is Artemis Seven. Powering up to 100%. Over." Lance sounded cool as a cucumber. I watched as he moved his right hand cleanly over to the control lever and nudged it up to full power. I immediately felt my body pushed back even harder into my seat. I tried lifting my hand but it felt like it was glued to the chair arm. These were the "G forces" Strider had told me about last night.

Our maximum speed – Escape Velocity Jonah had called it – was 24,000 miles per hour.

15

PLAYING WITH M&Ms

"He shoots," I said, with great expectation, tossing a green M&M gently through the air. It floated, end over end, weightlessly, in a straight line across the cabin. Jonah eased himself into position and opened his mouth. He focused on the M&M as it slowly and relentlessly sailed towards him. And then went cross-eyed as he watched it come closer, closer, closer and finally into his mouth.

"...and he scores!!!" I yelled. "The crowd goes crazy. Haaahhh. Haaahhh. The young man from Orlando wins the National Championship from three-point range!"

Lance was not amused.

"If anyone hits me with an M&M, I'll demote you to the Junior Junior Varsity," he snarled.

Trace flicked an M&M right towards the back of Lance's head, but I snatched it out of the air and mouthed "dummy" to her. She stuck out her tongue.

It had been about three hours since blastoff, and we were most certainly in outer space. Jonah kept saying "you are now free to unbuckle your seatbelts and move about the cabin," which I guess means something if you've been on an airplane. And I hadn't.

We realized, though, that we really had to keep our seatbelts buckled just to keep ourselves in our chairs. It was the weirdest thing. I unbuckled my seatbelt and would immediately start to drift up out of my seat. If I shifted my weight and gave just one little bump off the chair, that was enough ... that part of my body would rise slightly, slowly, steadily. With the slightest push of a pinkie, I could start moving and spinning in the other direction.

I looked back at Trace and she was completely mesmerized by a pen. She flicked it with her index finger and started it spinning like a propeller right in front of her nose. It kept spinning. And spinning. And spinning. I wondered if it would ever stop.

"Come on, Kat, what's your problem?" Jonah said, poking Kat with his elbow. Kat had been strangely quiet recently, and had shown no interest in our M&M game.

"Kat? Are you feeling all right?" asked Trace, sounding concerned.

I swiveled the other way to look at Kat. She did look a little green and had her eyes closed.

"Ungh. Not good," same the quiet reply. "Not good at all."

"Not good, like your head kind of hurts? Because mine does too. Or not good, like you might...." Jonah's voice trailed off. But I could almost hear his brain working overtime.

"Gee," he continued. "I wonder what would happen in space if you...."

Jonah didn't get to finish his sentence.

Right then, Kat made a lunge for an air sickness bag in the small pouch on the side of her chair. I saw her pull the bag up towards her mouth as she lurched forward and ... lets just say the next part was not pretty.

She threw up. Loudly. Big-time. She got some of it into the opening of the air sickness bag. When I say "some," I really mean "not much." A lot of orange-colored barf missed the opening and instead hit the side of the bag.

What happened next is hard to explain. I had never seen anything quite like it, and I hope I never see it again. The flying pool of barf hit the side of the bag and then started floating. There was a main glob of it that hovered, spinning slightly, about one foot in front of Kat's face.

But then there was a large break-away cloud of barf that slowly moved, spinning through the air, away from Kat and towards Trace. It was the strangest thing, watching this rotating galaxy of barf slowly but unstoppably inch its way through the air. There were medium-sized and small-sized drops of orangey liquid spinning around the central glob, like little moons. Each drop seemed to change shape from round, to oval, to flat coin-like shapes, and then kind of round again. A couple of the moon-things were connected to the blob by shiny, gooey tendrils.

I told you it wasn't pretty.

Suspended in the main glob were chunks ... bits of granola

bar and … yes … I could see clearly, a couple lumps of banana, no doubt about it. I remembered, Kat had definitely grabbed a banana on the ride up the hill to the rocket this morning. I was suddenly glad I had not grabbed a banana too.

The idea of a banana was very unappealing at that precise moment because the smell was something terrible.

While weightlessness did strange things to the shape of barf, it had no affect at all on its smell. I can assure you, it smells just as bad in space as it does on earth, maybe worse. Imagine going into a closet with four friends, and one of you throws up. That's how crowded it was, and that's how good it smelled.

Anyway, all five of us were watching this incredible slow-motion spectacle. The main blob was still hovering in front of Kat, but the break-away cloud was inching ever-closer to Trace, who was strapped into her seat and wedged into the corner of the tiny command module with nowhere to escape. And it was Trace who broke the silence.

"Aaaaggghhhh, it's coming straight at me! Stop, stop, stop, stop, stop" Trace yelled at the blob. "Go back! Reverse! Do a u-turn! Get away!"

The blob did not respond. It just kept moving, straight towards her face. I guess a barf blob has a mind of its own. If you know what I mean.

At this point, unable to move left or right, Trace did the only thing she could do. She put her hands up in front of her face, cupping her hands slightly, and allowed the blob to nestle into the bowl she had made with her hands. Then slowly and carefully and completely on purpose, she redirected it away from her … straight towards Jonah. Incredibly, the blob responded very well to this. It was a little more compact now, since Trace had focused it together a little bit, kind of packing it together like a snowball. She sent it, with a bit more speed, towards its next target. Jonah.

As it moved away from her, Trace looked at her hands. The blob had left its signature on them. They were covered.

"Nice one, Trace," I said, very impressed. "But DO NOT wipe those hands on your pants."

"Tell me you didn't just do that, Trace" said Jonah. "You've got to be kidding me. It's coming my way. You're gonna pay!"

Jonah frantically started to grasp at his safety belt buckles, but quickly realized there was nowhere for him to hide. He raised his hands to defend his face.

Our fearless leader finally spoke up. "Nice work Kat," said Lance. "Brilliant. If that gets into the controls, we're toast. How hard is it to throw up into a bag?"

"Ease off, Lance," I said, shooting him an angry look. "Why don't you try asking Kat how she feels? How do you feel by the way, Kat?"

"Amazingly better, thanks Mickey. Maybe not ready to eat another banana at this point, but amazingly better. I'm kind of wondering what to do about this, though." Kat pointed to the main blob of barf, which was now beginning to drift forward, towards the control panel.

"And a little help here too!" came a panicked squeak from Jonah. "It's closing in on me, I've got about 5 seconds until a really gross impact."

Spurred to action, I snapped open one of the overhead compartments, flicked aside a box of band aids and a small flashlight, and pulled out a tight roll of plastic bags. I quickly peeled off one and handed it to Kat before leaning back towards Jonah. I opened the plastic bag and, as though capturing a mouse or bug, scooped the unsuspecting barf blob out of the air.

Jonah breathed a sigh of relief.

The five of us spent the next couple of minutes catching stray mini-blobs with pieces of Kleenex and stuffing all of the disgusting bags and tissues into a single garbage bag.

All that was left was the smell.

Lance decided to call home. "Mission Control, this is Flight Commander Lance Marshall here. We're wondering if you packed any air freshener for us. Kat threw up, and thanks to her, our cabin smells like baby barf."

"Oh, go stick your head out the window," snapped Kat.

"Artemis Seven, this is Mission Control," came Looper's smooth, controlled voice. "How's Kat, is she all right?"

"She's fi…"

"I'm fine." Kat hit the TALK switch and cut Lance off. "I've been feeling a little sick since the launch and it finally caught up to me. But I feel better now that I … well … you know."

"Good. Let us know if it continues, Kat," Looper replied. "Now, did you get any fluids into the controls? That could cause a problem."

"Mission Control, we handled the situation," said Lance, regaining control. "The crew decided to play a little barf tennis at first, but then I made sure they performed a good clean-up. We're good. Over and out."

Trace let out a grunt of frustration. "Kat," said Trace to her friend. "Next time that happens, aim for our Flight Commander."

▲ ▼ ▲ ▼ ▲

If anyone tells you that space travel is exciting, give them my phone number. I'll set them straight.

Sure, the liftoff was insane. There were times when the rocket thrusters were so strong, I felt like my eyeballs were seriously going to be pulled back into my brain or that my teeth might pop out, backwards. When it was all over and we were drifting in space, I checked my seat to see if my body had made a permanent dent.

And sure, we were excited about what we would find on the moon. We had received only the quickest description of the moon base the night before blastoff. Strider had tried to describe the feeling of walking on the moon, but then stopped and stared off at the wall, saying "you'll just have to experience it. It's amazing."

But between blastoff and the destination, there were three days and three nights crammed inside our little command module. There was nothing to look at out the window. And it still smelled like barf.

"At least on road trips, you get to look forward to stopping at McDonald's," said Jonah, breaking a long silence.

"And you get to look at things out the window," I sighed.

"And when you're driving at night, you can play the padiddle game," Jonah sighed right back.

"You do WHAT in the car?" said Kat, joining in.

"Play the padiddle game.... Wait a minute. Don't tell me you've never played padiddle?" Jonah stared at Kat with a look of astonishment on his face. He turned to me, "can you believe that Mickey? Kat doesn't know what a padiddle is!?"

I gulped. "Oh, yeah," I said, pretending to know what he was talking about. "Amazing. I mean, all we talk about in Orlando is padiddles. I love them. I must have 50 padiddles in my room. I collect them."

I thought Jonah's mouth might get permanently stuck, it was

hanging open so wide.

"YOU DON'T KNOW ABOUT PADIDDLES EITHER!? First of all, you NO WAY have 50 of them in your room. Second of all, are you kidding me? Third of all, are you two sure you're from America?"

Kat and I both shrugged.

"A padiddle is a car with only one headlight. If you see one you've gotta yell 'padiddle.' Have you guys seriously never played?"

Kat and I both shrugged again.

"Well, you can look it up. But anyway," he paused as he stared out the window in to the starry sky, "I'm not counting on seeing any UFOs with headlights out here."

I joined him in staring out the window.

Kat was the one to break the silence again. "Um, Mickey ... Jonah ... I've got to ask you guys something." She glanced over at Lance, who was reclining in his seat with his eyes closed and his radio headphones on. I could just make out the sound of the Rolling Stones. Trace was asleep, curled up like a cat in her chair.

"When you were meeting with your astronaut tutors the night before liftoff ... you know, when they were telling us about what to expect? Did they tell you about something ... out there ... on the surface of the moon? You know, something strange?"

I just looked at her and shrugged. She continued. "Something on the far side of the canyon, a mile or so from Oblivion Base? Something they called 'The Glint'?"

Jonah leaned forward, suddenly alert. "Nooooooooo," he said, his voice falling and then rising again, as he drew out the word. "But I'm interested. Do keep going."

"Well, okay." Kat tapped her fingers on her chin. "Lets see.

I was paired with Major Austen. The tall, bony, bald guy who looks like some kind of zombie. Anyway, he didn't seem very interested in telling me about the space flight or the moon base. He hit the basic stuff ... how to drink something when you're in zero gravity without spilling on yourself, how you need to hop up a little bit when walking on the moon so you don't stub your toe and fall on your face, how you should never take off your helmet on the moon or else you'll totally die. You know, the basics."

"But then ... then he lowered his voice and kind of looked over his shoulder towards Riker. You know, to make sure he couldn't hear. He told me that, on the last trip, he and Riker had seen something fly overhead and actually crash land on the surface of the moon. I'm serious, I wouldn't make this up."

Jonah's eyes got big and he leaned even closer.

Kat was almost whispering by now. "They actually saw it flying and hit the ground."

"What did it look like?" I asked.

"Yeah, what was it?" asked Jonah eagerly. "Did it have wheels? An engine? LEGS!!??"

"Well," continued Kat, cracking a grin and enjoying Jonah's great interest in her story. "They didn't get a good look. And apparently, half of Mission Control thinks they made it up, or imagined it, or their minds were just playing tricks on them. But Austen swears they both saw it. Something big. Something fast. Something metal. Like the size of a refrigerator or a small car flying through the air and then crashing into the ground."

"And get this," Kat continued. "Austen said that NASA did some investigating. They confirmed that it wasn't something NASA had sent up there. They checked with the Soviets and the Chinese. Neither of them has a moon mission going on right now. So at this point, that shining speck, that reflection across the canyon is just a Glint of light. An UNIDENTIFIED Glint. And that's what they call it. The Glint."

Kat sat back, apparently quite pleased with her storytelling, and watched us speechless boys as we stared at her. "So anyway, Austen said this has been driving Riker half crazy. He didn't want any of us to know about it. You know, so we wouldn't get there before him. So THAT's why he never told us … I guess that's why NASA never told us."

Jonah, who hadn't buckled himself back into his seat, had been slowly spinning as Kat told the story and was now floating completely upside down with his head resting in the chair where his behind should have been. He let out a slow, cool whistle. "Ho-leeeeeeee cow," said Jonah. "The Glint. A genuine UFO."

Jonah grabbed the side of his seat and spun himself around.

"We've GOT to go check it out," Jonah continued, earnestly. "I mean, no question, we've got to find it. Don't you think, Mick? But wait … how will we find it? How will we even know where to look with our binoculars? Boy, it's going to take a long time and we probably won't have much free time. But we'll go out there every day with our binoculars and look for it. Unless … unless …."

Jonah stopped talking. His eyes were focused on a folded piece of paper Kat had pulled from a little zipper pocket on the sleeve of her coveralls. Jonah and I craned our necks forward to see the page as she unfolded it. It was a map.

"You asked how we would find it? Easy. If it exists, that is. Austen drew a map."

And there it was.

A piece of lined paper ripped from a spiral notebook, with the frilled edges still attached. The drawing was simple but good. I could identify the cluster of buildings representing Oblivion Base in the lower left-hand corner. In the bottom center of the page was a large circle labeled "Landing Pad." The middle of the page was a belt of black ... thick near the Oblivion Base at the center of the page, but narrowing slightly as it moved off to the right. The "Bottomless Canyon."

And then, on the far side of the canyon, right in the middle top of the page was a small X.

As the three of us stared intently at the map, studying the strange details, it was suddenly whisked out of Kat's hands and pulled up towards the front of the cabin.

Lance.

I couldn't hear the faint music coming out of his headphones any more. He had turned them off and had been listening to us.

"So you know about the Glint, do you?" his arrogant voice rang out in the cabin, just a little louder than necessary. "Riker warned me that some of you might pick up little pieces of Austen's crazy story. He told me to keep all of you focused on your mission and to make sure you just followed orders, and not to go chasing Austen's imagination."

Lance had carefully folded the map back into a small square and slipped it into his pocket. "You see," Lance continued, as though lecturing a class of preschoolers. "When you're up on the moon, your eyes sometimes play tricks on you. And your mind. As you know, the grown-ups on the last couple missions didn't do too well, once the Pleurinium mining started. So that's all the Glint is. They imagined it, and maybe the reflection is just a shiny rock." Lance yawned with perfect timing. "Case closed."

I could sense the outrage boiling up inside Jonah. "And you're going to believe Riker?" Jonah blurted out. "You've got to be kidding me. Did you hear what Kat said? According to Austen, Riker is obsessed with this thing, the Glint. He just doesn't want anybody to get there before him. He's curious too. Or maybe he even knows what it is! Either way, he knows it's important."

Lance raised his eyebrows, his eyelids drooping slightly, looking completely bored with the conversation. "Oh Jonah, you're a dreamer, too. Just like Austen."

The two of them stared at each other. "Well, guess what?" continued Lance, tapping the pocket holding the folded map with two fingers. "There's nothing you can do about it. Last time I checked, I'm Flight Commander and I don't give you permission to go wasting time on a wild goose chase. But when you get back home, you can start a UFO club with Major Austen, ok?"

Lance ended the conversation by popping his music headphones back on. He cranked up the volume and I could hear the rhythms of the Rolling Stones once again.

"C'mon guys! Do you believe that!?" Jonah turned back to us, appealing for support.

Kat spoke first. "You know, Lance might be right. Austen said nobody got a good look at it. Maybe their eyes were playing tricks on them. Maybe it was just a glint ... a reflection, you know. It could be anything."

"Kat, listen to yourself," said Jonah, exasperated. "This is real evidence of aliens and Riker is trying to keep us away from it. We have a duty to the human race! We've got to check this out!"

"Aliens?" said Trace, waking up from her nap. "Aliens? What did I miss, Mickey?"

"Hard to say Trace," I replied, suddenly distracted by what

was coming into view out the front window. "Right now, I've got something much more interesting for you. Check this out." I pointed out the front window. Just coming into view at the edge of the window, as our spacecraft streaked forward, was the Moon – bigger and closer and more detailed than I had ever dreamed it. Mountains gleamed white, casting enormous shadows over dark valleys. Huge craters, created by an ages-old meteors striking the surface.

So close I felt I could reach out and touch it.

16

TOUCHDOWN

The jolt of landing was much harder than I had expected.

The descent was so smooth and silent, I imagined we were drifting downward, almost motionless, and would alight like a feather on the powdery surface.

Lance had made a final adjustment to the booster rockets about twenty seconds earlier, following Looper's instructions perfectly. At least, I thought he was following them perfectly.

Instead of a feather, I should have imagined an anvil dropping from an airplane. The impact was a sickening jolt that I felt right up my spine, accompanied by a deep, echoing "WHAM." I felt certain that our spacecraft would split in two.

We bounced and there were a few seconds of silence until a second, softer impact. Then a third. Then a fourth.

Well, it wasn't pretty, but we had officially landed.

"Mission Control, this is Artemis Seven," Lance's voice filled the command module and crackled in our headphones. "Landing successful. Slight bounce."

I heard a loud "HAH!" coming from Trace's direction.

"Artemis Seven, Mission Control here. Did you have a hard impact?"

"Negative. We're good."

I turned and caught Lance's eye. He gave his head a slight shake. I raised my eyebrows in disbelief.

His response? He tapped the Flight Commander patch on his shoulder, shook his head again, and continued his discussion with Looper.

Great, I thought. I sure hope he knows what he's doing.

There was no time to argue, however, about whether to describe the landing as a bounce, a thud or a wham. Mission Control started giving all five of us instructions. We all had different dials to read and measurements to report. We had to put the rockets into "sleep" mode, find our helmets and gloves and other moon walk gear, and get ready to step outside.

We also had to get our radios ready. Looper explained about the radios we would use on the moon, and we tested them to make sure they worked properly. We each had a little radio sewn into our uniforms on the front of our left shoulder. It had a little volume dial, with a red "talk" button and a blue "talk" button. The red button was for Channel One or "long distance" – for talking to Mission Control. The blue button was for local radio, just between us kids on the moon.

Our space helmets had microphones and speakers in them

too, and our space suits had the "talk" buttons sewn into our gloves. A big button for Channel One to Mission Control. And a little button for local radio.

They told us to keep off Channel One as much as possible, so they could send important messages to us.

So, we tested the radios, checked each others' helmets and gloves, and about a thousand other things. And then, finally, they told us we were ready.

Though we had landed hard, we were right on target, inside a large landing circle marked by white rocks. Parked just outside the circle was a moon buggy, about the size of a large go-kart, but without walls or a roof. And off in the distance, about 200 yards away, was a small cluster of low-lying buildings. Oblivion Base. Our home for the next ... who knew? For the next week or so.

Trace, Jonah and I would go first. She would drive us over to the base in the moon buggy, then come back to get Lance and Kat.

In my full space suit and helmet, I squeezed through a small door located between Kat's and Jonah's seats in the back row of the crew cabin, and slid into a small "airlock." It was the gateway between the friendly oxygen-filled crew cabin and the harsh world outside. One at a time, we were supposed to slide into the airlock and tightly close the small door behind us, to protect the crew cabin when we opened the door to the outside.

So there I was, wedged into the small airlock with my hand on the heavy metal lever that opened the door to the outside. It had probably taken us 3 hours to prepare to leave the command module, but when it was finally time, my brain kept yelling "STOP!! THIS IS CRAZY!!"

"Mickey, you are clear to open the hatch," the radio crackled.

"Go ahead."

I took a deep breath, but stayed frozen in place.

"Mickey? Are you with us? Our sensors show the door is still closed. Is it stuck?"

"Negative," I responded. "More like, I'm stuck. I mean, I'm not really stuck. It's just that, you know ... aw, heck." I wrenched the lever downward and pushed hard. A brilliant sliver of light appeared at the edge of the hatch and grew larger as the door swung open.

I pushed my legs down through the opening. After two hops down the rungs of the little ladder, I was outside, standing on the white, powdery, dusty surface. I stomped my boots against the surface just to feel the impact and to make sure it was real. The surface of the moon stretched out in front of me, beside me, behind me. The surface was whiter and finer than sand. Completely lifeless, stretching out to a black sky that was filled with a million stars. It was so much to take in that it took my breath away.

"Mickey, report back please," came the voice through the radio. "Are you outside?"

"Guuuh, dummm, yeah.... I am SO outside. I'm ... wow ... TOTALLY outside, Mission Control."

"Okay, then. Shut the hatch, Mickey, and wait for Jonah and Trace."

I grabbed the outside handle on the hatch and locked it back into place with a sharp twist.

And then I realized that I'd totally blown it. Aw NUTS! For three days, for the whole trip up, I had thought about what brilliant and memorable words I would say when stepping out onto the moon.

Neil Armstrong had gone down in history with the first

moonwalk: "One small step for a man. One giant leap for mankind." Perfect!

And here I was. The very first kid to put his size 5 boots on the moon. I had decided to say something like: "Mickey Price – a humble step for kids everywhere – I'm Number One!" But it had totally slipped my mind.

What had I come up with instead? "Guuuh, dummm, yeah … I am SO outside?"

Ugh. So I blew my grand arrival onto the Moon. I decided I had to go to Mars sometime and have a better opening line.

Just then I saw a movement behind me and Jonah's feet appeared on the ladder.

When his feet hit the surface, the radio crackled with his voice: "Jonah Trotsky. Claiming the moon for Chicago Bears fans everywhere. Go Bears!" He hopped over towards me. "Nice one, Mickey. You're the first kid on the moon and the best you can come up with is 'Guh dum yeah?'"

I sighed, which steamed up the inside of my mask. "Okay, you're right Jonah. If only I had your gift of intelligence. Giving a shout out to the Bears is much more historic. What, didn't they win 2 and lose 12 last year? Come on."

"The Bears will be back," said Jonah confidently. "Mark my words."

"Oh yeah?" My mind raced for a good come-back. "By the time they're 'back,' we'll have cities with skyscrapers on the moon. There's no getting past my Dolphins as long as Bob Griese is playing quarterback."

Trace appeared next to us.

"Seriously, boys. I honestly can't understand why NASA didn't send five girls on this mission. We land on the moon, and the first thing you do is argue about your favorite football team?

Are you serious?"

There was silence. I think Jonah was yelling something back at her, but he had forgotten to press his radio talk switch.

"For the record," Trace continued, "Cleveland Browns rule. Their quarterback is a total hubba hubba. Now stop talking football and follow me."

Trace started moving in slow two-footed bunny hops away from the command module, towards a four-wheeled buggy about 30 yards away across the dusty surface.

I wanted to remind Trace that my Dolphins had beaten her Browns 42-10 the last time they had played. But I decided not to say anything because, seriously, I was on the moon. And for the first time in my life, I realized that there was something just as important as the Miami Dolphins. Or maybe ... *maybe* ... even more important.

My thoughts shifted quickly back to the moon. On the moon, we weren't weightless like we were in the command module on the way up, where there was no downward tug on objects. At least on the moon, you could tell what was up and what was down.

I started out doing bunny-hops like Trace, afraid to take a real step. But by the time I had gotten half way to the moon buggy, I was taking full, slow steps, pushing off hard with my back foot. Each time, I would glide several feet across the surface before being tugged gently back down by the moon's weak gravity.

I pressed the local talk button. "Hey Jonah, check this out," I said. Standing still, I bent my knees as far as I could in my stiff space suit and pushed up hard. The ground dropped away from me and I felt a lurch in my stomach like I was on a roller coaster. Two, three, four seconds then the small jolt of landing again on the ground.

"Sign that boy up for the Olympics!" shouted Jonah. "You were about 4 feet off the ground!"

"Trace, come on, measure how high our jumps are," I said excitedly. "Me versus Jonah. Come on, measure our jumps. See who wins."

"For the second time in two minutes," said Trace, "your boyness has amazed me. First an NFL argument. Now you're competing in the Leap Frog Olympics. Do I need to remind you that you have been sent here, by the United States of America, to save the moon from permanent destruction?"

Jonah and I hung our heads and looked at our feet through our gold-plated astronaut masks.

"Yes, ma'am," we said in unison.

"Now, get in the car," said Trace. "Lets go for a drive."

▲ ▼ ▲ ▼ ▲

Trace slowly, cautiously inched the zip buggy forwards, following tire tracks that curved around the edge of the landing area and cut across a dusty field towards the moon base.

"Uh, Trace. I admire your caution," I said into my radio. "But I don't want to die of old age on this trip. Can you step on it?"

"Yeah Trace," said Jonah. "Did you leave your racing skill back on earth?"

"Knock it off, passengers," said Trace, with a frustrated edge in her voice. "Believe it or not, this appears to be the top speed."

"Top speed!?" I exclaimed. "Are you kidding! I could walk faster than this."

"An ant could walk faster than this," laughed Jonah. "In

fact, I think I just saw one. A moon ant passed us and left us in the moon dust."

Trace decided to check in with home. She pressed the Channel One talk button in her glove. "Mission Control, this is Trace. Is there any way to give this zip buggy a little more ... zip?"

"Negative, Trace," came the reply from earth. "The zip buggy has a 30 horsepower engine, but that's way too much power for usual driving on the moon. So it has a little electronic box in the engine called a 'governor' that restricts the engine's power. The governor box limits how much power goes to the wheels, so it limits the top speed. Your maximum is 6 miles per hour."

"Six miles per hour! Oh, come on, I'm not a baby!" complained Trace as the zip buggy inched along the pathway towards the base.

"Six is plenty, trust me," came the reply from earth. "We've had a couple accidents on past trips. Having only a little gravity makes it A LOT harder to drive. Just think about walking on the moon. Any bump or jump would send you flying up in the air. Anyway, you're in no hurry."

Trace continued to grumble, but I was already done with that argument. Six miles an hour was just fine with me as I looked around. We had covered about half the distance between the command module and Oblivion Base, about the length of a football field. I could see thin, rectangular strip windows running along the edge of the nearest building to us. There were lights on inside, almost as if someone was there waiting for us.

As we started to come around the corner of one of the buildings, I could make out a small courtyard that looked like a parking lot. From a distance, I had seen the top of what looked like a huge orange truck peeking over the top of one of the moon base buildings. Now that we were coming around that building, I could see that it was indeed a truck. A ladder ran up the front side to the drivers' cabin. The enormous back door was open, and I could make out large bins – kind of like plastic trash cans – filled with something.

Even though he couldn't see my eyes through the reflecting gold visor, Jonah could tell what I was looking at.

"Pleurinium," he said. "They call that truck the MTV, the Mineral Transport Vehicle. It's loaded full of Pleurinium from the mine, ready to be hauled back to earth. Except they haven't been able to unload it."

Trace slowly maneuvered through the parking area towards a doorway in the far corner where two larger buildings were connected by a low hallway. Jonah and I clumsily pulled ourselves out of the zip buggy. I felt awkward and bulky, stiff-legged and stiff-armed. But light and bouncy at the same time. I was moving slowly and carefully, remembering what Strider had told me. It was easy to fall over, and you definitely did not want to fall over. It could tear your space suit and expose you to the harsh lunar atmosphere. That's something you definitely DID NOT want to happen.

Moving slowly, Jonah and I had no problems bouncing down the short pathway to the door, where we turned to wave goodbye to Trace. She expertly backed the zip buggy around and started the slow trip back to the command module to pick up Lance and Kat.

Leaving Jonah and me to head inside together.

Jonah paused a couple steps short of the door and raised his hand politely.

"After you, sir," he said through the radio.

"Oh, don't be silly. After YOU," I replied, giving him a slight bow.

"But you're the fancy-pants Co-Pilot!" I could imagine Jonah's big, goofy grin behind the gold visor. If he hadn't been wearing his helmet, I definitely would have grabbed his head and given him a noogie. The first human noogie in the history of the moon. Wow.

"Mickey." The radio in my helmet crackled. "Mickey, this is Mission Control. You will see a key pad on the right side of the door with three buttons. Press 3, 1, 3."

Luckily, the numbers were huge, because my space suit fingers were enormous. When I pressed the buttons, the door popped outward a few inches and then slid sideways, revealing a small room about the size of the downstairs bathroom at the Boys' Home. Except with no toilet.

A fluorescent light blinked on, and Jonah and I stepped inside the air lock.

"Mickey, you should see a large button that says 'CLOSE.' It should be flashing. Make sure you're standing away from the door and press it."

The door eased shut and snapped into place with a clang. Following instructions, Jonah and I pressed more buttons and headed through another door into a larger room with benches and hooks running along two of the walls. Just like the first room, it was lit by only a small emergency bulb at first. But as soon as we entered, the bright overhead lights flickered on automatically.

"Smart room!" I said to Jonah.

"Only the best. This is a taste of the future, Mickey. The future is a place without light switches. A place where the toilets flush by themselves. A place where...."

"Mickey," my radio interrupted, "look at the oxygen gauge on Jonah's chest. Is it green?"

"It's green, roger that, control," I replied.

"And Mickey, look at the pressure gauge next to the oxygen gauge. What does it say?"

"It reads 14.0, and it's flashing green."

"That means you're clear to take off your space suit. Mickey, you first."

After a full minute struggling with the complicated snaps and buckles on the side of my helmet, I was finally able to take it off. I felt a wave of cool, sweet air surround my head, and I realized how cramped and hot my helmet had been after just half an hour out on the moon. I helped Jonah take his helmet off and then we peeled off our suits and hung them on the hooks. "Man, I feel a thousand pounds lighter," said Jonah with relief.

Free from the helmets, we looked around the room again. And I think we both noticed them at the same time. There were several large, full-sized space suits with helmets hanging on the hooks at the far end. Waiting for owners who were thousands of miles away, back on earth.

A reminder that we were kids, alone, in a place too dangerous for adults.

17

WELCOME TO OBLIVION

At the end of a long hallway was a doorway to a large room. Through the dim glow of the emergency lighting I could see shapes of unidentifiable furniture lining the wall on the right side. I stepped into the room and the overhead lights automatically flickered on.

"The recreation room," I said, remembering the description from the maps Strider had shown me that evening before blastoff. On the right side of the room was a set of strange looking furniture – exercise equipment. There was a treadmill for walking and running in place, a stationary bicycle and three different weightlifting machines. On the other side of the room were clusters of chairs around a small table with games and playing cards piled in the middle, and a shelf of books.

"I don't think we'll have much time for hanging out here," I said.

"Yeah, and this won't do me any good," said Jonah as he strained to lift the heavy weightlifting bar. "Hey, move this outside onto the moon surface and I could probably lift it!"

"C'mon Jonah, let's explore some more." I was eager to see the rest of the moon base before the others arrived. "We have two doors to choose from … you pick."

Jonah made his way over to the door just beyond the stationary bicycle. Like all the others, it was grey metal, shiny and smooth. To the right of the door was a square pad about the size of a deck of playing cards, surrounded by glowing green light. The OPEN button. Below it was a keypad, like you would find on a telephone.

Jonah punched the OPEN button and the door opened with a shwoosh. We stood in the doorway and I waved my hand inside the entrance to turn on the automatic lights. The smell hit me a split second before the overhead light flashed on.

"Holy stinky cheese," Jonah exclaimed when he saw the mess. "What the heck happened here?"

"Um, I'd say the guys up here before us had a gi-normous food fight. What a mess! I haven't seen food fight wreckage this bad since Sister Rinaldi went to get a haircut and left Taco in charge. Ugh gross. Is that an old sandwich? Or some kind of fruit?"

Jonah looked closer. "No, I think it's … green Jell-O?" He

poked at it with his shoe, as if expecting it to move. Fortunately, it didn't.

There were boxes and plastic bags of food piled on the ground in front of two cabinets with more still on the shelves. Many of them were ripped open, with their contents spilling out onto the floor. The door of a refrigerator stood open. That's where most of the smell seemed to be coming from.

I pressed the TALK button on the small radio clipped to the front of my jumpsuit. "Uh, Mission Control. This is Mickey here. We hope you don't need us to clean up the kitchen. Over."

"Mickey, Mission Control here. We don't understand. Please explain."

"I mean the mess in the kitchen," I continued. "There's food everywhere. At least, what used to be food. The people before us were total pigs." I suddenly remembered Riker was probably listening on the other end of the radio. "I mean, no offense. They just didn't clean up. At all." Jonah was walking around the room, picking his way through the mess.

Riker's unmistakable, sharp voice crackled through the radio. "Riker here. Explain yourself, Mickey. That doesn't make any sense. What are you seeing?"

"Well, let's say this place gets the Bad Housekeeping Award. I've seen some food fights in my day, but this takes it to a whole new level. Back where I come from, this would be a three-week detention."

I felt a crunch under my feet and realized I was walking through a small pile of Froot Loops cereal.

"Mickey, I don't know what you're talking about," said Riker. "The kitchen was perfectly clean when I left it."

I looked at Jonah and he shrugged his shoulders. "These

162

guys are treating us like we're toddlers, or insane," I complained to Jonah. "I know a mess when I see one, and this...."

CRASH!

A chill ran up my spine.

I knew I had heard it because Jonah jumped at the same time I did.

A crash ... a one hundred percent definite crash ... had come from the next room, right ahead of us. There was no way the others had arrived yet. So that meant....

"Come on Jonah, lets go take a look," I said. "Time to earn our pay."

"Earn our pay?" asked Jonah. "Last time I checked we weren't getting paid. Let somebody else check."

"Somebody else? Like who? Come on, it's up to us. Lets check it out."

I headed across the room to the door on the far side, towards where the noise had come from, and punched the OPEN pad. The door slid aside with a "shwoop" revealing a short, dimly lit hallway. As I stepped inside, the main lights flickered on, activated by my movement, just like in the kitchen.

Jonah was right behind me. "You know, I never thought of that," he continued. "We're not getting paid. They sent us to the moon, and are we getting so much as a dime? Sheesh! I bet Riker and the rest of Team Varsity get huge salaries. But us? What's in it for us? I think we should just, um, sit and wait in that room with the games in it."

I had reached the door at the end of the hall, and paused to turn back to Jonah. "Are you listening to yourself? Just a few days ago, you said you felt like you had won the lottery, you were so lucky. 'An adventure in science,' you called it. And now you're holding out for money?"

Jonah looked glum. "Yeah. But now it's different. I wasn't exactly chasing mystery noises on the moon at that time." He sighed as he listened to what he had just said. "Okay, okay. Adventure in science. Go ahead. I'm ... um ... right behind you."

We had reached the door at the end of the hallway. I pressed OPEN and the door slid aside, revealing darkness. I took one, two, three steps inside, expecting the lights to flicker on at any second. Jonah was so close behind me I could feel him breathing on my ear. Smelled like peanut butter.

Then the door "shwooped" shut, leaving us in complete blackness.

"Um, Mick," Jonah whispered. "Um, this sucks. Do you think...."

"SHHH," I cut him off.

There was a mechanical hum and a steady, constant clicking coming from the right side of the room. Like some sort of machine or fan. But there was something else.

Irregular. Occasional. An unmistakable shuffling. Then silence. Then shuffling again. No doubt about it.

If something hadn't happened soon, I probably would have fainted. I was so nervous, I had forgotten to breathe and was holding my breath.

But something did happen. At the far end of the room, about 40 feet away, another door shwooped open. A dim glow of light spilled into the room. And right then, just as the door was sliding open, the faintest glimpse of a shadow ... or maybe it was a small shape ... no, definitely a shadow ... briefly flitting around the edge of the door.

Before I could do anything, the door shwooped shut, leaving us again in total blackness.

That's when I sprang into action. Not in the direction of the mysterious shape, of course, but back where we'd come from. Jonah and I obviously had the same idea at the same time. We both spun and dove backwards for the OPEN button, outlined in green light. I launched myself towards the sliver of bright light as the door opened, and so did Jonah, and we spilled back into the hallway, a tumbled mass of elbows and legs, knees and arms. Next thing I knew, I was crawling down the hallway as fast as I could, with Jonah riding on my back, like he was on a horse. Backwards. I dove for the OPEN button and felt Jonah's shoe on my ear as he propelled himself back into the kitchen. I was holding onto his belt, so I went right with him, doing a back flip and landing in a sitting position on Jonah's head.

After the door shwooped shut, we lay there on the floor for a while, panting. I rubbed the huge egg-shaped bump on my forehead where I'd accidentally run into the door.

Jonah finally broke the silence. He said it, but I was thinking it.

"An alien."

The word hung there in the still, stinky air of the kitchen.

"Definitely an alien. That's what we saw, and that's what made this mess. Mickey, do you know what this means? We're not alone in the universe. We're not alone on the moon. We're not even alone IN THIS BUILDING. Mickey. We've made contact with an alien!"

* * * * *

Tom was sitting up on his sleeping bag again, drenched with skepticism.

"Okay," he said, pointing a finger straight at his dad's nose. "I

was just starting to believe the story. But now, aliens? This is beginning to sound more like your regular stories now. Astronauts. Aliens. Next we'll probably have a couple moon dinosaurs, right? A good story. But it's a story, right?"

"What, you believed it through the whole space camp and rocket-to-the-moon part? But as soon as you think there's an alien involved, it's a tall tale? What's so impossible about an alien? Are you absolutely certain we're alone in the universe?"

"No," said Tom, still glaring with accusation at his dad, finger pointed. "There COULD be life on other planets. I just don't believe that you've ever met it."

Dad tilted his head as he thought about that one.

"Emph. Fair enough. So I've lost the Tom vote," he said, turning to Tess. "How about the Tess vote. Are you still with me?"

Tess's face looked tense, clearly showing the battle going on in her brain. "I don't KNOW!" she said with exasperation. "I want to believe you, but I just don't know!" She paused. "What did the alien look like. How many legs? What color? And did it talk? I need more information."

Dad smiled. "We'll get there, don't worry. Jonah and I lying in a twisted heap on the floor of the completely messy kitchen on the moon base. We had just discovered that we weren't alone. There was something else already at the moon base, waiting for us. And just then, Lance came waltzing in with Trace and Kat. And for the first time, I was actually glad to see him. Which lasted about three seconds."

18

WE ARE NOT ALONE

"Nice work, you two. You're the advance team with instructions to prepare the moon base for our arrival. And what do you do? Trash the kitchen and goof around wrestling. Top notch." Lance strode into the kitchen like he owned it.

Jonah and I were still lying in a mashed heap in the middle of the floor. I flung Jonah's leg off my chest and pulled myself upright.

"But wait ... you see," I started, "the kitchen was a total mess like this when we came in. All this food everywhere. And then we heard a noise. So we decided to investigate. So we went through that door and down a hall and you'll never guess what we saw! There was a...."

Lance's radio crackled to life and we heard Looper's voice.

"This is Mission Control. Please confirm that all five of you have arrived at Oblivion Base. Over."

"Mission Control, this is Flight Commander Marshall," replied Lance. "We have all arrived and the team is...," he cast an insulting sneer in my direction, "...the team is making itself at home here."

"Nice work so far, Artemis Seven. But don't get too comfortable, we need you to get right to work. Lance, lead the team down to the East Control Room. Kat, we need you to tap into the main computer running the nuclear reactor, locate the maintenance history, and send that information back to our scientists here at the space center. That maintenance history should contain the clues we need to figure out what's wrong, and how to shut down the reactor."

"Roger that, Mission Control," said Lance. "Over and out."

▲ ▼ ▲ ▼ ▲

"Aliens?" Trace stared incredulously at Jonah.

"Face it," said Jonah, crossing his arms and staring back at her. "It's the most logical explanation. The five of us are the only ones up here. And I definitely saw something alive."

"And you know what else?" Jonah continued. "MICKEY saw it too."

Trace turned to me, her eyes urging me to put an end to this craziness.

The thing is, I couldn't. As much as I didn't want to believe we had encountered an alien in our first 10 minutes at the moon base, I couldn't come up with any other possible explanation.

We were all crowded together in the East Control Room, watching Kat as she sat in front of a huge computer monitor. She alternated between tapping furiously at the keyboard and reading the dizzying scroll of computer code as it flashed up onto the screen. Lance hovered over her shoulder, occasionally saying "yeah" and "do that one" and "yup, that's right." Of course, none of us had any idea what Kat was doing, especially Lance. So fortunately, Kat completely ignored him.

As I thought about the strange thing we had encountered, I stared out the small windows above the control panel at the view. A flat, rocky area sloped up gently towards a ridge of rough boulders. Beyond that ridge, and out of our view, was the deep Bottomless Canyon. And still farther, lurking in the distance, was the dark grey mass of a massive mountain range.

I realized Trace was staring at me, waiting for a response. Oh yeah, aliens.

"Mickey?" prompted Trace again. "Mickey!? You're not buying Jonah's crazy theory, are you?"

"Well...." I didn't want to say it, but I had to. "I can't rule it out. We didn't see a ghost. It was something real. I think. Hey, why don't we ask Mission Control?"

Lance, who had been silently ignoring our conversation until now, suddenly spun to face us.

"Are you jerks serious? Ask Mission Control? Ask Riker? 'Hi, Mickey Price here. I think there are aliens on the Moon Base. And big purple elephants. And dancing fairies.' Mickey, you might be a stupid little kid, but at least don't act like one on my mission."

My cheeks flashed red. I was mad and embarrassed at the

same time. There should be a word for that. Mad-barrassed. Or emb-angry. I was both. Before my brain could reattach to my mouth, however, Kat surprised us all by speaking up.

"Done."

"Done with what, Kat?" asked Trace.

"Done with finding the nuclear reactor's maintenance records for the last three months, creating and running a program to decode them and eliminate the unnecessary information, compressing the file into something that can be transmitted, and then radioing it back to the engineers on Earth. I'm done."

We were speechless, except for Lance. He pressed his radio talk switch and said "Mission Control, Flight Commander Marshall here. My team and I have completed the computer work and have transmitted the information back to Earth."

"Nice work, Lance. Very good job. We're impressed with you. Oh, and tell your team they did a good job, too," came the immediate reply from 250,000 miles away.

Kat spun her chair and scowled at Lance. She hadn't missed the fact that he had just taken, and received, all the credit.

"One more thing, Flight Commander Marshall," said Kat. "I happen to agree with Jonah. He and Mickey saw something weird. They're not making it up. And right now, Jonah has the only explanation that makes any sense."

"Fine," said Lance. "I'm looking forward to doing my 'I TOLD YOU SO' dance when I prove we don't have little green aliens running around here with us. Come on, grab your travel packs and follow me over to the sleeping area. First one there gets their choice of beds. See you, suckers."

Our Flight Commander turned on his heels and broke into a very undignified sprint out of the room and down the hallway.

▲ ▼ ▲ ▼ ▲

Lance was first to arrive back in the kitchen area. He paused as he leaned over his backpack. Rather than pick it up, however, he drew back sharply. "Wait a minute...."

I noticed that the zipper of his pack was wide open and some clothes were hanging out the side. His toothbrush was lying on the floor nearby. Next to a candy bar wrapper. An EMPTY candy bar wrapper.

The other packs looked the same.

Something had rooted through our packs. And whoever it was ... or WHATEVER it was ... it was seemed to have a special hunger for our Butterfinger candy bars. There were five or six empty wrappers strewn about the floor next to our packs.

"Somebody laid a finger on my Butterfinger," said Trace.

"Believe me now?" said Jonah to Lance, who was poking nervously at his pack, as though it might still contain a mouse-sized burglar.

Before Lance could respond, we all heard a noise directly above us that sent a chill of terror through our bones.

It was a frantic, mad scrambling sound. Like the sound a dog makes when it scratches at the back door trying to get in. And it was coming from right above us, up in the crawl space above the ceiling panels.

Then it began to move away, down the hall.

There was something in the ceiling.

Something alive.

"Uhhhhhh, not good," Lance said, his voice shaking. He took several steps back towards the wall, moving behind Trace and holding Kat in front of him like a shield. "What-is-it, what-is-it, what-is-it, WHAT-IS-IT??" Then, composing himself slightly, he managed to squeak, "as Flight Commander, I order Mickey and ... um ... Jason to go follow that thing."

"Jason? Who's Jason?" said Jonah. He stuck out his arm towards Lance, as if to shake hands. "Nice to meet you, I'm Jonah. J-O-N-A-H. Are you a little scared of something, Flight Commander?"

We all laughed nervously. But to be honest, nobody was in the laughing mood. Truth be told, we were all seriously freaked out at this point.

The scraping sound was getting farther away. I knew we had to move fast. "Come on guys ... strength in numbers. Lets all go. Follow me!"

I set out down the hall at a slow jog, looking up for ... well ... I had no idea what I was looking for. I tilted my head for maximum ear exposure.

Down hallway after hallway, through laboratory rooms and back through the living room and the kitchen, we stayed a few steps behind the scraping, shuffling sound up in the ceiling.

The thing slowed as we neared the end of a long hallway and reached a sign marking the 'West Control Room.'

"Uh-oh," said Jonah. "Dead end. End of the line. Ground zero. Cornered. The big one. Showdown at the O-K Corral. No escape...."

"Jonah?" said Trace.

"Yes Trace?"

"Shut. Up. We get the picture."

We all stood there at the doorway to the West Control Room, our eyes riveted on the ceiling. Unless there was some kind of escape hatch in the roof, we had it cornered. The West Control Room wasn't that big, maybe the size of a ping pong table. The only way out was the way it had come, back down the hallway above us. Or through us.

I decided there was only one thing left to do. I had to take a look.

I had Lance and Trace get on all fours to make a ledge with their backs, and then Jonah stood with one foot on each back. I climbed up onto Jonah's shoulders, holding onto the wall with one hand as I wobbled to a standing position.

This seemed like a good idea when I imagined it, but now that I was standing with my head wedged against the ceiling it seemed slightly crazy. The ceiling was made up of square plastic panels, each one about two feet by two feet. The panel above my head tipped up easily when I pushed it, and I eased my head into the crawl space.

Total darkness.

I pulled my head back down into the hallway.

"Guys, it's totally dark," I whispered. "Anyone got a flashlight?"

I heard some rustling below and Kat handed one up to Jonah who passed it up to me. I flicked it on and saw that it cast a bright beam even in the lighted hallway. My eyes met Trace's, and she nodded in encouragement. Well, here goes nothing, I thought.

I poked my head back up into the crawl space and pointed the flashlight into the area above the West Control Room.

At first, all I saw was pipes and wires. The crawl space was only about a foot tall ... a little extra space between the ceiling panels and the hard cement that formed the outer wall of the moon base. I swung the beam towards the right. More pipes. More wires. And then....

Like a flash it came at me. Two glaring red eyes ... at first small but then getting suddenly larger as it came straight at my face. And teeth, gleaming teeth that flashed as they charged right at me. And I heard a scream. Maybe it was the creature's. Or maybe it was mine.

Forgetting that I was perched atop a human pyramid, I launched myself backwards. My arms and legs swung desperately but found nothing to grasp. As I sailed through the air, I was horrified to see that the charging creature had come through the ceiling panel and was still coming towards me.

As I sailed towards the ground, the last thing I saw before my head smacked onto the rock-hard floor of the hallway were the creature's legs and ... yes, no doubt about it ... a long, hairy alien's tail.

▲ ▼ ▲ ▼ ▲

A huge pair of eyes blinked above me, an inch away from mine.

Though the face was close, the voice sounded like it was coming from far away. "Wait guys. He's not dead. I think he's actually alive!"

I closed my eyes as a searing pain filled my skull and I emitted a good, long groan. When I opened my eyes again, I saw Trace leaning above me. She was patting my forehead with a warm washcloth.

I tilted my head and saw Jonah, who was looking at me with obvious concern. Next to him was Lance who looked ... unbelievable ... I'm sure I saw a look of disappointment when he realized I was alive.

I tipped my head the other way and saw Kat. On her shoulder was something I couldn't identify. I blinked hard.

OHMYGOSH, THE ALIEN!!!

I closed my eyes tight and blinked hard again.

When I looked back, there she was, clear as day. Kat. With, wait a minute....

I leaned up on one elbow. "Hey," I croaked, "can someone explain why Kat has a monkey on her shoulder?"

The monkey stared at me with small, intense eyes. When I met its gaze, it quickly buried its face in Kat's bushy hair. It certainly looked like an earth monkey, and not some sort of alien monkey. That's when I noticed that it was wearing a blue jumpsuit just like ours, with a little American flag sewn onto one of the arms. Under the flag was the name "Ziggy 3" in small, white letters.

The monkey pulled its head up and I saw one eye emerge from Kat's tangle of hair. It looked at me angrily and gave a shrill scream before it buried its head again in Kat's bushy hair.

"Guys," I said. "Can someone explain? Did I miss something?"

"Yeah, you kind of missed something when you fainted," said Lance, using his 'I'm talking to a pre-schooler' voice again. "After you freaked out and hit your head, I called down to Mission Control and confirmed that this monkey was part of an earlier mission. Riker said the Artemis Six team had to leave it behind when they evacuated the moon base three months ago."

"Hold on," I raised myself up onto one elbow. "You're saying I'M THE ONE who freaked out back there? I seem to remember a certain Flight Commander who was hiding at the back of the pack, using Kat as a human shield."

"I was giving you all a leadership opportunity," Lance replied, looking like he wanted to change the subject. "It's not fair to you if I'm always in front, making the decisions."

Jonah suddenly thumped himself on the forehead. "Oh, DUHHHH," he said up into the air, clearly frustrated. "As we were following the mystery noise, we passed a room with a sign that said 'Primate Room.' Now it makes sense."

"Excuse me?" I said in disbelief. "You saw a sign that said 'Primate Room' and you didn't bother telling us?"

"Well, it didn't seem important back then," said Jonah defensively. "We were busy chasing an ALIEN at the time, remember? If it had said 'Alien Room,' I might have commented."

Lance brightened up, realizing his chance to change the subject from him to Jonah. "Oh, right. Aliens. So, fantasy-boy, what do you have to say for yourself, now that your 'alien' has turned out to be a simple zoo animal? And 'The Glint'? Do you still think it's some alien space ship?"

"Well, it could be an alien space ship," said Jonah stubbornly. "Just because Ziggy turned out to be a monkey doesn't mean there's not an alien space ship out there. Ziggy has nothing to do with The Glint."

"Oh Jonah, don't you see. Ziggy has EVERYTHING to do with The Glint. They're the same thing. Something uncertain. Something unknown, in search of an explanation. Now, you're the kind of person who always thinks up the craziest, strangest explanation, and then actually believes it. But no matter how hard you believe in aliens, Jonah Trotsky, it doesn't make them real."

Jonah sighed. As much as I hated to admit it, Lance was probably right. I wondered whether Jonah realized this too.

19

PHONE HOME

The next day on the moon was probably the biggest disappointment in the history of humans. I was living the dream that millions upon millions of kids didn't even dare to dream. At age 12, I was an astronaut on a secret mission to the moon. Our mission was to save the moon from a nuclear accident that could contaminate it for a million years.

So how did we spend our first full day at Oblivion Base?

Cleaning the kitchen. One month worth of bad monkey table manners. Ziggy watched us clean his mess for a while with great interest. After about half an hour I walked over, handed him a dustpan and broom, and gestured towards the piles of food. Ziggy took one look at me, then chattered loudly and ran out of the room. "Hey, just 'cause you've got a tail doesn't mean you can't work. You're part of the team, fur-ball," I shouted.

Trace and Jonah shook their heads at me and went back to work. Great, now all of a sudden I'M the jerk for fighting with the monkey? Sheesh.

Meanwhile, Kat got a pass from kitchen duty and spent the day huddled over a computer monitor. Working with the engineers back on earth, she searched through line after line of computer code and ran dozens of tests, trying to figure out what was wrong with the nuclear reactor's shut-down mechanism.

And our Flight Commander? Well, he kept inventing a series of special projects for himself. Once, after he told us that Looper had ordered him outside to perform some complicated fix-it project, I took a break and went from window to window, trying to catch a glimpse of our team leader. I finally found him, out in the vehicle courtyard.

He was playing golf. He was actually playing golf. I could see three golf holes set up out there, with flagsticks and everything.

Jonah came up alongside me and squeezed his face into the small, round window. "Whatcha looking at?" he asked.

"Just watching our Flight Commander get a triple bogey," I answered. "Can you believe that guy? We're slaving away, ankle-deep in stinky old food, and he's outside playing golf!!??"

"Hmmm. Looks like he hit his ball into a sand trap," said Jonah with a laugh.

"Very funny," I answered. "This drives me crazy, I feel like going outside and dragging him back by the oxygen tank. We've still got hours left before we're done."

"Mick," said Jonah. "Before you go out there, think for a minute. You really want him in here with us? The only thing less pleasant than cleaning up month-old cheese is cleaning up month-old cheese with Lance Marshall. Come on, lets go back in there with Trace and continue our conversation about the greatest movies in the history of movies."

"You got a point," I conceded and followed him back into the kitchen.

Two hours later, the kitchen was sparkling like a photo from Good Housekeeping magazine. Lance had come back inside and gave our efforts a "B minus," saying he expected the kitchen to look better, given how long we had spent working on it.

Trace had just threatened to re-mop the entire kitchen with Lance's head when the radio crackled with a message from earth. Boy, Lance had some lucky timing.

We were surprised to hear Amanda Collins' voice through the loudspeaker. It was a welcome change from the no-nonsense messages we usually got from Looper and Riker and the others.

Amanda explained that they all understood how long we had been away from our families and how we might be homesick. She said she had arranged for each of us to have a 5 minute conversation with a family member.

"All of you head down to the East Control Room, where you can take the call in private," continued Amanda. "And Lance, honey, you're first."

We all rolled our eyes.

"The Director, your dad, is waiting to talk to you."

Lance, who had looked as excited as the rest of us for a minute, suddenly deflated. I was sure he had been looking forward to hearing from his mom, or grandmother, or even the mailman, rather than his dad.

"I almost feel sorry for him," I confided in Trace as the four of us waited in the hallway for our turn. "Imagine getting tucked in at night by Director Marshall."

"Dude," said Trace, sternly pointing a finger at me. "Don't you dare feel sorry for him. Remember the B-minus."

Lance emerged from the East Control Room only about two minutes after going in. "You're up Kat," he mumbled, before shuffling slowly away from us down the hall.

Trace caught my eye. "Okay. You're allowed to feel sorry for our Flight Commander for the next sixty seconds. But that's it."

Jonah and I smiled at each other as Trace crossed her arms defiantly, her jaw firm. I could tell she was allowing herself exactly one minute of sympathy for Lance, counting backwards from sixty.

Five minutes later, Kat came out into the hallway, her eyes red and puffy but with a huge smile on her face. "My Mom and Dad were both on the call!" The words burst out of her, followed by a giggle. "My Mom kept asking me if I was getting enough food. Enough food! Sure, Mom, I'm getting protein paste from a tube and plenty of powdered bananas. My Dad was speechless. Speechless! My Dad! All he could say was that I made him proud. Can you believe it?"

Kat walked right past us and kept on talking to the air.

Trace went next and then Jonah, both of them emerging from their phone call noticeably different from how they went in, as though they had received a burst of powerful medicine. I guess, in a way, they had.

And then came my turn. I imagined myself in Kat's place … or Jonah's … or Trace's. I wondered whether I would feel the same way as them after my five minutes with Sister Rinaldi. I felt a sudden pang of guilt, realizing that I wouldn't. Sister Rinaldi would probably make sure I was saying my prayers and obeying my orders and other important things like that. And sure, she cared about me and would want to hear me say I was doing just fine. And sure, she'd have some stories about what had been going on in the two weeks since I had left the house and it would be good to hear her voice. But still, curiously, I felt guilty.

"Mission Control? Mickey here, ready for my call."

"Roger that Mickey, we're making the connection." There were a series of clicks, and then the voice said "okay Mickey, you're on. You can proceed."

"Hey, Astro-boy," a familiar voice came through the speaker. "Come in Astro-boy. Are you there? I've been waiting on this phone for like half an hour and they keep telling me 'three more minutes' but it's never three more minutes. Are you there?"

I couldn't believe my ears. "TACO!!??"

"Yeah, who'd you think would call you? Awww, man. Don't tell me you were hoping for Big Linus, because that would reeee-ally hurt my feelings. Of course it's me you dingbat. How are you? How's the moon? How cool is it? Are you seriously on the moon, because if this is some sort of joke it's NOT FUNNY AT ALL."

"TACO!!?? Is that you??" I felt like I'd been transported thousands of miles and thousands of days away from the moon.

"Um, Mickey. Do you have some sort of Moon flu? Of course it's me. I said it's me. What's with you? I know you've been gone two weeks but it's not like my voice has changed or anything."

"Yeah, yeah. I know," I said, emerging from the fog of surprise. "It's just that I didn't expect you to be the one I got to talk to. I mean ... no offense ... but this is supposed to be some kind of secret mission. Super top-secret. Nobody is allowed to know about it. So, like I said, no offense ... but you're the worst secret-keeper on the planet."

"I know," said Taco with a nervous little laugh. "Sister Rinaldi told me it was a secret and I wasn't allowed to tell anybody. And I kept it a secret for about EIGHT WHOLE MINUTES. I swear. And I meant to keep it a secret longer. But then it kind of slipped out in a conversation. It totally wasn't my fault. And at that point ... well, once it wasn't a secret anymore, I just had to tell everybody in the whole house." He paused. "But do you know what stinks?"

"What?" I asked.

"NOBODY BELIEVES ME," he wailed. "Sheesh. They think it's all some big joke. When I asked Sister Rinaldi to back me up, she got this look on her face and said 'Why Taco, what a bunch of hogwash, where do you come up with this stuff?' And then she actually WINKED at me, kind of a 'SO THERE' wink."

"I think that's why the Sister told me about your secret mission, because she knew nobody would believe me. It's totally frustrating. Check this out. HEY ALVIN!!!!" I heard his yell echoing through what was probably the front hall of the big house.

"Yeah," came the muffled reply from the distance.

"I'm talking to Mickey and he's totally on the moon. He rode a rocket up there and now he's on the moon. Isn't that awesome?"

"Yeah, whatever Taco. Say hello to Mickey the astronaut. And when you get the Incredible Hulk and Batman on the line, let me know. THEN I'll care," came the distant reply.

"SEE!!?? Life's so unfair," sighed Taco. "So how was the

trip? Did you get to drive the rocket? Were you totally cruising? How long did it take you?"

"Lets see," I said, trying to remember his questions and answer them, in order. "Trip was great. No, I didn't get to drive. Yes, we were totally cruising faster than you can imagine. And it took three days."

"Three days?" said Taco, sounding disappointed. "That's totally slow. It only took us two days to drive all the way to Iowa that one time we went to camp. And that's like seven states away. I thought rockets were supposed to be fast!"

"Taco, I won't even bother to answer that one," I said. Sometimes I couldn't believe the things that came out of his mouth. "Oh wait," I said, "here's one cool thing. There's a monkey up here."

There was a long pause, then a tremendous shriek.

"ARE YOU SERIOUS? MONKEYS ON THE MOON!!?? I knew it, I knew it, I knew it, I totally knew it. Monkeys on the moon. I told you so. Or at least I should have told you because I totally thought it. I really did think it last week, I swear I did. Monkeys on the moon!!?? Are they like earth monkeys running around hairy and naked, or do they talk and wear clothes and fly space ships?"

"Taco," I interrupted. But he kept right on going.

"Oh my gosh, do they have cities? Do they have cities of tree houses with bedrooms out on the branches? Or wait, you're on the moon. Do you even have trees up there? If you don't have trees, where do the moon monkeys live? Some sort of monkey moon hotels? How does that work?"

"Taco," I interrupted again. But he hadn't stopped.

"Oh my gosh, and if there aren't any trees, what do they eat? Can you grow a banana without a tree? Now that would be crazy. Anyway, it doesn't matter, because YOU'VE discovered monkeys on the moon and now you'll be famous and...."

"TACO. STOP," I yelled. He stopped. "Taco, get a hold of yourself. No monkeys on the moon. I said monkey. MON-KEY. One monkey. An earth monkey. It's up here at the moon base. The astronauts before us brought it up. Sorry, but this isn't Planet of the Apes."

"Oh," came a small, disappointed voice.

"But he's completely cool and we're going to bring him back. He's friendly. And, no doubt, he's WAY smarter than you."

"Oh, you're gonna pay for that one Mickey. I'm totally smarter than any monkey. You can set up a test to prove it, I'm THAT confident. Seriously, set up a test, any time, any place. But just don't put any math on it, because that would be totally unfair and I'm not so sure I'd beat a monkey at math. GAH, you make me mad Mickey. I'm SO going to blow my nose on your bathrobe, which I just happen to be wearing right now. And you know what? You can't do anything about it."

I had to laugh as I heard a tremendous honk through the receiver, two hundred and sixty thousand miles away. At that point, I didn't care if he was kidding or if he had really just emptied both nostrils onto my bathrobe. I just had to laugh.

And that's when another voice broke into the line. "Moon base, this is Mission Control. We need to clear the line, Mickey. Time to say your goodbyes. We'll get you back to earth in less than a week and you can continue this ... um ... very fascinating conversation then."

"Awww man, come on," said Taco. "Mickey, that dude on the phone line sounds like a total drag. Are you going to put up with that? Does he boss you around all the time? You're totally an astronaut and I think you should call the shots. He's just some phone operator. You should be telling him what to do. You can...."

"Taco. Slow down. Take a breath. Breathe. Now, I gotta go. There's one thing I've learned on this trip: I've gotta listen to the people on the other end of the radio. They call the shots. But like the man said, I'll see you in a few days. Can you make it?

Taco heard my question.

But I was really asking myself.

20

HARD TO RESIST
A GALLANT MONKEY

"Snap to it," Lance barked as he strode quickly into the room. Jonah looked up for just a second, and then returned his attention to a thick book of moon maps he had been reviewing. He had given up asking Lance for the map showing the location of the Glint, but hadn't given up on the idea that he would solve the mystery.

Kat, Trace and I decided to ignore Lance and continued with our card game.

The only person or creature to move was Ziggy, who jumped

to his feet and snapped a crisp salute.

"Monkey one, humans zero," pouted Lance. "How am I supposed to work with you guys if you don't give me the respect I deserve?"

"Oh, I'll give you what you deserve," said Trace, shooting Lance an angry glare.

Lance let that comment go and stood at the front of the room, puffing out his chest as he continued.

"I just got off the radio with Mission Control and have our orders for the afternoon. The engineers back home have analyzed the computer information we sent back to earth and have figured out how to shut off the nuclear reactor. Kat and Mickey, you are making a short moon walk over to the reactor and will turn it off, following instructions from Earth. Jonah, you will do some basic maintenance tasks, following instructions from Major Austen on radio channel seven. And Trace," he said with a spiteful grin, "guess what? You're making our dinner."

"You're kidding," said Trace.

"Nope. Orders straight from Riker, as a matter of fact. Kat and Mickey, you'd better go get suited up and get on the radio with Mission Control, they're waiting for your call."

As much as I felt bad for Trace, I have to admit that my surge of anger at Lance didn't last long. Kat and I had been chosen for the most important part of our mission. A risky trip outside on the surface of the moon to the faulty nuclear reactor and then … somehow … who knew how? … we were supposed to do something that a half dozen adult astronauts before us had failed to do.

Trace kept her emotions in check, but she couldn't control her curiosity.

"So you've given the four of us our orders," she said as she stood facing Lance. "What about you?"

Yeah, what about Lance?

"Oh, I have my own instructions," he said, looking away quickly and then bending over to tie his shoes. "Nothing much. Just like Jonah is doing some routine fix-it things inside the Moon Base, I'm doing some routine fix-it things on the outside. Nothing to get excited about."

I had learned a few things from Poker Night at the boys' home. One was to be patient and not to bet all your chips on your first good hand. Another was how to tell when someone wasn't telling the truth. Lance was as easy to read as a big-print book for kindergarteners. I knew he was hiding something. He always wanted to be doing the most important task. So why wasn't he upset that Kat and I had been chosen for the biggest job of all?

Trace gave me a quick sideways look and raised her eyebrows, so I knew she noticed it too. Lance was up to something, but neither of us could figure it out.

▲ ▼ ▲ ▼ ▲

Ziggy followed Kat and me to the locker room. I spent the next several minutes carefully pulling on my moon suit, and helping Kat put on hers. This was pretty much a two-person job. The oxygen tanks were slotted into a bulky built-in backpack, attached to the main suit. Out on the moon, with the lower gravity, they seemed lighter. But inside the Moon Base, this backpack was extremely heavy.

I lifted Kat's backpack as she squirmed her arms into the suit. Kat grunted as she heaved my heavy suit up onto my back.

And then came the helmets.

Each one weighed as much as a bowling ball.

And then came the checking and re-checking of the snaps and buckles and gauges, to make sure the suits were completely air-tight.

Finally, about 10 minutes after we had started, we were ready to head outside. Turning to the air lock door, I remembered Ziggy. There he was, sitting on a chair with his legs crossed, waiting patiently by the door. His moon suit and helmet were on and ... did he really do that? I think he flashed me the thumbs-up sign.

"No way, Ziggy. You're staying here," said Kat emphatically, more sure of herself that I had ever heard her about anything. "This is way too dangerous for a monkey." She shook her head, pointed at Ziggy, and then pointed back towards the door to the kitchen.

A sharp chatter of angry monkey sounds came through the speaker in my helmet and Ziggy thumped the door to the air lock with his little fist.

"Ummm, Kat," I said hesitantly. "I'm not sure you want to fight this battle. Let him come."

"No way," Kat said, almost pleading. "I won't allow it. This poor monkey has been through enough already. It would be cruel and dangerous for us to drag him outside onto the moon. And besides, what if he runs away or something? We don't have time to chase him around. And besides besides, Mission Control didn't tell us to take him."

I looked at Ziggy for a while, standing by the door. He was standing at attention like a soldier. Then, he gave us a salute. Okay, that did it.

"Kat, who said anybody else needs to know we're taking him? They won't have a clue if we don't mention it. And look, we're a team here and every team member has to contribute. We don't know what Ziggy can do, but he's been here way longer than either one of us. He might just know something we don't."

Kat was clearly torn. But when Ziggy pressed the green "OPEN" button and held out his paw to Kat to lead her into the air lock, the struggle was over. "Looks like WE'RE going with HIM, rather than the other way around," I said. "Lets hit it."

I heard Kat sigh. She just couldn't resist a gallant monkey.

We stepped into the air lock. The door back to the locker room slid shut with a clang and we heard the air whistling out of the room as the pressure changed to the harsh lunar level.

"Mission Control," I said, pressing the long range radio button inside my right glove. "This is Mickey and Kat, reporting for duty in the South Air Lock. We're ready to head outside."

"Roger that, astronauts. Proceed outside when you're ready."

With that, the exterior door slid open and the small room was filled with brilliant sunlight. With an excited squeak, our pint-sized companion led us out onto the dusty surface of the moon.

▲ ▼ ▲ ▼ ▲

The entrance to the nuclear reactor looked like a port-a-potty, rising up from the moon dust. As we bounce-walked across the vehicle courtyard towards it, Looper explained that astronauts on earlier trips had affectionately named it "the outhouse." But he also explained that, of course, there was more to the nuclear reactor than meets the eye. Behind the door was a ladder that led deep down into the ground, to a series of rooms and equipment that provided power to the moon base. Enough for several moon bases, some day, if it could be fixed.

Looper explained that the reactor was powered by uranium, a very powerful but very dangerous material that had to be handled with extreme caution. When the reactor was working, the uranium fuel rods were moved into the middle part of the reactor and created an incredible amount of power. When the reactor was not working, these fuel rods had to be pulled out of the reactor and "parked" in a safe position so that they would cool down.

That was the problem.

One of the fuel rods was stuck in the reactor. The tiny motor that pushed the fuel rod into place was jammed in the "on" position. Nothing had worked to pull it out of and it was getting dangerously overheated. The solution? We would just reprogram the main computer, turn off the little motor that was causing the problem, and then the fuel rod would slide easily out of the reactor and into the "park" position.

"You make it sound easy," I said as we bounce-walked over to the outhouse.

"That's because it is easy," said Looper. "Kat will log into the reactor's main computer. And if she does just what we tell her to, this whole thing could be over in 10 minutes."

With that confident prediction ringing in our ears, we entered the outhouse. One by one, we descended the ladder, down a narrow tube illuminated by a string of lights running along one side. Ziggy and I waited at the bottom as Kat's legs slowly emerged, and then we bounce-stepped across a small room to an air lock and shut the heavy door behind us, sealing out the harsh moon environment. After only a few minutes in my suit, I was already sweaty and couldn't wait to get my helmet off.

I didn't have to wait long. After a short wait, the "WARNING" sign in the air lock turned off, replaced by a green "READY" sign. We unclipped our helmets and slipped off our suits.

As soon as my helmet was off, I was greeted by cool, fresh air ... but also by an ear-splitting alarm that pulsed one second on, one second off. Like a truck's horn. Only harsher and sharper.

It was so loud we couldn't talk normally. We could only communicate during the one-second gaps of silence.

"Step [HONK] one [HONK]" I said, filling the silence with words. "Turn [HONK] off [HONK] this [HONK] dumb [HONK] alarm!"

"Seriously [HONK]," Kat yelled back. "I [HONK] think [HONK] we [HONK] get [HONK] the [HONK] picture [HONK] there's [HONK] an [HONK] emergency [HONK] right!!?? [HONK] [HONK] Duh!!??"

As soon as Ziggy stripped off his bulky space suit he scampered over to Kat and extended both hands upwards to her. Of course, she was happy to give him a ride. He hugged her hard with his legs, and squeezed her neck with his elbows. His paws were firmly clamped over his ears and his eyes were shut tight. The loud noise of the alarm was clearly bothering the little guy. Heck, it was bothering me too.

We gave up trying to speak and wended our way through a maze of tunnels.

We knew we had found the Main Control Room when we stepped in through the low door. There was a bank of computer equipment along one wall, set in front of a long, low window overlooking the reactor in the next room.

Kat struggled to set Ziggy down, who reluctantly relented

and grasped her leg. After a few quick taps on a keyboard, the brain-rattling alarm suddenly stopped mid-honk. My ears were still ringing.

Ziggy cautiously removed his paws from his ears. He looked at me angrily and let out a loud shriek.

"What?" I blurted incredulously. "You're not blaming me for the alarm, are you?"

Ziggy kept staring at me angrily as he gripped Kat's leg.

"Eeeeeeep."

"Oh come on, monkey. It hurt my ears too. I would have…."

"Um, Mickey," interrupted Kat. "Please stop arguing with the monkey. Can you do something useful, like call back home?"

"This isn't over, Ziggy," I called out as he turned his back on me and jumped up onto Kat's lap. "We'll talk more about this later."

Kat cleared her throat. "Em-hem."

"Okay, okay," I said, trying not to get irritated at a 10-pound monkey.

I contacted Mission Control and, for the next few minutes, I watched and listened as Looper led Kat through a series of complicated procedures on the computer. It turns out, logging onto the computer system and turning off the alarm was the easy part. After that, nothing seemed to go right.

It was soon clear that the plan designed by the NASA scientists wasn't going to work. No matter what they did, the fuel rod remained stuck in the reactor. Which meant the reactor's temperature kept rising.

Just because we had turned off the sound part of the alarm didn't mean the problem had gone away. In fact, it was getting steadily worse. If we didn't get this fixed soon, we were going to have to accept defeat and abandon the moon base.

"That," said a new voice over the radio, "is NOT an option. Director Marshall here. Time for the Hail Mary."

Kat looked up at me. "I have a feeling that's a sports term, am I right? Please translate."

"Right," I smiled, "here's the translation. A Hail Mary is a prayer that the priests and nuns make you say a lot in Catholic church. And on a football field, it's kind of a prayer too: a last-second desperation long-bomb pass when all else has failed. Like for example, two years ago in the last game of the regular season, the Miami Dolphins were playing the Denver Broncos. The beloved Dolphins were down by six late in the fourth quarter. Things looked bleak, but Bob Griese ... he's the Dolphins' quarterback, you know ... he called a play named Eagle-Duck Left Seventeen Hook, where two receivers line up wide on the left side and run this crossing pattern. Here, let me draw this out for you...."

"Mickey?"

"Yes."

"Mickey, I get the picture. And I don't think Marshall is going to call Eagle-Duck Left Seventeen Hook, okay? Let's hear HIS Hail Mary plan."

I sighed. "Director Marshall, please proceed. We're ready for your Hail Mary."

"Roger that, Mickey," came the NASA Director's reply. "The little motor keeping the fuel rod in place is stuck in the 'on' position and we can't turn it off. We've tried every imaginable way to cut the power. The only thing left is a total shutdown."

"All right," I said. "Just say the word and Kat can do it."

"Well, we tried a total shutdown using the computer, but it

didn't work. All that's left is doing this the old fashioned way. We need you to cut the power wire somewhere between the master panel and the generator. Just clip it with a pair of wire cutters. With all power off, the engine that keeps the uranium fuel rod in place can't keep running, it's impossible. So the fuel rod will just slip back down the tube out of the reactor and slide into the safe "park" position."

Sounded easy enough.

"But I told you, this is a Hail Mary," continued Marshall. "It's our only hope, but we don't usually do this. It has other consequences. When we say it shuts off all power, I mean ALL power in your part of the base. Even the emergency power. Even the power that runs the oxygen pumps. Once you cut the power, you will have about 5 minutes to get back to the air lock and get your suits on before the oxygen runs out. You think you can do that?"

"Roger that," Kat and I said together. Not because we felt any confidence. But because, really, we didn't have any choice.

After tearing apart the control room for ten minutes, digging through every drawer and closet, we finally found the wire clippers. The three of us, two kids and a monkey, then followed Marshall's directions to a short hallway two levels down below the control room.

We removed the floor panel and exposed a maze of pipes and strand after strand of wires. "This is it, Mickey," said Marshall. "You only get one chance. If you can't do it, we're evacuating the moon base and bringing you home."

I looked over at Kat. "He really knows how to calm a guy down, doesn't he," I laughed nervously.

"I don't think he was trying to calm you down Mickey," said Kat, completely missing my sarcasm. "I think he was trying to tell you that if you don't cut the right wire, we all may die and the moon will be a toxic disaster area for a million years."

I sighed and shook my head. At that moment, Ziggy tiptoed over to me and put one paw on my shoulder. With his other, he made a thumbs-up sign and nodded his head.

"Kat, you see that? Take a few lessons from Ziggy here about how to calm a guy down."

I turned back to the spaghetti of wires and called back to Mission Control. "Is it ok with you if I just start clipping randomly? I'll eventually get the correct one, right?"

A chorus of voices immediately blasted through the radio. "NO!!!!"

I got the picture.

"Mickey," Marshall explained, "if you cut the wrong wire, it could have a disastrous result. We don't know what it would do. It could start or stop one system or another, and that could cause things to spin out of control. We don't have time to create new problems. You have to clip the Aqua-colored wire in bundle number seven underneath the main water tube. Not the dark blue wire. Not the baby blue wire. Not the royal blue wire. The aquamarine blue-green one. Aqua. Can you do that?"

I leaned down into the mess of pipes and wires and reached down … way down … snaking my arm downward, firmly grasping the pair of wire cutters.

And then I could see it. A twisted cluster of multicolored wires, way down near the bottom of the utility duct. And one of them, sticking out to one side, was definitely aqua. I reached down through the tangle of pipes.

Not even close.

"You got it yet? Mickey? You got it?"

I wedged my shoulder hard against the row of pipes at the

top of the duct, shoving my arm down as far as it would go. My hand swung down and the wire cutters snipped the open air. It was just out of reach.

"Mickey, you got it?" Marshall asked again.

"I ... can't ... reach." I replied, disappointed. "I just can't reach. How long do you think my arm is after all?"

There was a long pause. "You're right, Mickey," came Marshall's reply. "The utility duct was made with a full-grown astronaut in mind. A full-grown astronaut could reach down to those wires. By our calculations, you need to reach about 32 inches down into the duct. Your arm just isn't long enough."

I pulled the clippers up and rolled over onto my back. Kat crawled over and reached her hand down into the duct. Again, not even close.

We didn't say anything to each other, however, because we had a lot to listen to. Somehow, Looper and Marshall had left the radio channel open, and we could hear a confused, chaotic argument coming through the radio.

Somebody, maybe Looper, suggested that Lance had the best shot at reaching the wire, since he was by far the tallest member of our team. We heard Looper call for Lance over another radio channel without getting a response. Marshall started yelling "where the heck is Riker?" And some other voices started arguing about whether we could use a saw to cut away two of the pipes, so that I could reach down farther.

Kat looked at me with a tinge of desperation in her eyes. "That does not inspire confidence," she said quite simply.

I agreed.

"Eeeep," said Ziggy, brandishing the wire cutters.

Kat reached to grab the tool from the monkey, saying "Ziggy, don't wave those around. You might poke out your little monkey eye."

I looked at Ziggy, who was angrily pulling the wire cutters back from Kat. And I looked at the utility duct. There was no way for Ziggy to fit between the pipes. But maybe ... just maybe ....

"Kat, let go of the wire cutters. Ziggy's trying to tell you something. He can do this. HE'S our real Hail Mary."

Kat let go, and Ziggy stood in front of me, holding the wire cutters in both paws. They were looked huge in his hands, like he was holding a guitar.

"Okay, Mickey, maybe he can get down there. And maybe he knows you need him to clip a wire. But how on earth are you going to tell him which wire? Remember, he can't just cut all of them. What's monkey for 'aqua'?"

Kat must have thought I was going crazy as I started to unzip my space suit. And even crazier when all I could say was "my underpants, my underpants, my underpants."

You see, as I explained earlier, the Miami Dolphins are my favorite football team on earth. And the team's colors are orange and aqua. And I happened to be wearing my lucky underpants that day. My glorious orange and aqua Miami Dolphins underpants.

With the wire clippers I snipped a hole in the fabric and tore off a strip. Ziggy looked about as confused as Kat, but when I handed him the one-inch by one-inch square of aqua material ... and pointed down to the utility duct ... and pointed to the wire cutters ... I thought, just for a split second, that I sensed a glimmer of understanding in Ziggy's little monkey eyes.

He grabbed the wire cutters from my hand and tore off down the hallway to the far end of the duct and disappeared into the tangle of pipes and wires.

"Kat. Do you think ... maybe ... you think he gets it?"

Kat sighed deeply and shook her head. "Mickey, I think you're a dreamer who needs a new pair of underpants. I think it's very, very unlikely that Ziggy understood your crazy sign language."

A minute passed. Then two. Kat and I strained our ears, but we didn't hear any shuffling or movement from down in the duct.

"He should be there by now," Kat said nervously. "He should be there and he should have cut the wire already. Something's wrong. Something's wrong, I just...."

She stopped talking because everything went suddenly black. Really, really black. I don't think I'd ever really seen black like that before.

At night, back in Orlando, there was always a glimmer of light coming in through my bedroom window from a street lamp or the moon or some stars. Playing hide and seek in a closet, you usually have a little sliver of light coming from under the door. Or at least, you know that light is just the turn of a doorknob away.

But this was something else. Complete blackness.

"I guess he found the right wire," I said into the muffled silence.

"I never doubted him for a minute," said Kat. "That was a joke by the way."

"I know," I said, waiting for something to happen. "It was pretty funny. Remind me to laugh when we get out of this, okay? So ... now what?"

Our long-range radios crackled and emitted a faint, choppy sound. Knocking out the power must have affected the signal ... maybe turning off a booster antenna that helped the radio reach us under ground.

"Mission Control," I said very slowly and loudly. "The lights are out. Repeat, the lights are out. Please repeat what you said," I said.

All I could make out was "good job" and "hurry, hurry, hurry" and then something that sounded like "flashlights."

"Mission Control, you're hard to understand. But yes, a flashlight would be useful now. Where can I get one?"

There was a pause.

Between crackles I heard "flashlight pocket" and "your right hip."

I patted my right hip, finding nothing but a flat, empty pocket.

"I don't have one Kat, do you?" I said, feeling a jolt of panic.

"No … but … oh no … I remember the flashlights clipped to those charging stations in the locker room back at the moon base. I remember looking at them thinking 'when would we ever need those dumb things?'"

The radio crackled again and I heard "hurry, hurry" and "losing oxygen."

They didn't need to tell us again.

I remembered back to the last thing I saw before the lights went out. I was pretty much facing the wall, straight ahead. That meant that I should turn left … a full, square left turn … and then walk straight ahead, feeling for a door on the right side about 10 or 15 steps down the narrow passageway.

I turned and took a step forward, smacking immediately into Kat's forehead. Hard. We both fell backwards. As I lay on my back in the hallway, it was so dark that I wondered for a second whether I was standing or lying down. I reached out with my hand and patted the floor next to my head. Definitely lying down.

I heard Kat scrambling along the hallway. "Mickey, follow my voice. Hurry."

I flipped over and started crawling towards the part of the blackness that had emitted Kat's voice. "Wait," I heard her say, close up ahead. I started crawling faster and then – SMACK – we clunked heads and ended up on the floor again.

Great. 30 seconds in the dark and all we'd managed to do was smash heads twice. And we were about 10 tunnels, 5 rooms and 100 yards from the air lock where our suits were waiting. In the pitch black.

With a sinking feeling I could feel the air getting colder and heard a steady hiss. The sound of our precious oxygen leaking out of the tunnel. We were officially toast.

The second blow to the head must have been harder than the first, because I sensed a glowing over to the right side. I thought maybe I was seeing stars. Because I could definitely see a glow down the hallway ... I could see the shine of the polished floor and a couple pipes hanging from the ceiling.

"ZIGGY!!" Kat yelled.

Turning the corner, scampering quickly towards us, was Ziggy, carrying a little flashlight and clutching three inch strip of aqua wire.

"You cut the aqua one!" squealed Kat. "Good monkey!"

I made a trade with Ziggy. A handful of banana chips in exchange for his life-saving flashlight.

"Work now, party later," I said quickly. "We've got to move it, move it."

We took off down the hallway at a full sprint, with Ziggy leading the way. And thank goodness for that. Several times, I would have picked a right turn instead of a left. But Ziggy got us back to the air lock and we threw ourselves into our space suits, breathing heavily in the thinning air.

This time, it was a relief to get my helmet on, and I gulped down the sweet oxygen that poured in from the tank.

As we bounced back across the parking area towards the main buildings, my heart was still pounding from the excitement of our successful Hail Mary. "Kids and monkeys 1, impossible task ZERO!" I announced triumphantly.

Mission accomplished! It's all easy from here, I thought.

I was wrong.

21

Don't Forget the Parking Break

Once Kat, Ziggy and I got back to the main base, we found the others gathered in the kitchen area. Trace had made a huge batch of Mac and Cheese. The food at Oblivion Base was pretty terrible. The powdered eggs tasted just like the powdered potatoes, which tasted just like the cream of wheat.

But this Mac and Cheese was going to be different, I just knew it. Even by earth standards, it smelled awesome. Lance wasn't back yet, but we were all starving, so we took a quick vote. I'm not sure Ziggy knew what he was voting for, but he raised his hand when the rest of us did. Eat now, 5; wait for Lance, 0.

The Mac and Cheese tasted even better than it looked. Between bites, Kat and I told the full details of our adventure, including how Ziggy had saved the day and how I needed a new pair of underpants. When we finally finished our story, we had put a large dent in the Mac and Cheese. Ziggy gathered up our plates and carried them over to the sink. The rest of us looked at each other, unable to ignore the empty chair at the head of the table any more.

"Okay," I said, leaning back in my chair and patting my satisfied belly. "Is anybody besides me wondering where our Flight Commander is?"

"Jonah and I were talking about that while you guys were gone," said Trace. "Of course, Jonah has a crazy theory about it. And this time, I think he's right. And the longer Lance is gone, the more it makes sense."

"Wow, call the newspapers!" I said, raising my eyebrows. "I can see the headline: 'Miracles do happen. Trace agrees with Jonah.'"

"Very funny, Mickey," said Jonah. "But this one's obvious. I'll forgive you for not figuring it out because you were, kind of, busy saving the moon from total destruction."

"Mick, we think he went out looking for the Glint," Trace blurted out. "He went outside … he took a zip buggy … and remember, he has Major Austen's map. He's out there looking for the Glint, we're sure of it."

As soon as I heard it, it made so much sense I knew it had to be true.

"How long has he been out there?" I asked.

"Almost two hours," replied Jonah. "And not a peep on the radio."

"Well, I don't know about you guys," I said, scrambling to

my feet. "But I'm going to the West Control Room and try to find him with my binoculars." I scrambled out of the kitchen with the others hot on my heels.

▲ ▼ ▲ ▼ ▲

Thirty minutes later, we were ready to give up. We took turns with the binoculars, scanning the ridge and the hills beyond, looking for the mystery glint of light or looking for a zip buggy. There was only grey dust and rocks. We even tried calling him on the local radio channel, but got no answer.

The silence was finally broken by the radio. But it wasn't Lance. It was his father.

"Artemis Seven, Mission Control here. Put Lance on, please." The four of us froze and we exchanged nervous glances. Who would move to the microphone first?

"Lance, this is your ... this is the Director." The Director's voice was more insistent this time. "Please reply."

I stepped over to the microphone. Pressing the red button, I said "Mickey here. Lance is...," I looked over to Jonah for inspiration, but he just shrugged. "Uh, he's in the bathroom."

Jonah rolled his eyes. "Now *that's* creative," he whispered sarcastically.

"Come on, man," I said, defensively. "Could you come up with anything better?" I pointed up at the speaker where Marshall's voice had crackled a few seconds earlier. "Anyway, it seems like that took care of him. Right?"

Wrong.

"Mickey ... Marshall here." The Director's normally no-nonsense voice sounded even more serious, if that was possible. "We can't wait for Lance. This is urgent. We have discovered an issue with the oxygen tanks on the command module. Your oxygen for the ride home. I need you to confirm the readings."

Kat scooted over to my side and started tapping the keyboard. A few seconds later, a picture of four dials popped up onto the computer screen. Kind of like the gas tank indicators on a car. "There you go," said Kat. "The oxygen tank levels. Tell Marshall you're looking at them now."

I pressed the talk button to open the line again with the adults back on Earth. "Okay, Mission Control, I've got it up on the screen. I'm looking at the four oxygen tank levels for the command module. What can I tell you?"

"Very good, Mickey. Tell me what they say."

"Here we go, I'll read them to you," I responded, happy to be in control. "Number one says 'EMPTY.' Number two says 80%. Numbers three and four both say 'EMPTY.'" I felt the others scrunching up next to me to see for themselves. I realized that, now that I had said the words, it didn't sound good. Three tanks were empty with just one left?

"Is that a problem?" I asked.

"Mickey, remember, we don't have problems. Just challenges. We can deal with this one. Kids ... we're bringing you home right now."

"Mission Control, can you repeat that? When you say 'now,' you mean, like, today?" I glanced nervously at the others.

"Negative, Mickey. Now means this instant, without delay. In fact, we have already started the launch sequence for the command module. You don't have any time to waste. You will lift off in 30 minutes."

Trace grabbed my arm and mouthed the word 'Lance!!' and stared at me with huge, terrified eyes.

"Hey, that's cool," I said, as casually as I could. "We have a few other things to do, though. We'd rather leave in two hours. Over." I made a face and waited for the response. I had a feeling I wouldn't like it.

"Negative, Mickey. You can't wait two hours. Tank three is empty: that was supposed to be your oxygen for the trip home. Tank four is empty: that was your emergency spare. The only oxygen left for the command module is what's in tank two, but the level is slowly dropping. Right now, it has enough for about 72 hours ... and if you leave right now, that's just enough to get you home."

Marshall went on to explain that the tanks must have come loose with the hard impact of our landing and the system had been slowly but steadily leaking away oxygen for the last few days. He explained that we needed to launch right away because of the earth's rotation. If we waited any longer, we would have to do another whole orbit of Earth to hit our landing zone, and we didn't have enough oxygen for that.

He didn't need to explain what would happen if we ran out of oxygen in the command module while we were still in space.

As he talked, Trace nervously squeezed my arm until her fingernails dug into my skin and I yelled "OW!!! THAT HURTS!!"

I didn't realize I was holding down the "TALK" button while I yelled. Director Marshall said "Yes Mickey, I know that hurts. I know there are things you still wanted to do up there. But you kids have completed the mission. You need to leave, and you need to leave now."

"Roger that. Gotta go tell the others. I'll be right back." I switched off the "TALK" switch and grabbed for the moon radio. But Trace already had it.

"Lance, this is Trace. Come in Lance. Emergency.

Emergency. Code Red. The sky is falling. Come in Lance."

This time ... finally ... there was a response. "Lance here. I leave for an hour and you guys can't survive without me? Really, do you require adult supervision every minute of the day? What is...."

Trace cut him off. "LANCE, GET BACK HERE NOW!! The command module is low on oxygen. They've started the launch process. Blastoff is in 30 minutes. We can't delay."

Lance's voice came through the radio immediately. "Did you say 30 minutes? Is this an order from Mission Control?"

"Yes, Lance, of course it's an order from Mission Control. I'm not sitting here making stuff up. We leave in 30 minutes, so GET ... BACK ... HERE ... NOW!!!"

"Roger that, Trace. I've found what I was looking for anyway. I'm returning right now, I'll be back in 20 minutes. Walking back to my zip buggy ... it's parked right on the other side of this little hill."

"I deserve a serious award for this solo moon walk and treasure hunt. I got an excellent ... rock sample." Lance just couldn't help himself. If that guy went an hour without bragging, it would just spill out the first time he opened his mouth.

"Deserve?" fumed Trace. "You deserve a serious slap on the forehead, that's what you deserve, you giant meathead showoff. You're giving us a heart attack. HURRY UP."

I rolled my eyes and waited for Lance's reply. But it didn't come. The radio remained silent.

"Are you still there, hero?" said Trace, mockingly. "How long until you get back here?"

"Where the...? What the...? How the...?" Lance did not sound happy. "Who STOLE MY ZIP BUGGY?"

"Very funny, hero," said Trace. "You'll be here in, what ... 20 minutes?"

"This can't be." There was no mistaking the panic that had crept into Lance's voice. "This just can't be. I parked right hear this little rock pile. I stopped. I got out. I walked up this little hill for, maybe, 5 minutes."

"Lance, did you put on the parking brake?" asked Trace.

There was a pause.

"Of course I put on the parking brake," said Lance, uncertainly. "Do you think I'm stupid?"

There was another pause.

"I mean, I ALWAYS put on the brake. Everyone knows you're supposed to put on the brake when you stop. And I always do what I'm supposed to. Right?"

Nobody answered.

"Well, almost always," he continued. Now he was talking to himself. "Come on, Lance. Come on, zip buggy. Aw, come on ... don't tell me ... awww ...."

Silence again. Then, "AW NUTS!!!!!" The voice was so loud that the moon radio seemed to jump from Trace's hand and it hit the floor with a loud crack.

"AW NUTS, NUTS, NUTS!!!!!!!" Lance's voice was a little quieter, since the radio had scooted under the table. Kat bent down to fish it out. "The stupid brake must have broken." We could hear Lance huffing and puffing, as he apparently was bounce-running along. "My zip buggy rolled back down this little hill ... I'm following the tracks ... rolled down ... and now it's ... AW NUTS AGAIN!!!!!! It's nose-down in a ditch."

"Lance, now it's your turn to relax," said Trace. "Can't you back it out? You can still drive it, right?"

"OF COURSE I CAN'T. It's totally in a ditch. A real ditch.

Like a 20 foot deep hole. It's down there so far, I can't even reach down and touch it."

Silence again. I knew what was coming next.

"Somebody's got to come get me." Said Lance. "Please. Somebody's got to come. Who's coming to get me?"

"Lance, where are you," asked Trace slowly.

"I'm … I'm on the other side of the canyon. I'm about 20 minutes away. I'm … I'm at the Glint."

The words crackled like a jolt of electricity through the speaker and right through the four of us gathered in the West Control Room. The Glint. 20 MINUTES.

I looked at my watch, but didn't really need to. A first grader could have done that math. The zip buggies couldn't go more than 6 miles per hour. 20 minutes to get there, 20 minutes to get back. And the command module was leaving in less than 30 minutes.

I didn't need to explain it to Jonah or Kat either. Trace was obviously so freaked out that she sprinted from the control room as soon as she heard where he was.

AW NUTS was right. I couldn't see any way around this.

"Mickey," whispered Jonah. "You know what you need to do. We can't cover for Lance any more. We've got to tell Marshall."

I knew he was right. I handed the moon radio to Jonah and said "you deal with Lance. I'll tell his dad." I stared at the microphone. How was I going to say this?

▲ ▼ ▲ ▼ ▲

"Mission Control, Mickey here. Director Marshall, please."

"Marshall here," came the immediate reply. "Good timing.

We have started the launch sequence and confirmed that you are all set for an easy trip. Everything looks clear and good to go. We need you to make your way to the air lock, and then immediately out to the command module. Congratulations Artemis 7, you're coming home."

It sounded so simple. I hated to do this.

"Um, just one slight … little … one little thing going on here. Not a problem. Just a little challenge, as you'd say." I took a deep breath and just let the words roll out. "You see, about an hour ago Lance took a zip buggy out to … uh … he told us he was going to collect rock samples. I know, I know, we told him not to go but he really thought he was doing the right thing and he's in charge up here (and what were we supposed to do, stop him?). Well anyway it turns out he went looking for this thing called the Glint and that's where he is now, but something happened with his brakes and his zip buggy is in a ditch and he can't get it out so now he's stuck at the Glint and it's going to take almost an hour to go get him." I paused to take a breath. But then I didn't dare start up again.

Director Marshall had a simple, short reply. "Roger that."

The radio was silent.

We didn't realize it at the time, but although the radio was silent, there was absolute chaos at Mission Control. My radio transmission had been broadcast over the loudspeakers in the command center room, so all of the scientists and engineers and assistants, and all of Team Varsity, had heard what I said.

Everybody had a reaction. Everybody had an opinion. And they all started talking and yelling at once. People were running across the room. Some of them whipped out calculators and started punching numbers like crazy, trying to calculate a solution to our impossible problem. Others heaved huge maps of the moon onto tables and started measuring different routes with rulers. Still others dove for bookshelves and grabbed huge books and manuals about rockets and orbiting the earth and reentry and oxygen tanks and everything in between.

As I said, it was complete, total chaos.

People in Mission Control told me later that, at that moment, Director Marshall stood up on his chair, put two fingers into his mouth, and gave a whistle so loud, it could have called a dog from three states over. It cut through the noise and brought everybody to a screeching halt. He told the assembled scientists, engineers and mission specialists to calm down. He told them to please keep working, but just do it more quietly.

Apparently, while Jonah, Kat, Ziggy and I were staring nervously at the silent radio, Marshall was explaining to the workers at Mission Control that the lunar module needed to blast off in 30 minutes ... no, 28 minutes, to be exact ... and if it didn't leave then, it wasn't coming back to Earth. And his boy was trapped two miles and 40 minutes away from Oblivion Base. And for the first time, he used the word "problem." He said "this is a problem. And because I'm the dad of the stranded astronaut, I can't be the one to decide what to do. I just can't."

So, Director Marshall quit. He explained that, with his own son in danger, he might make decisions based on protecting Lance, rather than on what was best for the entire team. So he was stepping down as the Director and was turning over the job to Commander Riker.

We didn't realize it at the time, but as we sat there waiting, Marshall was climbing down off his chair and quietly walking out of the silent room, out into the Florida sunshine.

All we heard over the radio was silence. Two full minutes of silence.

And then, Commander Riker's voice.

"Artemis Seven, this is Mission Control. DIRECTOR Riker here." He spoke that part slowly and clearly, relishing the sound of the words. "The launch clock shows 26 minutes to liftoff. Proceed directly to the outer air lock, put on your suits, and head to the command module. No detours."

"Roger that," I said. "But what about Lance. Can't we...."

"Negative, Artemis Seven. This is an order. Your safety is our primary mission. And to get back to earth alive, the command module needs to blast off in ... 26 minutes."

"But Mission Control..." I started.

"Artemis Seven, you need to start following orders or else you risk the four lives that can still be saved. The best scientists on planet earth are working on how to save your other crew member. Leave that to the adults down here. That's not your job. Your job is to follow orders. So I repeat: go directly to the outer air lock; put on your suits; and head to the command module."

"But Mission Control...," I tried one last time.

"No buts," came Riker's voice, razor-sharp and ice-cold from 238,000 miles away.

"And one more thing," he added. "Leave the monkey behind."

▲ ▼ ▲ ▼ ▲

Kat, Jonah and I argued half-heartedly for a minute but we realized there was no hope. With only 26 minutes ... no, 25 minutes left ... it would be just impossible to drive four miles, round trip.

Our one act of rebellion, as we left the control room, was to take Ziggy. He gripped Kat's shirt hard with his little hands, holding folds of fabric tight in his furry fists. His legs were latched around her middle too, squeezing her tight. And he wedged his head under her chin. I'm not sure Kat could have followed Riker's instructions even if she had tried.

I wondered for a minute whether Ziggy had understood what Riker had said. Or maybe he just sensed that we were nervous and scared. Either way, he knew something bad had happened, and sensed that his people were about to leave.

We jogged back through the moon base, calling Trace's name, heading towards the air lock. I felt suddenly disoriented and confused. In two short days, the moon base had come to feel like home, and now we were leaving it without any chance to say goodbye. You might not think it makes sense to say goodbye to a building, but I think it does. I certainly felt like the moon base deserved a real goodbye. It was our protector, our sanctuary on a cold, barren rock out in space. But some part of me felt, as we sped through the hallways and rooms on our way to the air lock, that I was saying "see you later," and not "goodbye." And that somehow made it feel better.

As we came through the kitchen and into the little hallway at the air lock, I realized that we had something more important to worry about.

Trace.

Where the heck was Trace?

We had come through the entire moon base, yelling her name, without so much as a peep in response. As I entered the locker room, I saw the suits lined up on the wall. Mine. Kat's. Jonah's. And at the end, on the lowest hook, the little suit belonging to Ziggy. But the two hooks in between were empty. Lance's and Trace's. Trace's suit was gone!

Oh, no, I thought. Not Trace, too. Even if she had left immediately in a zip buggy after dropping the moon radio, that was only about 5 minutes ago. There was no way she could make the round trip in one of those zip buggies before liftoff. Not even Trace, winner of the 1977 KF-3 Go-Kart International Cup. I ran to the small window that looked out onto the courtyard.

There was Trace, wearing her space suit, bent over one of the zip buggies with its engine cover opened up. On the ground next to her was a tool box.

At that moment, I saw her pull a small object about as big as a mini-size candy bar out of the engine compartment. Two wires dangled from either side of it. She turned to look back at the air lock and must have seen my face in the window. She pumped her hand with the candy-bar-wire thing above her head, in a gesture of triumph. Then, with her free hand, she beckoned to me frantically.

As I stood there, frozen, she threw the candy-bar-wire thing carelessly over her shoulder and jumped into the driver's seat.

What the heck was she doing to the engine of the zip buggy? As I jumped into my space suit and barked at Jonah to zip me up, it hit me.

I realized what Trace was doing to the moon buggy. Would the 1977 KF-3 Go-Kart International Cup winner allow this mission to fail because the moon buggy was too slow? Would she seriously be satisfied with a top speed of 6 miles per hour?

Of course not.

She was doing what she'd wanted to do since the day we landed on the moon. Since the first time she had stepped on the accelerator and felt the zip buggy creep forward at walking speed.

The small object she had thrown over her shoulder must have been the governor, the device that limited the top speed of the zip buggy. Through the window, I saw Trace tearing around the courtyard, throwing up huge clouds of dust, doing 'donuts' like a NASCAR driver after winning a race.

"Kat, Jonah ... Ziggy ...," I said, "take the other zip buggy to the command module and prepare for launch. Do whatever Riker tells you to do. Jonah, when you talk to Riker, you can pretend you're me if you want to. We're going after Lance, and we'll meet you there."

Kat, Jonah ... and Ziggy ... all exchanged confused looks.

I didn't have time to explain.

As I disappeared into the outer air lock and prepared to put on my helmet, I yelled back over my shoulder. "We'll see you in 24 minutes. At least, we'll see you if Trace is as good as she says she is."

22

DRIVE LIKE THERE'S
NO TOMORROW

Trace and I left the courtyard at top speed, the rear tires kicking up clouds of dust behind us, and started barreling up the hill away from the moon base. And towards Lance.

I quickly understood why they had put governors on the zip-buggies. This was absolutely insane.

Remember, the moon has about one sixth the gravity of earth. A one foot jump on earth turns into a six foot jump on the moon. A six foot jump turns into a ... well, you get the picture.

Every time a wheel hit a rock or a bump, the wheel would fly up in the air. On the trip from the landing area to the moon base at 6 miles per hour, the moon seemed smooth and flat. Now that we were going fast, the moon seemed like it was *all rocks and bumps.*

The zip buggy was soaring 10 ... 20 ... sometimes 30 feet in the air. And it would bounce when it landed. We lost speed whenever we bounced, as the buggy's engine could only push us along when the wheels were touching the surface.

Sometimes if we didn't hit a bump straight-on, the zip buggy would tilt dangerously to one side or the other. To stay balanced, I had to throw my weight to the left side, leaning behind Trace as far as I could go. Or to the right side, leaning as far out into the thin air as I dared. Whatever it took to tip us back and level us out.

It didn't take long for Trace to get the hang of it, though. She was always looking 30 yards ahead, picking her way between the larger boulders and flooring it on the flat parts.

In almost no time we reached the top of the first hill and had an amazing view.

In front of us, stretching from right to left as far as we could see, was a huge, dark canyon. Black like a scar across the light gray surface of the moon. The canyon was about 70 or 80 yards wide ... almost the length of a football field. And I could only guess how deep it was. The sun was at a steep angle, so the shadows were long, like you would get at sunset on earth. Because the sun was so low on the horizon, only a few feet of the canyon wall on the other side was visible. The rest of the canyon was blackness. A deep, murky blackness far darker than the star-studded sky that spread out above the lunar surface. The thought of this deep, murky blackness caused me to lean away from the canyon as we sped along its edge.

After about a mile, just as we remembered from Major Austen's map, the canyon narrowed suddenly. I tapped Trace on the arm when I saw our target ... a tiny strip where the canyon walls came so close together they touched, before spreading out again on the other side. It was a thin natural bridge, stretching over the narrowest part of the canyon. A graceful, fragile arch of rock, only about 10 feet wide.

When we reached the land bridge, Trace slowed sharply. No reason to risk things here. We crept across the narrow pathway, and I peered to my right, down over the side and into the deep canyon. I glanced nervously at Trace, who fortunately was not looking down into the abyss. I couldn't see her eyes, but her helmet was pointed straight ahead and both hands clutched the steering wheel.

When we reached the far side, I instinctively grabbed the side of the zip buggy. And just in time. Trace put all of her weight on the accelerator and the machine lurched forward, swerving to the left, back along the far side of the ravine.

"Lance, we're ... OOF ... across the canyon bridge," I announced across the local radio channel, my voice choppy as we bounced and skipped along at top speed. "We're coming ... baAAAAACCKKK ... along the canyon ... UFFFFFF ... towards you. Come to the top ... PUHHHHH ... of the hill and wave so we see you."

"Roger that, Mickey," came Lance's reply. "Hurry."

Yeah, right, I thought. He didn't need to add the last part.

From time to time, we would see the tire tracks Lance had left, where he had driven an hour earlier. Sometimes Trace picked a different, smoother path. And sometimes our zip buggy would leap clear over Lance's tracks as we raced the clock.

Trace's eyes were locked on the surface ahead of our buggy. I was staring farther ahead, scanning every hill and ridge for a sign of Lance or his zip buggy … or The Glint.

THERE.

Around the edge of a rocky outcropping, there was Lance, standing still and staring straight up at the distant earth above us.

When he saw us, he started going nuts, waving his hands over his head and jumping up in the air. It was pretty impressive, I think his first jump was about six feet straight up.

Oh, to have that ability back on earth.

I squeezed the little TALK button in my left glove. "See him, Trace?"

"Got it," was her simple reply.

Lance kept leaping straight up into the air.

My helmet was filled with Lance's whoops of excitement, coming in over the radio. The only words I picked up were "awesome" and maybe "you rock!" but otherwise it was just whoops and yahoos.

Although his jumps were impressive … freakish, in fact … I was distracted by the shape lying in the dust next to him. At first I assumed it was his zip buggy. It was about the right size. As we got closer, however, I realized that it wasn't his buggy. The zip buggies were clunky-looking things perched on top of four big rubber tires.

This thing was gray, shiny and mysteriously elegant. Its surface was perfectly smooth, like a giant metal egg. But as we got closer, I could tell that it was broken. Its top part was smooth and intact, but the bottom was jagged and cracked, as though it had landed with a hard impact. And its surface was shiny and reflective, like metal. The Glint.

Even as we got closer, it was hard to get a good look at it because Trace was driving the zip buggy like a maniac, and my biggest concern was just holding on.

When we screeched to a halt at Lance's side, with a puff of dust, I stepped out and bent down to take a closer look. Whatever it was, it had definitely crashed into the ground, with the bottom part buried in the dusty surface. There were no markings on the side. No American flag. Or Soviet flag. Or Chinese flag. In fact, no words or letters at all. There were several long cracks in the side, zigzagging up from the bottom. One of them was large, almost splitting the object into two pieces.

"Nice work, team," shouted Lance. "Trace, how'd you get that thing to go so fast? Mine drove like a golf cart. You were FLYING!!!"

"Lance," I took a couple steps towards the strange object lying in the lunar dust 5 feet away. "What the heck? What is it?"

"No idea, Mickey. Absolutely no idea. But look." He held up a jagged piece of metal with wires and pieces hanging off of it, and waved it in front of us. "I've got a souvenir!"

"Guys, let's GO," urged Trace.

"I can tell you one thing," said Lance, gesturing towards the Glint. "It's not one of ours. It doesn't belong to NASA. I can't tell who it belongs to. Or what it is."

I leaned forward and peered closely at the mystery object. I could see inside the crack now ... what was it? Wires! And small parts. It was definitely a machine. Some sort of machine. And on the ground next to it lay a few pieces. One of them, about four inches by four inches. And shiny. With strange markings on it and bumps on one end....

"Mickey, NOW!!" yelled Trace. I felt a tug on the back of my space suit. "We've got to go. AND YOU KNOW IT."

Yes, I knew it. I glanced up and saw Trace and Lance turn their backs on me and climb back into the zip buggy.

I paused ... taking one last look at the Glint ... leaning over one more time and reaching out my hand....

Then I followed them back onto the zip buggy.

Before I had settled back onto the seat, Trace already had her foot on the accelerator and we surged away from the strange and beautiful pile of metal and turned back towards the canyon.

I was jolted back to reality as my brain reminded me what was most important right now. The time.

I looked down at my right wrist and couldn't believe what I saw.

My countdown timer had shown 23 minutes until liftoff when we left the moon base courtyard. Even though Trace had driven like a champion, up the hill, along the canyon, across the land bridge and back to the Glint, the clock had run all the way down to 10 minutes.

We were toast.

"Trace, we're 10 minutes from liftoff. Aw shoot, now it's 9 ... 9 minutes. It took us 13 minutes to get here. And once we get back, we need at least a minute or two for the three of us to climb into the command module. Can you make it back in time?"

My question hung in the thin lunar air. From this point on the hill, I could just make out the top of the command module in the distance, straight across on the other side of the canyon. It seemed so close. Teasing us. But we still had to turn left and travel a mile up the canyon to the land bridge, and then a mile back again to the moon base and the rocket.

I knew the answer to my question before Trace spoke. "Mick, I'm sorry." Her reply was soft, but certain. "I can't make it. Especially with Lance's added weight. All I can do is try, but I'm sorry, I can't cut our time in half."

The truth sank in for all of us.

"We'll still be driving when Kat and Jonah lift off," Trace continued. "But at least we'll have a good view of them going home."

"What!?" yelled Lance. "Are you kidding me? How can that be! What took you so long then? I thought you were some driving champ. You can't even...."

"Lance-one-more-word-and-I-swear-I'm ... THROWING ... YOU ... INTO ... THE ... CANYON," Trace yelled back, spitting each word angrily into the radio. All the time, we kept careening down the hill, following the tracks we had laid on the way up.

The black canyon yawned in front of us.

The canyon, separating us from our ride home.

The tire tracks turned away to the left, towards the land bridge. But Trace kept pointing the zip buggy straight ahead.

"Trace, you gonna turn left and head up the canyon to the land bridge?" asked Lance.

Our zip buggy continued straight forward, picking up speed.

"Trace ... um ... put on your blinker." Lance was starting to sound nervous. "Ah, left turn please. You might have noticed the enormous BOTTOMLESS PIT straight ahead?"

"Lance," I said hoarsely. "You obviously don't know Trace very well. You might want to be quiet and fasten your seat belt."

We must have been going almost 70 miles an hour at this

point, flying down the hill, straight to our doom.

I could hear the engine screaming under my seat. Trace had steered towards a flat, smooth stretch leading up to the lip of the canyon, which was fortunately hard-packed and dust-free, allowing the wheels to grip the ground with perfect traction.

The canyon must have been 60 yards wide at this point

This was crazy. Absolutely crazy.

"NOOOOOO! Let me off!" screamed Lance.

It was too late for that.

The black lip hurtled towards us, relentlessly, until finally the ground gave way and there was just blackness beneath us. The screaming of the engine stopped. Trace had taken her foot off the accelerator.

We were flying.

Up, up and steadily out. I was pressed back into my seat, hard, with the same sensation as when we had lifted off from earth at the beginning of our mission.

We were flying.

And spinning.

When we took off, it felt like the right side of the buggy hit a bump and kicked up harder than the left side. So, as we soared, the horizon line tipped and then rotated before our eyes. Up and to my right was the bright, starry sky. Down and to the left was the deep, lifeless, total blackness of the canyon.

Then, the blackness was above us. We were upside down.

As we soared and spun, I saw a flash of metal as something slipped off Lance's lap and spun away from the zip buggy, flipping end-over-end down into the canyon. His souvenir was gone.

We kept spinning. The horizon line was now vertical again, with the blackness of the canyon on the right side. I could see a strip of bright white moon surface straight ahead. And the starry sky was on the left.

By now, I had no idea which end was up any more, but I could definitely feel we were no longer rising. We were beginning to fall. My body strained against the seatbelt and I was aware that the moon buggy was pulling us down, down, down towards the beckoning blackness of the canyon.

"Come ONNNN," Trace urged. She jammed her foot onto the accelerator and the engine roared, spinning the wheels uselessly in the air. I leaned forward, willing our buggy to just keep moving.

Then there was something white rushing towards us. The white powdery surface of the far side of the canyon was rushing towards us as fast as we fell. It was a race to that far side of the canyon, with the deep blackness pulling us down and the white moon surface pulling us forward.

And the darkness lost the fight.

The impact was unbelievable. My butt was already bruised and my neck was already sore after more than 20 minutes of bumps and lumps of our mad dash. But this next impact was something else. I'm serious, 30 years later and sometimes I think I can still feel the bruise when I sit down on a hard wooden chair.

WHAM!! The front wheels cracked hard into the ground and my heavy, helmeted head was pitched forward and slammed into my knees. Then the buggy bounced skyward, tipping back and landing on the rear bumper, pointing straight up, before pitching forwards again.

The impact was loud, hard and painful. But exactly what I was hoping for. The most welcome impact of solid ground I had ever felt in my life. There were several more enormous hops, back-to-front and side-to-side. But we didn't tip over. And finally we skidded to a stop in a massive cloud of dust.

I broke the total silence with a huge whoop.

"Trace, that was AWESOME!!!!! Lets do it again!!!!!"

"Not a chance, Mick." Trace's voice quavered. "That's a one-time ride. In fact, I might just stick to bicycles for the rest of my life."

"That was an all-universe moon record jump, Trace. That has Guinness Book of World Records written all over it. Or Guinness Book of Universe Records! Lance, you ok?" I slapped him on the arm, surprised by his silence.

"Did anybody else pee their pants?" asked Lance.

"Wait ... you serious?" I asked. "Really?"

"Yeah, didn't you guys...." Lance caught himself. "I mean, I'm kidding of course. I didn't...." He sighed. "Aw, man."

As much as I wanted to take this opportunity to discuss the dampness of Lance's pants, I realized I would have to wait.

I looked at my watch. "6 minutes 'til liftoff. Start 'er up, Trace, it's just over that hill."

The engine whirred to life but then whined with no result. I saw Trace press the accelerator with her right foot. Nothing.

Trace floored it and the engine screamed, just like it had during our mad dash towards the canyon less than a minute ago. But this time ... nothing.

"Bad news boys," said Trace, her voice firm again. "The impact broke our axel. Maybe both. We're not going anywhere. I hope you have your track shoes on."

"Oh, no. It just keeps getting better, doesn't it?" I said, unbuckling my belt and leaping from the buggy onto the surface. My legs were like jelly after that incredible jump and I had to catch myself with my hand from falling face-first.

"Lance, move it. Last one to the command module is a rotten egg. Or a dead duck."

▲ ▼ ▲ ▼ ▲

I remember every detail of that mad dash down the hill. Every jump. Every stumble. Every slip. Just like it was yesterday.

Trace led us up the hill. At the top, we had a great view of the moon base below, down and to the right. I could see the rooftops, and the dock area, and the huge transport vehicle filled with Pleurinium. Straight ahead, just a little farther away than the moon base, was the command module, with a zip buggy parked a few yards away. The one that had carried Kat, Jonah and Ziggy a few minutes earlier.

A thin stream of white gas billowed from the rocket engine beneath the command module. The launch sequence had begun. We didn't have much time.

While Trace had led the way going up the hill, Lance quickly shot into the lead on our way down. His long legs carried him swiftly down the hill with big, graceful hops.

He paused half-way down and turned to watch us picking our way down the slope, with me second and Trace in the rear. He pressed his radio TALK switch.

"Come on guys. You can … you can do it." His voice was confident and encouraging. "Copy me, take long steps. Concentrate on taking long steps … make each one count."

That was the perfect advice. Taking long, soaring steps, Trace and I moved much quicker and could almost keep up with Lance now.

When we came off the hill and were on level ground again, I

noticed that more cloudy white gas was billowing out of the command module. The pre-launch process was moving to the next stage.

The radio crackled and Kat's voice filled my helmet. We were close enough for the local radio to reach us. "I see you guys," she said excitedly. "HURRY! We're at two minutes to launch. If we don't have the door closed when the timer reaches zero I'll have to hit the 'CANCEL' button and stop the launch. HURRY!"

"Roger," was all I said. Neither Lance nor Trace responded. We were putting 100% of our effort into running. I was breathing hard and the inside of my mask was starting to steam up. I was so hot and sweaty it felt like I was running on the sun, instead of the moon.

"One minute ten," came Kat's voice.

"One minute. Come on guys," she pleaded, "the door has to be closed in one minute!"

We were now following the tire tracks from the zip buggies. The ground was packed hard in the tire tracks, so it was easier to get a good grip without slipping in the powdery moon dust. Lance was in first place, Trace right behind him running in the left tire track, with me running alongside in the right track.

"Fifty…. Forty-five."

Suddenly, Trace disappeared from the corner of my eye. It took me a couple steps to stop and turn my body around towards her. I saw with horror that she was lying face-first on the ground, her hands flopping out beside her, and her feet scrambling in the dust. She had tripped.

"Forty!"

Without thinking, I took four quick hops back towards her, grabbed her hand and pulled with all my might.

"Thirty five!"

As I pulled her up, I felt myself tumbling backwards and stuck my foot behind me just in time to stop myself from falling.

"THIRTY!"

There was no time to talk on the radio. No need to talk. We only had....

"TWENTY!"

Ahead of us, we saw Lance's boots disappearing up through the hatch on the bottom of the command module. Trace and I continued to run, taking huge, desperate leaps.

Trace reached the ladder just before me, and as she climbed I put one hand on her belt and shoved her upwards with all my might.

I paused, knowing I had to give her a few seconds to move out of the air lock and into the crew cabin before I could start up the ladder.

"NOW MICKEY. NOW!" came Trace's voice, sharp with fear.

"Don't stop," I yelled, "I'll make it I'll make it I'll make it...."

"SIX ... FIVE ... FOUR ...."

I don't think my feet touched the rungs of the ladder. I pushed off the ground and soared straight up into the air lock, grabbing the large metal handle and pulling the door closed behind me with one motion. My helmet cracked hard against the far wall of the cramped air lock.

"I'M IN ... GO-GO-GO ..." I yelled, as I was suddenly slammed backwards sharply against the floor of the air lock and the hatch door.

At first I wondered why Trace had pushed me back so hard. But then I realized I hadn't been pushed back. The floor had been pushed up.

We had lifted off.
We had made it.

23

RETURN

I lay there in the air lock, breathing heavily, as I listened to the chatter of the radio.

Jonah's voice came through, loud and clear. "Mission Control, we have power up and liftoff from the moon surface. We're coming home."

"Roger that Artemis Seven." Looper's voice squawked through the cabin's speakers. "Our instruments show a good liftoff. Um, we heard a lot of commotion and background noise before launch. Confirm your status please. Do you have all four with you?"

"That's a negative, Mission Control, we're not four," replied Jonah.

"Roger that, Artemis Seven," came Looper's reply. "Who are you missing, over?"

"Nobody. We don't have four," said Jonah, looking back at the rest of us with a huge grin. "We have five. Mickey and Trace had the crazy idea of going to save Lance. They got him and they all made it back. As I said, we're coming home."

We could hear the sound of cheers and celebration erupting through the command center in the background, but Looper's voice remained calm, cool and unflappable as ever. "Nice work, Artemis Seven. Nice work. Over."

Since then, I have imagined how Looper would react ... calm, cool and unflappable ... if he won the Megabucks lottery. The head of the lottery prize patrol would show up at Looper's front door with cheerleaders holding balloons and a marching band and TV cameras. Looper would open the door, wearing his pajamas and holding a cup of coffee. The announcer would scream "YOU'VE JUST WON ONE HUNDRED AND TWENTY MILLION DOLLARS!!!!" Looper would slowly take another sip of coffee, blink, and say "Roger that, Megabucks lottery guy. 1-2-Zero million. Nice work. Over."

The next voice on the radio brought me back to reality. It wasn't Looper, but instead was the steely, sharp voice of Commander Riker ... DIRECTOR Riker, actually.

"Artemis Seven, we will take a full report of your activities later. Nice ... uh... nice job. Lance Marshall, are you there?"

"Yes, sir, here." Lance's shoulders slumped and his voice lacked its usual cocky tone.

"Lance," continued Riker. "Did you ... did you get the sample?"

Lance's head sagged another few inches. He pressed the TALK switch. "Negative. I had it. I had the sample in my hand. But then it slipped out and I lost it. You see, we had to hurry back and...."

"Roger that, Lance," Riker cut in. "You and I will talk when you get back. Mission Control out."

As I pulled myself up through the small door into the main cabin, I realized that the air was filled with spinning brown, green, yellow and red objects. It took me a few seconds to realize what they were. M&Ms. Hundreds of them. Maybe a thousand. Trace had emptied an entire bag into the weightless air of the crew cabin.

It was like confetti dropping on New Year's Eve, or balloons at the end of the Super Bowl. Or a swarm of fat, wingless, delicious bumble bees.

I started singing "We Are the Champions" at the top of my lungs. Trace, Kat and Jonah joined in. Jonah was so far off-key, it was like he was singing a different song. But at that point, the tune didn't matter. It was all about the words. Without any question, we were the champions.

And then, out of nowhere, somebody joined in with an awesome, jamming imitation of a guitar solo. It was Lance, who had the first real, honest smile I had ever seen on his face. He then opened his mouth and grabbed about 15 M&Ms in a single bite.

▲ ▼ ▲ ▼ ▲

We galloped through space at a nice speed of about 5,000 miles per hour.

I did some quick math in my head. The Miami Dolphins

football stadium was about 250 miles from my house in Orlando. Driving at 50 miles an hour, which was the fastest Sister Rinaldi was willing to drive, even on the highway, the trip would take 5 hours. At 500 miles an hour, you could drive 250 miles there and 250 miles back in an hour…so that meant it would only take half an hour to get to Miami.

50 miles an hour, 5 hours. 500 miles an hour, 30 minutes. So, at 5,000 miles an hour, it would take 3 minutes to go from my house to the stadium.

Wow, 3 minutes. If only I could put this speed in a bottle and take it home with me. With that kind of speed, I could go to every game. I could even go to church in the morning, which Sister Rinaldi made sure we did every single Sunday, and still make it to Miami in time for a one o'clock game!

Then I started thinking about the problems this would cause. With this kind of power, you'd step on the accelerator to back out of the driveway and end up two towns over before you realized it. If you saw a red light 10 miles away, you would have to stop in … um … um … how many seconds?

Ow. My head started to hurt. Any further math would require a calculator, so I abandoned the math daydream and stared out the window at the Earth, beautiful and blue and white and growing larger by the minute.

I was curled up in a back row seat between Jonah and Trace. I had traded seats for a while with Kat, who had moved up to the front row with Ziggy on her lap. She had wanted to spend some time looking out the front window, watching the European continent swung into view.

Every few minutes I looked out the front window at the Earth, just to make sure it was still there. And every few minutes I tapped the object zipped into the right side pocket of my space suit.

"Pssst, Mick," whispered Jonah. He glanced over his shoulder at Lance, who had his eyes closed and his earphones on again. "Mick. You've never told me about The Glint. Did you actually see it? It was an alien space ship, wasn't it?"

I pressed my finger to my lips in a "shhhh" movement and tilted my eyes towards Lance. Then I shrugged my shoulders. What the heck, I thought. Lance was fast asleep, and Jonah looked like he might die if I didn't tell him the story. So I described it to him, in every detail I could remember. The polished, shiny, perfectly smooth surface like a metal egg. The crumpled, torn section at the bottom, suggesting it had landed or crashed. The crack down the center revealing some sort if machinery inside.

"So," I concluded, "I guess it's a machine. Some sort of mining equipment, or satellite, or piece off of a space ship. But alien? I just don't know."

Jonah furrowed his brow, thinking hard.

"And that 'sample' Riker asked Lance about?" asked Jonah. "It wasn't a rock sample, was it? Riker ordered him to bring back something from the Glint, didn't he?"

I looked at Lance, who still hadn't moved. I nodded my head.

"I knew it," whispered Jonah loudly. "I knew it, I knew it. So what was it? And why didn't he bring it back? He had it but then ... what ... he *lost it* on the way back? Are you serious?"

I glanced up at Lance again. His mouth was open and a little drool was spilling out of the corner and running down onto his coveralls as he slept.

"Okay," I said, leaning in. "Lance had something at first. He had pulled a piece off of the Glint, or pulled something from the inside. His 'sample' was metal and was about, I don't know, maybe the size of a phone book." I gestured in the air, making the shape I remembered. "I didn't get a good look at it. There were other things to worry about at the time ... like MAKING IT BACK ALIVE, remember? But I did see it. It was ... I don't know ... it's hard to describe. It had markings on it and bumps at one end. It was dusty ... but under the dust it was shiny. A super-shiny silver color."

"Go on!" pleaded Jonah, as I paused. "What else? What kind of markings? What kind of bumps on the end? What did it do? What else?"

"I don't know. Like I said, I didn't get a chance to really examine it. He had it in his lap when we were riding back in the zip buggy. And then, when we jumped over the canyon ... it just slipped off his lap, down into the darkness."

"Are you sure? You're sure it's gone!?" Jonah said, disappointed and incredulous at the same time.

"Yes, I'm sure. Positive. I saw it slip off and fall into the million foot deep chasm we jumped over in the moon buggy. It's gone. That's it."

"That's IT?" His whisper was curious but also angry. "That's IT? Oh, come on. He finds proof of alien life ... finally, finally we have proof, after all this time ... and then he goes and drops his alien souvenir into the first canyon he can find? And you come back empty-handed? And all you can say is 'That's it'?"

He was breathing hard as he stared me down with a poisonous glare.

I couldn't help but crack a slight grin, which only seemed to make him madder.

"Who said anything about empty-handed?" I asked.

The words hung there, like an M&M floating in the weightless air.

Jonah's eyes got huge. His mouth opened. He watched as I unzipped my hip pocket and pulled out, just for a peek, the small metal tube that had been sitting in my pocket since I left the Glint. Shiny. Silver. About the size of a TV remote controller. With strange markings on one end and lines, like a little doorway or compartment, on the other end.

You see, I had grabbed a souvenir, too. Except I had enough sense to shove it in my pocket before we started the trip back in the zip buggy.

"WHAT THE......!!!!!!" Yelled Jonah at the top of his lungs.

Everyone in the cabin jumped, including Lance, who lifted off his earphones and turned to face us.

"WHAT THE..." I repeated loudly, as I shoved the strange object back into my pocket. "What the ... what's the ... what's the. WHAT'S THE first think I'm going to do when we get back to Earth?" I asked quickly. "Great question, Jonah. You sure know how to ask the right question at the right time. What's the first thing I'm going to do? I think I have a trip to McDonalds in my future. Big Mac, fries ... and two chocolate shakes."

I looked up at Lance who was eyeing me suspiciously. I kept my hand on my hip, hiding the strange, unidentified souvenir in my pocket.

"How about you Lance?" I said, with all the innocent curiosity I could muster. "What's your first stop when you get home?"

"I dunno," said Lance, slumping back into his seat and facing forwards. "I'll probably be grounded for a month for having disobeyed orders. My dad might let me go to McDonalds again when I'm a senior in high school." He sighed heavily.

I almost felt sorry for him.

Almost.

▲ ▼ ▲ ▼ ▲

Lance was right about being grounded. His punishment started only a few hours later. When Looper announced that it was time to begin our reentry procedure, he ordered Jonah and me up to the front row, with me in the Flight Commander's chair. Lance protested at first, but then lurched sulkily to the back row.

Flight Commander Price, steering the Artemis command module through the atmosphere. Flight Commander Price, bringing the command module home.

Things just kept getting better, I thought to myself.

"Price, I'll walk you through a few simple steps," Looper said. "There's not much for you to do."

Phew, I thought.

"Program 64 is the computer program that controls your reentry," Looper continued. "Once you start Program 64, the computer will do the rest. It knows when to fire the booster rockets and how much to fire them. It knows the correct direction and angle for the command module's reentry, to put it on track for a perfect landing in the Pacific. You're familiar with this procedure. You practiced it in the simulation center before your mission."

I heard panting and barking from the back row. "Oh great, the Captain Chihuahua strikes again" said Lance. "Next stop, Mexican desert."

Boy, that guy was annoying. But, I'll have to say, he did have a point.

I clicked the TALK switch. "Um, Mission Control, Program 64 and I didn't get along too well the first time we met. Remember? Can you say something to boost our confidence here?"

"The simulator is always harder than real life," came Looper's steady voice. "We threw you a few curve balls in the simulator. No curve balls this time. This is a baby pitch, right over home plate. You are on a perfect flight path. Program 64 will make a few adjustments, it will handle your reentry and will deploy your parachutes, all at exactly the right time. And we'll be watching your progress every step of the way."

"Kat," I called to the back row. "How confident are you in Program 64?"

"I don't know. I would feel better if I had written it," she said. I had to laugh to myself. Kat lacked self confidence about most things. But when it came to computers, she could take on the world.

"I know one thing, Kat," I said back over my shoulder, "next time, I want you to check all the computer programs before we go on a mission, okay?"

I heard an immediate hoot from Trace. "Next time!!?? Mickey, I told you, if you get us back to Earth, it's all bicycles for me for the rest of my life. I'm serious. Anything with an engine or a rocket ... forget about it!"

Following Looper's instructions, I read him the information on a series of dials and displays. Every time I read him a number, he said "Check" or "Copy that," which meant that he agreed with me and everything was on-track.

And then, on his command, feeling the eyes of my fellow astronauts staring intently at me, I hit a green button marked "GO" on the right side of the main computer screen. Program 64 was now underway. And I sat back for the ride.

"Artemis Seven, we're 'GO' for final reentry," reported Looper. "In T minus 60 seconds, LSR booster will fire for 17.5 seconds. Rotation adjustment into position 1-4-4-2-9 at angle 7.22 degrees. Service Module will detach, pushing the Command Module into the outer atmosphere."

"Mick, did you follow all that," asked Trace. "Could you please repeat the part after he said 'Artemis Seven'?" I couldn't see her face, but I could tell she was smiling.

"Trace," I said, "this is not the right time to tease the Flight Commander. Remember, I have the power to make you walk the plank."

"Aye, aye, Captain," came her immediate reply from the back row. "But, um, can we get a translation from Einstein here? What's happening now?" I could always count on Trace to ask the question I wanted to ask.

Jonah was happy to explain. "A translation for those of you who didn't pay the slightest bit of attention on the flight simulator. The main thrusters on the Service Module will fire and put us into the desired position. Then the Service Module … the back half of our spacecraft … will detach, leaving just this little command module to fall through the atmosphere back to Earth."

"Oh, and," he continued, "now a translation for Trace: big rocket go boom, command module fall down."

A comment like that would have cost Lance two of his front teeth. But Jonah knew he could joke with Trace. A little.

"Watch it Einstein, you can't run from me in here," Trace threatened without any actual malice.

I don't think Jonah was listening, though. I heard him muttering "coming … right … about …."

A sharp thrust pushed us forward as the main booster rockets kicked into overdrive.

"Now," said Jonah.

As the booster fired, I watched as the small sliver of earth visible through the front window disappeared. The rockets had turned us so that the front window was pointed straight out into space. We were now backing our way home.

Then there was a loud boom and jolt, which must have been the Service Module detaching. The big piece of our spacecraft, containing our booster rockets, the air lock and other equipment was now officially a piece of space junk.

"Service Module has detached," said Jonah. "It's just us in this little command module now. All lights on the main panel are green. We're now like a brick, falling down into the atmosphere."

"Artemis Seven, you should feel some light chop right now," Looper warned us.

Right on cue, our Command Module began to shake lightly, as we entered the Earth's outer atmosphere. Boy, this was happening fast. It was hard to believe that we'd be floating in the Pacific Ocean in about fifteen minutes.

The Pacific Ocean.

I had lived near the Atlantic Ocean my entire life but had never seen the Pacific. I wondered if it would look the same.

"Mission Control, copy that," I said. "We're feeling light chop." Instinctively, I checked my seatbelt.

"Artemis Seven, in 30 seconds you will enter the second layer of atmosphere and you will lose radio contact for about four minutes."

"Which means some serious rock-and-roll," said Jonah from the Co-Pilot's seat. "Hang on to your underpants."

As I scanned the main display panel one more time, I noticed something change in the top right corner, followed by a rapid beeping.

"Mission Control, I have a flashing red light on the upper right. It says 'Pitch Alert.'"

Looper's reply came right away. "Mickey, read me the number, left of the light."

"Radio loss in ten seconds," said Jonah from my right.

"Eight-two-two, it says eight-two-two," I said.

"Eight-two-two? Should be seven-two-two," said Looper. The cabin had started to shake harder now. The warning beep, which had been sharp and clear just a few seconds ago, was now almost drowned out by the rattling of every piece of metal inside the command module.

"Too steep ... too steep ..." said another voice on the loudspeaker.

That was the last thing we heard from Mission Control.

The light chops had turned into full-blown thumps. Like driving over a speed bump at 50 miles an hour. Backwards.

The rattling sound in the cabin was now drowned out by a roaring sound, louder than the sound of the rocket at blastoff. A red glow appeared in the window ahead of me as we hurtled backwards at 2,000 miles per hour. Flames. There were red, orange, yellow and white flames shooting backwards from our module as we streaked down like a comet. It seemed for a moment that we were actually hurtling backwards into the sun, instead of returning to earth.

With nothing left to do but ride it out, my mind raced. Pitch alert? Too steep? What did that mean? Hadn't the booster rockets set our course at the perfect angle? Too steep meant ... what did it mean? Too steep meant too hot. Too hot meant we could flare out. Burst into flames like a marshmallow at a campfire. Oh, great.

And then I felt the heat. It was definitely getting hot inside the command module. I felt like I was being slow-roasted in my space suit. Through the bone-crunching shaking, I could see that the window in front of me had completely fogged up. I couldn't see the flames anymore, but could still see the bright glow of the raw, angry heat.

And through all this, I could still see the flashing red light that said "Pitch Alert."

I squeezed my eyes shut, blocking out the vision of searing heat through our front window and the view of the warning light, alerting us to some uncertain danger. Up until that point in my life, I had loved roller coasters. The scarier the better. I vowed, at that point, never to ride one again.

▲ ▼ ▲ ▼ ▲

And then, almost as quickly as it started, the worst of it was over. It was still a little choppy, but the command module was only skipping and wobbling, instead of shaking insanely. And, unlike the completely weightless sensation of outer space, I now had the stomach-tickling feeling like we were falling. Falling hard and falling fast.

"Um, is anyone else alive?" Jonah called out. "Because I'm not completely sure whether I am."

"That was SO not fun," answered Trace. "Kat, seriously, tell me you didn't throw up."

The radio crackled.

"… respond … Artemis Seven please respond … Artemis Seven please respond …." Looper's no-nonsense voice droned over and over again. My hand jumped up to the TALK switch.

"Mission Control, Artemis Seven here. Please tell us we're through the worst of it, over."

We heard cheering and applause in the background as Looper replied, "Good to hear you Artemis Seven, we knew you'd make it. Yes, reentry is over, you only need to go through that part once. But listen carefully. There was a problem with Program 64. We don't know why, but you're off-course and you won't be landing at the Pacific Ocean landing site. We show you coming down much farther east. Much."

I glanced over at Jonah. He mouthed "MUCH!!??"

"Um, Mission Control," I replied, "can you explain 'much'? Where exactly are we coming down."

My heart sank when the answer didn't come immediately. They must have been debating what to tell us. I slapped the TALK switch again. "Hey, this little tidbit of information is pretty important to the five of us right now. Where are we coming down? Tell me we're hitting water."

It was Riker's voice that responded. Two words. "Dayton. Ohio."

24

DESTINATION DAYTON

Now, I don't have anything against Dayton. Jimmy Jankowitz, who had played shortstop on our baseball team the last season, had been adopted by a family in Dayton, so he moved out of our house. Jimmy and I had written a couple postcards back and forth and he invited me to come visit sometime.

But crash landing like a meteor in his back yard was NOT how I wanted to visit.

I remembered back to my disastrous experience in the flight simulator. How could this be happening again?

"Mission Control, what do I do. How do I change course? What's the emergency plan. I've got all these controls, I've got a million buttons. There's got to be something I can do."

Silence. The only answer came from Jonah. "Mick, we don't have any booster rockets. Those were on the Service Module. We have no wings. We're falling like a rock. You can't steer a rock. We've played all our cards."

"The computer will deploy parachutes in sixty seconds," came Looper's flat, steady voice.

"Mission Control," I repeated. I must have been yelling. How can you NOT yell in a situation like that. "I've got to try something. What buttons should I hit. What should I do?"

"DO. NOTHING." Riker barked the reply back to me. "DO ABSOLUTELY NOTHING. The computer is in control, Program 64. You have to let it do its job and get you down to the ground. Prepare for ELCI. Emergency Land Crash Impact."

"Okay, what does that mean? What do I do?"

"The computer is in control," Riker's cold voice continued. "It will deploy your parachutes. The three main chutes will come out, and you will impact the ground at about 40 miles per hour. You would prefer to land in water, but it is possible to survive an emergency land crash. After impact, if anybody is able to move, try to open the escape hatch. Do not bother trying to put out the fire. If you can, just try to save yourself. Crawl as far away as you can to escape the explosions. Ambulances will arrive within 30 minutes."

"Great plan, Mission Control!" I yelled, trying to pump as much sarcasm into the radio transmission as possible, as though that would save us. "Way to go. You guys are awesome!"

"Parachutes in ten seconds," said Looper.

"Mick," came Trace's voice. "It's not your fault."

"Price, do your crew a favor. Don't do anything stupid. No other options," barked Riker.

No other options? Oh yeah? Jonah was wrong, I hadn't played all my cards. I still had one left. And I decided to play it.

Looper's calm voice came over the speaker. "Computer will deploy parachutes in three ... two ... one...."

I reached up and slapped the large, circular orange button on the top left side of the control panel. The one marked "OVERRIDE."

I had just turned off Program 64.

"Parachutes have deployed," said Looper.

But the falling sensation continued and the small command module kept whistling downward towards the earth.

"Think again, Mission Control," I said to my crew mates, without hitting the TALK switch.

"Um, Mick?" said Trace casually from the back. "I respect your protest here. But we kind of need those parachutes. Know what I mean?"

Lance wasn't quite as casual. "YOU TOTAL IDIOT!!!" he screamed. "YOU'VE RUINED EVERYTHING!!! We're not going to hit the ground at 40 miles per hour. Without those parachutes, we're going to hit the ground at 400 miles per hour!!!"

There was a sudden commotion from the back row. I heard the clicks of a seat belt unbuckling and saw Lance start to climb towards the front row, a determined look on his face. "Mickey, move over. I'm taking command," Lance threatened as he advanced.

Quick as a ninja, Trace was on him. What she did next confirmed something I had thought in the back of my mind since the first time I met her. Never get into a fight with that girl.

With one hand, she grabbed Lance's jumpsuit and pulled him sharply backwards. With her other hand, she put his head into a crazy wrestling move. And with still another hand ... wait, how many hands did this girl have? ... she yanked on his ear, causing him to give a sharp yelp. Meanwhile, with another crazy wrestling move, she looped her leg around his waist and slammed his head into the wall with a sharp thud. Oh, I wish I had this on video.

Anyway, in about two seconds, Lance was back in his seat, face-down, whining "oh quit it quit it quit it quit it ... ow!!"

Trace eased herself back into her seat. "Flight Commander Price, the mutiny has been defeated. Now, can you please tell us what the heck you're doing?"

Still amazed by her lightning-quick ninja moves, all I could say was "I'm playing my card."

"Artemis Seven, your parachutes have not opened," said Looper. "You're at 13,000 feet and falling. Push the manual parachute button. Push the manual parachute button." His voice was calm as always. But insistent.

"You're doing what?" asked Trace, ignoring Looper.

"He's playing his last card," answered Jonah for me. He was looking at me with a look of ... what was that? I thought I saw a glimmer of understanding in his eyes. At least, it wasn't a look of panic or disbelief, which I had expected to see.

"Let me explain this way," continued Jonah. "Lets say you have a long and complicated math problem. You have all these numbers being added and subtracted and multiplied and divided. And the one thing you know is, you don't like the answer. You want a different answer. What do you do?"

"What do you do? You push the stupid parachute button, that's what you do," squeaked Lance, still face-down in his seat.

"12,000 feet. You're falling fast. Deploy the parachute," said Looper.

"You want a different answer, what do you do?" repeated Jonah with a smile. "You change one of the numbers in the math problem, and you get a different answer. That's what you do."

"Ahhh," said Kat. "I get it. Mick, I'll use the term you taught me yesterday. This is a Hail Mary, right?"

"Guys," interrupted Trace. "You're talking about cards and math and football plays. Stop playing word games and explain the plan, ok? You do understand that we'll hit the earth in about a minute and turn into a big metal Frisbee, don't you?"

"Roger that, Trace," I jumped in. "I'm waiting to pull the parachute at the last possible second. The computer projected that we would land in Dayton if we pulled the parachute at 15,000 feet. If we pull it later, then we'll land somewhere else. Right Jonah?"

I hoped Jonah would agree with me. Because I really had no idea if this would actually work.

"Mickey's right," said Jonah. "The computer calculated that we would land in Dayton based on how far the command module would float with the parachute, pushed by the wind. If we don't pull the chute until much later, we'll fall straight down for longer and will drift less. Meaning, we'll end up … well … we'll end up somewhere else."

"But where?" squeaked Lance. "How do you know where?"

"I don't," I replied. "But it can't get any worse than Dayton. No offense to Dayton. And it just might get better. We might get lucky. Jonah … Einstein … just tell me one thing. When do I push the button?"

As we continued to plummet towards the earth, Jonah frantically scribbled numbers on a piece of paper. He had covered the front side of the page with numbers so he flipped it over and started making more calculations on the back.

"Um, Jonah, we're kind of in a hurry here. Just give me your best guess. More or less. We're at 10,000 feet right now. When do I push the button? When we're at 8,000 feet? 3,000 feet?"

"Artemis Seven," Riker's voice cut through the cabin like a knife. "You have disobeyed orders and have hit the manual override. You're below 10,000 feet. Deploy parachutes NOW. Respond NOW."

"Mission Control, thanks for your suggestion," I said. "We're doing a little math problem up here and having a nice debate about wind speed. Meanwhile, can someone at Mission Control please tell us, what's the last possible moment we can deploy our parachutes and still live?"

"DEPLOY NOW!" screamed Riker. "That's an order, you pipsqueak!"

"4,900 feet," said Jonah. "That's my final answer. Pull it at 4,900 feet and the three parachutes will have still be able to do their job and slow us down to about 40 miles per hour. Any later, they won't have time to slow us down and we'll be going faster when we smack into the ground. And that's not good."

"Mission Control," I repeated. "The last possible moment we can deploy our parachutes?"

This time it wasn't Riker's voice on the radio, it was Looper. "Artemis Seven, our engineers tell us 5,000 feet. Don't go below that. Pull at 5,000."

"Eh," Jonah shrugged, glancing down at his complicated math work. "I still think 4,900 will work. They're being a little too cautious, but you'd expect that from grown-ups. Plus, they didn't have as much time as me to do the math. Pull it at 4,900 feet."

The altitude dial was spinning like a clock racing backwards. We were at 6,000 feet. Through the front window, the bright blue sky had given way to some light clouds. I could almost feel the Earth looming behind us, like a big bully lurking over my shoulder, ready to wham me with something heavy.

"Mick, how about hitting that parachute button now," suggested Kat. "To be safe. Not that we don't trust you, Jonah."

The numbers flew by, 5,500 feet from the ground and getting closer.

I reached up and placed my finger on the button.

"Artemis Seven, push the dang button," snapped Looper. "YOU'RE GIVING ME A HEART ATTACK!!"

Wow, we had finally caused Mr. Cool Cucumber to crack!

The dial hit 5,000 and continued to race downward.

"All right, Mick," said Jonah. "I'd appreciate some parachute right about now."

I slammed the button marked PC-MASTER with all my might. There was an agonizing delay, which probably lasted only about one second. Then, with a tremendous lurch, we were all pressed down and backwards into our seats as the parachutes engaged.

I could see the parachutes out the front window, a series of strong cords reaching up towards two enormous red and white parachutes that spread out and filled with air. They were glorious, straining hard to slow our command module and save our lives.

"Mission Control, parachutes have deployed," I reported. "Repeat, parachutes have deployed."

"Thank you for that Artemis Seven," said Looper. "You saved me from a heart attack. Prepare for impact in two minutes. We are tracking you on radar and recalculating your crash site. I mean LANDING site."

I breathed a heavy sigh. I had played the last card, in a desperate attempt to improve our landing location. I watched as the two parachutes billowed in the air above us, with several stray strings flapping on one side.

Stray strings.

Two parachutes.

"Um, Jonah. How many parachutes are we supposed to have?" I asked nervously.

"Yeah, you noticed?" he replied from the seat next to me. "The Artemis master parachute array is designed to have three parachutes for maximum drag. It looks like parachute number three had different plans today."

"And what does that mean?" asked Trace from the back row.

Jonah took a look at the complicated math equations on the paper in front of him, and then crumpled the paper with his right hand. "It means you can throw my math out the window. Two parachutes won't slow us down as much as three parachutes."

"Which means, prepare for impact," I said. "Really hard impact. Sorry guys."

"SORRY GUYS!!??" Lance shouted. "That's all you've got? Sorry guys! Lets get that on your tomb stone: 'Here lies lousy Astronaut Mickey Price, 1964-1977. Famous last words: Sorry Guys.' I mean, really, what kind of...."

His voice trailed off at the sound of Trace cracking her knuckles.

"We might only have a minute left to live," said Trace threateningly. "But I can't think of a better way to spend my last minute...."

"Come on guys, focus," I said. "You remember what Riker

said. On impact, head for the escape hatch. First one there, try to open it. Second person, grab a fire extinguisher. We have three on board. After that, we try to get everyone out of here. Everyone. Nobody gets left behind."

The dial was spinning a little slower now, but still too quickly for comfort. We were below 1,000 feet. But because we were heading backwards, and the only window was at the top, we still couldn't see where we were headed.

I was about to continue with my speech about "nobody gets left behind" when Looper cut me off.

"Artemis Seven, listen closely. Impact in less than a minute. With two parachutes, your impact speed will be about 50 miles an hour. We are tracking your position on radar and have recalculated your landing spot. We checked it and checked it again. And we can't believe it. Your impact location is near Chicago, about one mile from downtown."

"Sweet," said Jonah. "Maybe I can walk home."

I held my breath. I crossed my fingers. "Exactly where … near Chicago?" I asked. "Any chance…?"

"Yes, Mickey," said Looper. "You gambled and you hit the jackpot. Impact location, Lake Michigan."

25

THE LUCKY DOLLAR

I have to admit, even after going to the moon and back, riding in an army helicopter over Chicago was even cooler. The police speedboat that picked us up from the broken command module headed south on the lake, away from Chicago, towards an industrial area with grimy docks with big Great Lakes barges being loaded and unloaded.

As we pulled into a particularly dirty, empty dock, I saw a huge green helicopter streaking along the tops of the warehouse buildings, coming straight towards us. It slowed when it reached our dock and touched down at exactly the same time as our boat arrived. The day was already windy, but the blast of air from the rotors made it almost impossible to stand upright.

The pilot didn't even turn off the engine, and we were rushed on board up a small ladder in the back. Ziggy clung tight to Kat and buried his furry little head into her shoulder. I think the reentry, splashdown, boat ride and now being rushed into this screaming beast of a helicopter was a bit much for a monkey … even a highly-trained veteran of the space program like Ziggy.

Less than one minute after the boat pulled up to the dock, we were lifting off again into the sky.

There were several doctors wearing white coats who were waiting for us in the helicopter. As soon as we lifted off, they started poking and prodding us and took our temperature and pulse. They also peppered us with questions, but none of us felt much like answering so we each just gave the thumbs up sign and smiled. That seemed to do the trick.

Aside from feeling absolutely exhausted and wobbly-legged, none of us were hurt. Amazingly. The impact of hitting the water was bone-jarring but surely not as bad as slamming into solid ground. The command module hadn't fared so well, though. It had started sinking almost as soon as we landed in the water. If the police boat hadn't arrived in just a few seconds, we would have had a long swim. In space gear. Not a pleasant thought.

Jonah pointed out landmarks as the chopper raced back up the coastline towards Chicago. We saw the enormous Sears Tower in the distance, with its two giant radio antennas reaching up towards the heavens.

"And look over there! Soldier's Field! Look, home of the Bears!" Jonah shouted into my ear. We passed directly over the stadium, then banked hard to the left. I could see cars backed up on the expressway heading into the city, and even a few joggers in a park, looking at us with upturned faces.

An arm came shooting over my shoulder from the left. It was Trace, giving me a big hug, leaning her face next to mine as we looked out the window at the city streaking past beneath us. Our breath steamed up the inside of the small, round window.

"Did that really just happen, Mick?" she asked, speaking quietly into my right ear.

"You better believe it," I said. "We just saved the moon. You, me, Jonah, Kat and Ziggy." I smiled. "Oh yeah, I seem to remember some guy named Lance kicking around too. We saved the moon and lived to tell the tale."

▲ ▼ ▲ ▼ ▲

Director Marshall paused and seemed like he was waiting for something. He had called each of us over, one at a time, to sit with him in the back row of the 10-seat Lear jet that was carrying us back to Florida. Back to Florida, where our families were gathering. Or, for me, where the adventure would end and I would return to the Boys' Home.

Not that there was anything wrong with that. At that moment, there was nowhere else I wanted to be. And to be honest, even though we were under strict instructions not to tell anybody about our secret mission, I didn't even feel like telling my friends back home anyway. Except for Taco, who would make me tell him stories about the trip over and over again until my voice was hoarse.

I just wanted a heaping plate of normal ... and my own bed.

But that would have to wait. At that moment, I was sitting in the back of the airplane next to Director Marshall, who had apparently re-claimed his job from Riker as soon as the command module touched down. He paused and looked at me, expectantly.

I paused too, hesitating with that uncertain feeling you get when you're deciding whether to jump into a cold pool. In the end, I knew I was going to jump … I just had to ask the question that had been haunting me for the past two weeks.

"Director Marshall," I said.

"Please," he drawled in his heavy Arkansas accent, leaning across the narrow airplane aisle towards me, "call me Bob."

"Um, with all due respect, I think I need to keep calling you Director Marshall if that's all right with you."

The big man nodded and raised his eyebrows. "Roger that. You were saying…?"

"I need to know something," I said. "Why did you pick me? Out of everyone at the camp and out of every kid in the country, why me? I mean, I know why you picked the others … their special talents. And Lance. I mean, that's an obvious one. He's big, he's strong, he's your SON…."

"Hold on right there, Mickey," said Marshall. He peered forward down the aisle, like he was making sure nobody else was listening. He lowered his voice. "I know it might look like I was playing favorites, but let me explain why I picked Lance." He sighed. "You don't understand how difficult it was to send you kids on such a dangerous mission. It was the hardest thing I have ever done, asking parents for permission to send their sons and daughters up into space. I sent Lance because … well … because I couldn't ask other parents to do something I wasn't willing to do myself. If I wasn't willing to send my own boy up to the moon, and make sure he got back okay, how could I ask them to?"

As soon as he said that, it made sense. Perfect sense. Not just his decision to send Lance, but his decision to send me.

"Ohhhhhh," I said slowly. "That's why. I get it now. You sent me because I don't have any parents. That made it easy for you. You just picked me because you didn't have to convince a mom or a dad ... or both. This was a dangerous mission, and you sent me because you knew nobody would miss me."

I saw a little smile at the corner of Marshall's mouth. "Mickey," he said, "you think you've got it all figured out, don't you?"

That must be it, then. He was about to confirm what I had suspected. But then, the Director's smile grew broader before he pressed on.

"Mickey, I'm happy to say that you're totally wrong about that. True, getting permission from the parents before the trip was not easy. But if you think it's hard to get a green light from parents, you should try dealing with the Florida Department of Children's Services. And Sister Rinaldi. I almost gave up trying to get their approval. But as you might have figured, I'm a very stubborn man. And in the end, I got what I wanted."

He regarded me with his piercing slate grey eyes. "No, you're wrong about why I picked you. If you really want to know, it's because I knew you kids would face some unexpected challenges up there. And I knew that you, Mickey ... out of everyone up there ... would be able to face those unexpected challenges and defeat them one by one. You ... out of everyone up there ... wouldn't expect the adults down at Mission Control to have all the answers. You would figure things out for yourself. That's how it's been your whole life."

"Do you know how I know that?" asked Marshall.

I gave him a shrug.

"Because you remind me of myself 40 years ago. My parents both died when I was a baby and I was raised by ... well ... I don't know how many people, in I don't know how many homes. I lived in an orphanage for a while, not unlike your Boys' Home over in Orlando. So when we were looking for a team of kids to send up to the Moon, I knew just where to look. I went looking for someone who was like me."

Director Marshall paused to catch my reaction.

After a while I looked up. "But why me? Out of all the options in Florida, out of all the orphanages in the United States, why did you pick the Boys' Home in Orlando? How did you pick me?"

"Well, that one's easy," said the Director. "Your Boys' Home was the closest one to Kennedy Space Center, and we didn't have time to look anywhere else. As I've always said," as he flipped a silver dollar coin in his hand, "sometimes in this business you've got to rely on luck. I took a chance on you. And I guess I got lucky."

"Wait a minute," I said, cutting in. I had caught the great Director Marshall bending the truth. "On the night before launch you said you didn't believe in luck. You said something like 'Luck is what saves you when you fail,' and 'Never rely on luck.' You said...."

Director Marshall winked and shook his head. "That was just a pep talk. I was trying to give you all a little confidence. I didn't want you all to know that I had my fingers crossed, and my toes too, and carried a lucky silver dollar for seven straight days while you were up there."

"Here," the big man continued. "I feel like I've used up all the luck in this one. Let's see how far it takes you." With that, he flipped the silver dollar into the air and it sailed end over end across the center aisle of the airplane. My hand shot out before I could think, and I caught the heavy silver coin perfectly, mid-flight.

As I walked up the aisle towards my seat, I slipped the coin into my hip pocket. I smiled as I heard it clink against the small, heavy metal object I had been carrying in my pocket for the last three days. The one I had lifted from the fine, white, powdery surface of the moon. So now I had two souvenirs. One could buy me a large sundae at the Dairy Queen, though I decided I would never spend it. The other ... well ... I would just have to wait and see.

26

SUNRISE

The faint but definite glow of morning spread across the waters of the glass-still lake and crept into the campsite. Tom let out an emphatic "grrr-afffff" as he stretched the night out of his joints. His sister stared disbelievingly at the dim light in the eastern sky, amazed that … yes … indeed … her dad's story had lasted from bedtime all the way until dawn.

"So," said Tom, finally daring to inject his voice into the pause that was growing longer and longer. "Is that it? The end?"

"Well," said Dad, "I'm not sure I can go on." He faked a faint, bad-cold voice and rubbed a hand over his throat. Come to think of it,

the twins realized that his voice had been getting a bit scratchy after talking for about eight hours.

"But anyway," Dad continued, "it does seem like an appropriate place to stop. We all got back safely. Mission accomplished."

Tom sat up and faced him. "Ooooo-kaaaaay," he said slowly. "So now, the moment of truth. The tire swing incident, the men with sunglasses, the space camp, the mystery metal, the trip to the moon. After all that ... are you STILL telling us this was a true story?"

"Does it need to be true to be a good story?" asked Dad. "The great Greek myths are perhaps the greatest stories of all times. They have super-powered gods living on a magical mountaintop, half-human monster-creatures, fantastic battles, flying shoes and all sorts of special effects. Or a gripping tale of wizards, dragons, flying broomsticks and a school of magic? All of these, great stories, but do you need them to be true?" asked Dad.

"No, I suppose not," said Tom. "A story can be a total fib and still be enjoyable. But this one," he paused. "This one would be extra interesting if it was true, you know what I mean? With you ... supposedly ... as the real life hero?" He stared at his dad with eyebrows raised. "Am I right?"

"Maybe," Dad shrugged. "What do you say, Tess. Truth or fib?"

Tess stared at him intently. "Dad," she said. "Look at me right in the eye and tell me it's true."

"True, every word," said Dad right back.

"Then, yes," Tess said with a glorious, instant smile. "I've got a few questions for you, mister, but I believe you."

"And Tom?" asked Dad. "You know what, I won't make you vote. Lets just call it a 'good story' and I can start up the camp fire again and make us all some pancakes."

Tom frowned.

"Come on, Tom," said Tess. "Pancakes." She looked pleadingly at her brother.

"Okay," Tom finally said, deliberately, like a lawyer on TV. "On one hand, we have your statement that your story is true."

"And on the OTHER hand," he said as he held his two hands out in front of him like a set of scales, and tipped one hand down sharply, "we have your history of telling wildly untrue stories. Like that one about the girl who jumped out of an airplane without a parachute and landed safely on a cactus. Well, not exactly safely, but she supposedly landed on the cactus and lived to play a starring role in more of your made-up stories."

Tom was on a roll.

"And on this same other hand," he tipped the low hand still lower, "we have the details of your story. Your tall tale. A bunch of kids who were practically kidnapped by NASA, prepared for a space mission that adults could not take due to some mystery metal we've never heard of, launched up into space, saved the moon from nuclear destruction, and found an alien device."

He paused and pointed at his dad. "Which, by the way, you haven't fully explained."

Dad shrugged and started to say "that's another story...," but Tom kept right on with his speech.

"And on top of all that, the hero overcomes a fatal error in the navigation system and manages to find ... oh, miracle of miracles ... he manages to find Lake Michigan by complete luck, rather than crashing and burning in a shopping mall parking lot outside Dayton. And all of this," he said grandly, reaching the conclusion of his compelling argument. "All of this, even landing a space ship right in the middle of Chicago, without ANYBODY finding out about it. No fame or fortune for the hero. No career as an astronaut. No parade or huge welcome home. The best-kept secret ever. No media coverage. No newspaper articles. Nothing."

The last part was said emphatically. Oh, he had his dad on the ropes.

"Well, Tom," said Dad, "if you describe it THAT way I guess it's pretty incredible."

And that's when Tess saw the envelope.

She had actually noticed it, in the faint firelight, at some point earlier in the night. A regular white envelope, slightly worn and crumpled at the corners, sitting in the pine straw next to her dad. It hadn't seemed important at the time. But now....

"Dad?" asked Tess, pointing at the envelope. "What's that?"

"Oh, this? Hmmm. Yes, good point. We have this envelope here. Now, I'm trying to remember what you said, Tom. Something like: "'No media coverage. No newspaper articles'?"

The words hung there in the air.

"Well," Tom finally said. "I think I said it, kind of, as a question. Didn't I? Let me rephrase it. 'No media coverage? No newspaper articles?'"

Dad leaned forward and prodded the smoldering embers with a long stick. The faint glow of dawn had now grown brighter and the clearing around the campfire was starting to come into focus. Looking straight up, he stared at the moon, full and beautifully round, sitting majestically in the sky far above the tall pines surrounding the campsite.

He scooped up the envelope and handed it to Tess.

"I'll see if I can figure out Mom's recipe for pancakes. Meanwhile, you go ahead and read what's in the envelope."

The Envelope

New York Times

Another NASA Success: Artemis Returns Safely

Honolulu Naval Station, November 2, 1977.

At 7:15AM Eastern Time Tuesday, the command module for the Artemis Seven mission splashed down in the Pacific Ocean 150 miles southeast of Honolulu. The US Navy vessel Durham was nearby to collect the five-member crew.

"I cannot comment on the details of the mission other than to say it was a complete success, and that Commander Riker and his crew all returned safely," said NASA spokeswoman Amanda Collins.

The mission was shrouded in secrecy from the beginning, starting with its surprise launch on October 25th. The reason for the mission was not made public. One source inside NASA, who asked not to be named, told reporters that the crew was sent to the moon to repair a broken refrigerator in the moon base kitchen.

Reporters were not allowed to take their usual place onboard the U.S.S. Durham to watch the splashdown. No photos of the landing are available. NASA explained that the astronauts had endured a particularly difficult reentry procedure and were immediately hospitalized. The only member of the crew to speak to the press was Captain Frank Riker, the veteran Flight Commander, who talked to reporters by telephone.

"The other members of my crew are extremely tired and asked me to speak on their behalf," said Riker. "They are tired, but I feel great, like I could go to the moon again tomorrow. Seriously. If NASA approves it, I'll go tomorrow."

NASA has not yet announced the date of the next Artemis mission.

Weekly Tattler

NASA Space Craft Crash Lands in Lake Michigan
By Lacy McKenzie

Chicago, November 1, 1977.

An unidentified flying object plunged into Lake Michigan less than a mile from Chicago early yesterday morning, witnessed by several citizens. Local police boats were seen heading out to the landing spot shortly after the strange craft hit the surface of the lake.

Eyewitnesses described seeing a large object pulling red and white parachutes falling through the sky into the lake.

"The object was a shiny gold color, definitely metal. It was flat on the bottom and then narrower the top, with windows on the side," said Ms. McKenzie, the beautiful, intelligent and reliable Senior Reporter for *The Weekly Tattler* magazine, who happened to be taking her dog for an early-morning walk in Lakeshore Park.

Another eyewitness, Mr. Egbert Winzel, offered an identical description. "It looked exactly like an Artemis command module," reported Mr. Winzel. "It had those huge red and white parachutes. Except all those pictures in the papers show three parachutes. Strange ... this one only had two."

At the time this article was printed, no photographs of the spectacular event were available. Anyone who witnessed this strange sight, and especially anyone with a photograph, is urged to contact the newspaper immediately.

An eyewitnesses reported one more odd twist. Using binoculars belonging to Mr. Winzel, the eyewitness spotted police boats removing what appeared to be five very short people, quite possibly CHILDREN, from the strange craft. The five seemed to be wearing matching astronauts' suits.

And, as strange as this may sound, one of the female astronauts was seen carrying what appeared to be a small baby, also wearing an astronaut suit.

Officials at NASA refused to confirm that this was the Artemis Seven space craft. Instead, they claimed that the command module had landed, at approximately the same time, in the Pacific Ocean. NASA's claim cannot be confirmed because reporters were not allowed anywhere near the recovery area, and were not allowed to photograph or interview the astronauts when they returned.

The Daily Tattler contacted NASA for a comment about whether the Artemis Seven module had actually landed in Lake Michigan. NASA spokeswoman Amanda Collins said "Oh my gosh, how did you find out ... um ... how did you find out ... my telephone number?"

Pressed for a formal response, Ms. Collins said "Look, the Artemis Seven mission was led by Commander Frank Riker. Everything he does is strictly by the book. Trust me, with Frank Riker at the controls, that space craft would never have landed in Lake Michigan."

AUTHOR'S NOTE

The space program and the race to land astronauts on the moon was one of the greatest seat-of-your-pants adventures in human history. Figuring out how to get humans to the moon and back took years of teamwork by dreamers, metal-workers, professors, mathematicians, computer programmers, daredevil test pilots, chefs (who do you think invented Orange Tang and freeze-dried ice cream?) and, of course, rocket scientists. There were terrible setbacks, including unmanned rockets blasting off at strange angles and, tragically, astronauts losing their lives on the launch pad and in space. But there were also amazing successes, including Yuri Gagarin's historic first trip into space and Neil Armstrong's famous stroll on the surface of the moon. And there will be others.

If you want to learn more about the history and science of the space program, ask the librarian at your school or local public library. Hopefully, you already know that librarians are an excellent source of information. Even better than the Internet because they can help filter out the junk and lead you to what you're looking for. Or ask at your local bookstore, because they can help you find any book on the planet. Try it.

If you read more about the space program, you will recognize a lot of things from this book. The parts about the early Mercury, Gemini and Apollo missions are true. I wasn't kidding: the average distance from the earth to the moon really is 238,000 miles, although it varies by a few thousand miles depending on the moon's orbit. Also, I didn't make up the top speed of a rocket leaving the earth's atmosphere, a scalding 25,000 miles per hour.

There are, however, a few things you won't find in other books. You won't find any mention of an astronaut named Mickey Price, or about the Artemis Program, or about a mining center built on the moon or a special metal called Pleurinium. Neither will you find any description of any NASA command module making a "direct descent," landing straight on the moon and then blasting off again for the trip home. In the Apollo program, NASA scientists figured out that taking the entire command module down to the surface of the moon and then back up again uses way too much fuel. So instead, they decided to send the command module *almost* all the way, putting it into orbit around the moon. From this position, the Apollo astronauts rode in a small, lightweight landing craft to the moon's surface, and then back again to their orbiting command module for the return trip home. Much more fuel efficient.

Does that mean it's impossible to build a space craft that lands directly on the moon? Impossible to erect buildings on the moon? Inconceivable that a group of young astronauts could have led a glorious mission to save the moon?

Just because none of this can be found in any of the excellent books your librarian shows you, does it mean that it can't happen? Or that it didn't happen?

Mickey Price and a handful of others know the secret of what happened at that space camp back in 1977. And now, you do too.

▲ ▼ ▲ ▼ ▲

There are a number of people whom I need to thank profusely for their help on this book. Sara, for helping conceive the idea and for encouragement at every step of the way. Freddy & Joey for laughing out loud when I first read the book to them and for not complaining when I changed the names of their characters. Ryan Kirschner, Willie King, Alex Hoffman, and Maggie and David Hacker-Donoghue for being enthusiastic Test Readers. All the Dellingers for their unwavering support. Aviva Goldfarb, Suzy Yalof-Schwartz, Brad Meltzer and Dan Abrams for expert advice and strategery. And Paul Forsyth, for bringing the characters and scenes to life with inspired drawings.